Hi! x

Before & After You

Copyright © 2020 by Michelle Chamberland

All rights reserved.

Cover design by Maria Spada of Marie Spada Book Cover Design

This book is a work of fiction. Names, characters, places, and incidents are either products of the author's imagination or are used fictitiously. Any resemblance to actual persons, living or dead, business establishments, events, or locales is entirely coincidental.

No part of this book may be reproduced or transmitted in any form or by any means, electronic or mechanical, including photocopying, recording, or by any information storage or retrieval system, without express written permission by the author, except for the use of brief quotations in a book review.

All rights reserved.

ISBN: 9798620789238

For my husband,
who picked up all of my broken pieces,
held them in the palm of his hands,
and showed me the way the light shined on them
and made them beautiful.
♥

One *Before*

I KNEW IT from the very first moment I saw him. He walked into the classroom, and I swear he wore a golden halo around his head. It could have been the absolutely ridiculous, yet somehow completely charming bleached-blond mop of hair he wore and the sun illuminating it from behind him, but I'm going with halo.

Because he was perfect.

I twisted around, fully turned in my seat at the front of the classroom as I watched his every move. I couldn't take my eyes off of him. His fingers as they tightened around the straps of his backpack, the muscles in his arms tensing from the grip; the way his jawline moved as he licked his lips; the way he ran his fingers through his hair, as if it were purely out of habit and he had no idea that it made his hair settle across his forehead in just the right way.

When his green eyes finally stopped on mine, my stomach swarmed with butterflies. I felt time slow down. I felt the world around me shift and fade out. My heart beat faster, my lungs closed in on me, my mouth dried up like the desert—*all of it*—because those moments they talk about, where your eyes meet across a room and you just know that that very moment has changed everything you ever knew? Those moments are real. I felt it in those few short seconds he was looking at me. I felt it in the way my walls were already beginning to crumble with just that one encounter.

That alone should've had me running for my life in the opposite direction, but by the time he had smiled at me and ducked his head as he lowered into his seat, I had already dreamt up a hundred different lifetimes with him. It didn't matter who he was. It didn't matter that I'd never seen him before, that I didn't know his name, where he came from, how old he was, that I really didn't know anything about him at all. It didn't matter that I was all wrong for him, that I was broken.

I wanted him.

I wanted his love; I wanted it desperately.

Two *Before*

WE WERE WORLDS apart. Light-years, universes. He was so far out of my reach, there was no way he could ever be mine. He was the sun and I was the moon. He was the light, and I was the darkness. I knew this, but I didn't care.

He had that crazy, bleached-blond hair, expensive clothes and clean, white Converses, and that smile. That smile that turned up slightly more on the right side than it did on the left. I'd noticed because he threw at least a half a dozen of them my way that morning. And I'd even smiled back a few times—*okay, every time*. And it was something I was immediately suspicious of. Nobody made me smile like that, like I could feel its warmth from the inside out.

Besides, who smiled that much? And was happy about it? Because he did seem happy. *Happy, happy, happy.* It radiated off of him like sunshine. I'd even caught him smiling at himself a few times. At something he was reading, and again at some joke he must have been telling himself inside his head. Who did that? It wasn't normal.

And then I found myself smiling again at how weird he was. *What the hell was wrong with me?*

I forced myself to stay still and stare straight ahead for the rest of the class period. I couldn't keep looking back there at him; I was being so obvious. But it was torture, *pure torture,* not to turn around and steal another look at him. It's like when you walk into a room and someone screams, "Don't look!"—and it feels literally, physically impossible *not* to look. That's how it felt keeping still even though I could feel his eyes burning holes into the back of my head.

It excited me, and at the same time, it terrified me.

So much, that when the bell rang, I jumped from my seat and booked it out the door without a backward glance. I'd suck up the courage to talk to him another day, because one more look at him, and I'd beg him to let me have his babies someday, or something equally embarrassing. I needed to get it together first.

"Jess!" Sara yelled for me across the grassy quad between school buildings. Sara was one of my best friends, my only girlfriend, and while we didn't know too much about each other beyond the surface of our friendship, choosing not to dig too deep and ask about all the dirty and dark we immediately recognized in each other, we were still super close. As close as two people like us could be. And we had fun together; we knew when to shut up and make life disappear for each other in the moments that we could.

I ran over to her and straight into her arms, squeezing her tight. "Sara. Sara, I'm in love."

She laughed. It wasn't the first time I'd said this, or the hundredth. But usually, I was only talking about some dark and brooding, hot and barely famous new band member I'd discovered. Rarely did I swoon over some guy I'd actually come across in real life. But this was different.

"No, I mean it this time." I pulled away, looking her in the eyes. "I'm dead serious. The hottest guy is in my class, and I mean, *the hottest guy I have ever seen in my life* is in my first period, and I'm pretty sure I'm going to marry him one day."

She smiled and looped her arm through mine as we walked to second period. It was the only class we had together that semester, which totally sucked. "Hottest guy you've ever seen in all your sixteen years, huh?"

"*Yeesss*," I whined. "He's beautiful. Too beautiful. And he smiles way too much, but *God,* Sare, I couldn't stop staring at him."

She snorted, flipping her wavy blond hair over her shoulder. "So, you're playing hard to get?"

"From now on I am."

She laughed again. "Good luck with that."

"Shut up." I shoved her halfheartedly.

We walked into photography and found two seats next to each other.

"So, what does he look like?" she asked.

I thought it over for a minute, images of this morning tumbling through my mind: the clear green of his eyes, rimmed by a deep, forest green; the perfect, pouty shape of his lips. "Nope. No way. I'm not even going to try. I won't do him justice. You'll just have to see him for yourself."

"Oh, it's like that?!" She poked me.

"Yes. Yes, it is very much like that. So you understand what I'm saying now."

She smirked. "Yeah, I think I do."

Three *Before*

THE BELL RANG for first period the next morning, but he was nowhere to be seen. I tried not to feel as disappointed as I did, but I'd taken the few extra minutes of effort to get ready, and he wasn't even here. I had on a clean black shirt, mascara. I'd fingered through my short, usually unruly, black hair. I'd even put a bobby pin in it, sweeping a small piece to the side. And he. Wasn't. Even. Here.

Was he not in this class anymore? Did he get switched? Did I imagine the whole thing? Was he even real? Definitely not. That would make so much more sense. Things that beautiful didn't happen to me.

I kicked his empty desk with my ratty black Converse and cursed Satan himself as I made my way over to my desk. But then I saw it. *Him.* That halo. He was pulling at the locked classroom door. Not a single thought processed through my brain as I walked over to it and opened it for him. And then that smile, that perfectly lopsided smile, and those eyes.

Real. Definitely real.

"Both of you to the front office! You know the rules!" our teacher yelled from the front of the classroom, causing me to jump back from the door.

I turned. "What?"

"Tardy passes, now!" he yelled again with fully bugged eyes.

"I wasn't even late," I replied like an idiot. *Thanks, brain.*

"Now!" he reiterated, completely irritated.

I swiped my backpack off my desk and muttered a, *"Jesus,"* under my breath as I headed outside, golden halo following closely behind.

We walked silently side by side for at least a full minute, or for what felt like forever. An eternity. I kept my eyes trained on the ground in front of me, severely aware of his presence beside me.

Speak, mouth! But I had nothing. I couldn't think of a single thing to say. I picked at the black nail polish on my fingers instead.

"Sorry about that. Didn't mean to get you in trouble," his deep and gravelly voice slid into my consciousness, burning itself there.

I looked up at him. "It's okay." I shrugged.

More than okay. Totally worth it.

He smirked; I smiled.

It was ridiculous, the warmth swirling itself around inside my body.

"I'm Greyson, by the way." He'd stopped on the sidewalk, sliding his hands into his pockets.

I stared up at him a second too long before finally replying, "Jessica, but my friends call me Jess."

"Jess." He nodded, a slow smile forming on his lips, and then he turned away, back toward the office, and continued walking.

Fast; my heart was beating way too fast.

Greyson. Even his name was perfect. And the way he said my name, the way his tongue slid over the single-syllabled word: *Jess.*

Jess, Jess, Jess.

I'd burn that one to memory, too.

We reached the front office, grabbed our tardy passes, and made it back to class entirely too fast for my liking.

"Good luck," he said, holding the door open for me. And then? He winked at me. *Winked* at me. Fast and subtle, and completely pulling it off.

And in that very moment, I remember thinking, *God, I know you don't like me all that much, but maybe I could have this one thing? Please? Just this one thing. I swear it won't make me too happy.*

But that was a lie, because I wanted Greyson more than I had wanted anything in my entire life.

Four *After*

A NAKED MAN with a bleeding heart in the palm of his hands stares back at me from the canvas. He grips it as if it's his life force. He's on his knees, blurred faces surrounding him in a chaos of colors and streaks of paint marring their features. They lean toward the heart—possibly curious, possibly hungry for the chance to snatch it away from the man and rip it to shreds.

That's up to the observer to decide, but I'd like to think that if any of those faces dared to try, he would rip them to shreds instead, fiercely protecting the heart with his life.

I blow my hair away from my face, wiping my paint-streaked fingers across my apron, and take a step away from the painting. Something's missing, but I'm not sure what.

Caffeine.

I need more caffeine.

And supplies.

I quickly down the rest of my green juice and slip my apron off, draping it over the empty easel beside me. I don't bother changing out of my paint-stained clothes. I'll be gone and back too quick for it to matter.

Shutting the double doors of my studio behind me, I step off the wooded patio and into the overgrown grass of my backyard. I like it this way. It makes me feel like I'm in a mystical faery meadow, or the never-ending rolling hills of wildland somewhere far away and foreign. At least that's what I tell myself, since I don't have the care enough to cut it as often as I should. But it's mine—*all mine*—and it makes for perfect grounding energy. Again, this is what I tell myself.

I sink my toes into the moist soil beneath the grass, close my eyes, and tilt my face toward the sun; pull in a deep, determined breath; fill my lungs with air and inspiration and will the answers I need to magically come to me through divine intervention.

Color? Maybe the painting needs more color. Or less color. More vibrancy? Muted tones?

Less contrast? More contrast? Hell, I don't know.

I mentally shrug, and then physically shrug.

Thanks anyway, Universe.

Ten minutes later, I'm browsing the aisle of acrylic paints at a local hole in the wall art supply, still unsure of which direction to take in finishing this one. The one I've secretly named *"Mine."* Because no one will ever know for certain that the heart on that canvas is mine, or that the man protecting it has been holding onto it, in reality, for the past eight years.

He was supposed to be mine, too.

I will the thought away, throwing almost every color there is into my basket. Problem solved. I can figure out the rest later; I always do.

And then I smile, because *this,* this is my life. Colors, and feeling, and the complexities of life streaked and splattered and meticulously stroked onto a canvas, releasing whatever it is that needs releasing, freeing me for hours and hours on end.

I've been lucky enough to be successful at something I love. At something I can pour my heart and soul into. A place where I can dump all of my demons.

No, not lucky. I've never believed in luck.

Except for maybe twenty minutes from now, when I've randomly decided to be mildly social for once and walk down to the coffee shop instead of opting for the drive-thru like I normally do; when I turn around after picking up my order of one venti mocha iced coffee and come face to face with the one person from my past I never expected to see again. Least of all in my busy, chaotic hometown of Seattle, Washington.

Because this can't be anything but dumb luck, right?

To be not ten feet away from him after all of these years.

My fingers tighten their grip on my coffee, lest it fall to the ground in an overly dramatic fashion. Because nothing about this is all that dramatic, aside from the raging chaos going on inside my head. And the way my heart refuses to stop racing. And my hands to stop shaking.

Surely my eyes are playing tricks on me.

It isn't him. It can't be. This isn't happening.

He looks up at me, and I squeeze my eyes closed. No. *No, no, no.* No way. *There's no way.*

"Jess?"

Okay, there's definitely a way.

Five *Before*

"**WE'RE GOING TO** be partnering up for this assignment," our first-period teacher announced a few days later.

Everyone immediately began turning in their seats, subtly and not so subtly pairing up into twos. I felt that pull, the one that constantly drew my eyes to him. He was doodling something in his notebook, lost to the world. I watched him, also subtly or not so subtly, also lost to the world. He bit and released his bottom lip over and over again, deep in concentration, and I imagined what it would feel like for him to bite my lip like that, or for me to bite his, or to simply feel his lips on mine.

"Mr. Hayes," our teacher called.

Greyson looked up at him. "Yes, sir?"

Ah, Greyson *Hayes*. A second perfect name for a perfect face.

"You and Ms. Martinez will be working together, and since you're the only two students not paying any attention in class this morning, it seems you'll make the perfect pair."

Ms. Martinez, that was me, but all I really heard was *perfect pair, perfect pair, perfect pair.* Yes. Yes, we absolutely would make a perfect pair.

Greyson looked at me, raising an eyebrow in question. I nodded, letting him know that, *yep, that's me. I'm your partner.* The corner of his mouth tugged up in a small smile, and he nodded back, quickly looking back down and losing himself in his notebook again.

"Go ahead and get together and begin talking about what direction you think you'll be heading in for this assignment," our teacher said to the class. "And remember, poetry is open to interpretation, so there are no wrong answers, but I also want to hear some conviction in your presentations. Not only should you believe what you're telling me, but you should also be able to convince me of it, too. Got it?"

A wave of nods and *yeses* chorused around the room. I grabbed my backpack and stood up, making my way over to Greyson. I plopped down into the seat next to him, but he was so lost in that notebook of his that he didn't even notice me. At least I didn't think he did.

I leaned forward, resting my elbow on the desktop and my head in my hand, watching him sketch away. *Was he an artist, too?* When I looked closer, I saw that he wasn't drawing, but writing. Words all over the page, on the lines, in the margins.

"What's that for?" I asked.

"Just a song that keeps playing in my head. Wanted to get the words down before I forgot them," he answered without looking up, still writing. So, he was writing a song? His own song, or someone else's? Was he in a band? Did he sing? Could I survive it if I ever heard him sing? There were a million questions on the tip of my tongue, but I kept them all to myself.

Pairs were murmuring all around us, but the only sounds that really registered were the inhale and exhale of his steady breaths and the familiar scratch of pencil on paper. I closed my eyes, listening, inexplicably soothed by it.

After a long while, it stopped. I opened my eyes, and he was staring at me.

"Tired?" he asked.

"No. Well, yeah, a little," I admitted.

He smiled. "So, I guess we should pick a poem."

I turned to the board, to the long list of names and titles written across it. "Poe," I answered right away. I liked Poe, was drawn to the darkness of his words.

"Okay, cool." He turned toward me. "You want to meet after school one day this week to get started?"

I was melting away in his stare. "Yeah, sure. What day?"

"Friday good?"

"Works for me." I bit the tip of my thumb, suddenly nervous under his gaze.

"Friday it is."

His eyes.

His eyes, his eyes, his eyes.

"Friday it is," I agreed.

And his smile, his fingers tugging at the bottom of it.

I was such a goner.

Six *Before*

THAT FRIDAY, AFTER school had cleared out for the day and I had successfully managed to dodge my friends, I found myself lying in the middle of the quad, sprawled out across the grass, thinking that maybe the warmth of the sun would somehow seep its way into my bones and worm its way into my soul.

I couldn't explain it—*I didn't understand it*—but I felt numb, hopeless. It was like this shadow that followed me around sometimes, clouding the world in a haze I didn't care to see through. It sheltered me from the outside, protected me. But sometimes it felt like I was drowning.

I opened my eyes and saw Greyson walking across the quad, watched his sure and confident steps as he headed right toward me, smiling. I wished I felt the kind of happiness that radiated off of him. I couldn't even find it in me to smile back. I was still reeling. Still lost in the darkness I couldn't seem to claw my way out of.

"You ready?" he asked.

"Ready?" *Ready for what?*

"It's Friday."

Friday?

"Poetry assignment?" He rocked back on his heels, gripping the straps of his backpack, looking down at me expectantly.

And then it dawned on me, or more like violently smacked me in the face. "Oh, shit! I almost forgot. I'm sorry. Yes, I'm…I'm ready. Do you want to head up to the library, or something?"

"You hungry? We could go to Maddie's Diner," he suggested instead.

"Oh...I don't have a car, actually." I did have a car, I just refused to drive it.

He smiled, pulling his keys out of his pocket and dangling them from his fingertips. "I'll take you. Come on."

I stood from the ground and wordlessly followed him to his car. He opened the door for me, and I slid in. He drove a nice car—a really nice car, actually. Clean-cut lines, smooth leather, and the smell of old, classic car.

"This car is so beautiful it's disgusting," I said.

"Shh, earmuffs, baby girl." He laughed, petting the dashboard before turning toward me. "There's nothing disgusting about Lady."

So, he was one of *those* types. The kind that treasured a purring engine like it was a beating heart; the kind that felt it necessary to name their car. So, he wasn't perfect after all.

Ah, hell. Who was I kidding? The way he'd just pet his car and called her *baby girl* was hot as hell. I wanted to be his *"baby"*...and I might've had the passing thought of wanting him to pet me like that, too.

I smiled to myself. "Sorry, Lady," I said with a hand on the dashboard.

Greyson groaned, lip caught between his teeth. It was the most beautiful sound. I wanted to hear it again, and again and again. "Careful, Jess. Lady will get attached if you keep sweet-talking her like that."

"She sounds awfully moody."

He laughed, and with his foot to the pedal, I was sucked back into my seat. Lady purred—no, *growled*—as we made our way across town. The music was turned way up, something soft and catchy, seductive. So, Greyson had great taste in music, too. Was there anything he sucked at? I doubted it.

We arrived at Maddie's Diner, and Greyson turned back the key, Lady's motor shuddering to a halt. I went for the door handle, but Greyson stopped me with a hand on my arm.

"Lady would be highly offended if I didn't get the door for you," he said.

I laughed. "Really? I totally had her pegged as a feminist."

"Nope. She's old-fashioned. Believes a pretty girl should never open their own door."

And *holy shit,* but the blushing of my cheeks. I didn't do blushing. He noticed and smiled softly, opening his door and coming around the car for mine.

When he opened my door, my gaze locked onto his. *Such a strange place to feel so familiar, so comfortable,* I remember thinking.

He reached his hand out for me, his fingers gliding over mine achingly slow, and it was like a drug—that excitement, the awareness of a first touch that stirred like butterflies in my stomach and made my heart beat just that much faster. I was already addicted.

I was aware of every movement, every twitch of his hand, every glide of his thumb across my fingers. If holding his hand felt that good, I could only imagine what everything else with him would feel like. If his arms were wrapped around me, if his lips were to ever touch mine.

It had to happen.

I didn't care what I had to do, I was going to make him mine.

Seven *Before*

NOTEBOOKS, FOLDERS, PAPERS, pens, and pencils were strewn across the table in front of us, our devoured burgers, fries, and shakes pushed to the outer edges.

We'd already tackled the first few sections of The Raven when I found myself spaced out again, staring at Greyson's profile—for what felt like the hundredth time. But I couldn't help it. The way his brows furrowed in concentration and the way he absentmindedly licked his lips when writing something down in his notebook made it completely his fault I'd lost concentration so many times.

His face turned toward mine, half-smile, eyebrows raised. "Jess?"

"Hmm?"

He laughed, shaking his head and flipping his notebook shut. "I guess we should stop here. We did get a lot done already."

What? No! I didn't want to leave; I wasn't ready to leave yet.

Thankfully, it didn't seem like Greyson was in any rush to leave either. He slid his things into his backpack and turned toward me, crooked smile on full display. "Dessert?" he asked, pulling out the menu and silently reading over the options.

"Is that a serious question?" I scoffed playfully. "What the hell is this life without dessert? Nothing. The answer is nothing."

He whistled, eyebrows sky-high, playfully mocking me in return. "Wow. Jess takes her dessert seriously. Noted."

I laughed, nudging him with my elbow, and he nudged me back, and somehow, we ended up even closer to each other than we already had been. Our shoulders were now touching—our arms, our hips, our legs. The entire right side of my body tingled with awareness.

"Want to share something?" he asked.

"Okay," I replied, immediately embarrassed at how soft it had come out. Could he tell how affected I was, how desperate I was?

If he noticed, he didn't show it. "Hot fudge sundae?"

I nodded, not able to get the words past my lips without embarrassing myself again.

When our sundae came, we dug into it, falling into an easy conversation. I felt an ease with him I'd never felt before. It was unsettling—or more accurately, *scary as hell*—but also... comfortable, *warm*.

I told him about my love for art and photography, and he told me about his for football and music. He'd already joined the team at our school, but his real passion was music—*and yes*, I found out that he *did* sing, and I almost died at the thought of hearing his voice belt out the words he'd been writing in his notebook the other day.

Also? He played the drums and guitar, too. *Swoon.*

I tried my best not to stare at him as he took his last few bites of ice cream, but like much else in my life, it was a total failure. He dropped his spoon into the bowl, licked his lips, and relaxed back into the booth, turning his face toward mine.

"I've been meaning to ask," he started, his eyes narrowing just a bit. "Have you always lived here?"

I rubbed my hand along the base of my throat. A habit; a nervous tic. "No." It was like a security blanket, giving me the illusion that I felt choked by myself and not by the outside world. "I just moved here over the summer."

He nodded, looking as if he might have expected that answer. "Where from?"

I swallowed past the thickness quickly building in my throat. I swear I could almost feel the pressure of it sliding past my palm. "Washington."

He nodded again, tapping a beat against the table with his fingers, completely oblivious to the raging of my heart inside my ribcage. Oblivious to the anxiety slowly trickling its way through my body. But then again, I was pretty good at hiding these things. "That's pretty far. Why here, of all places?" he asked.

I didn't know why, but I forced the truth past my lips even though I could feel that familiar weight pressing down on my chest. It was a question I anticipated every time someone asked me where I moved from, but it wasn't one I had ever planned on actually answering until then. "My mom died last year, so...after that I didn't really have any choice but to move out here with my dad," I told him.

I didn't say the other words that were on the tip of my tongue, words that begged to be released.

That I'd hated my mom. That she'd been a drug addict with a rotating door of men who took advantage and stole from us, men who only ever pulled her deeper into her addictions, and who tended to pay more attention to her daughter than to her.

I didn't tell him that we'd been homeless more often than not. That I'd gone hungry too many times to count. That she'd been a mean, and miserable, and hateful person, or that she'd never really been a mom to me at all.

I didn't tell him that in many ways her death had felt like a relief.

He winced. "I'm sorry; that's shitty."

I nodded, shrugging. It was shitty, just not for the reasons he was thinking of. "What about you?" I deflected. That was enough about me. "You just moved here too, right?"

He shifted in his seat. "I was raised here, actually. My family and I just uh," he paused, almost too quick to notice, and cleared his throat, "we moved away for a little while, for some family stuff."

If I hadn't been so familiar with that kind of pain, I wouldn't have recognized it in him, but I did. His eyes had clouded over, infinitesimally, a little distant, some hidden pain showing itself momentarily before it was gone.

It knocked the breath straight from my lungs.

"You ready to go?" he quickly said, smiling as he slid his backpack over his shoulder.

I wanted to reach out and touch him, tell him I recognized his pain because I held it inside of myself, too. But I couldn't do it; I didn't do it, but I'd never wanted to tell somebody my truths more than I wanted Greyson to know them.

"Yeah, I'm ready," I replied.

That crooked smile of his grew brighter—light, happy. *How did he do that?* And then he grabbed my hand, and all of it, all of the heaviness, fell away.

And by the end of that day, I had learned three things about the boy I was going to marry someday:

One, he was smart as hell.

Two, he was charming as hell, too.

And three, he was hiding something dark inside of himself; he was just a lot better at hiding it than I was.

Eight *After*

"JESS?" HE STEPS closer, this grown-man version of who Greyson used to be. He's taller, older, wiser. There's no way I could actually know that just from looking at him, but somehow, I know it's true. This man in front of me knows things he didn't all those years ago, has lived things, seen things too, maybe.

And he is definitely, *definitely,* leaps and bounds sexier than I remember him being.

It's almost too overwhelming to handle—his familiar eyes, that same tilted smile, the angular line of his scruffy jaw, and above it all, the fact that he's even here, in *my* hometown, in *my* coffee shop.

I watch him, and he watches me, and neither of us says anything for far too long. I think it's because we're both in shock.

He looks good. *Really good.* So good it's almost too painful to look at him.

His hair is buzzed short on the sides, the top longer and thrown back in a perfect mess. It's no longer bleach-blond. Just dark. *Black, black, black.* His army-green tee perfectly fits the form of his sculpted arms and broad chest, and he's wearing these dark shit-kicker boots and ripped black jeans and is clenching and unclenching hands that have touched and healed and broken so many different parts of me.

Emotion lodges itself in my throat. I want to run out that door and launch myself into his arms all at the same time.

I don't miss the way he studies me as intently as I do him, a flood of emotions raging behind his eyes that match the ones playing in mine—fear, joy, excitement, regret.

"How are you?" he asks.

So, this is going to be the point where we start talking and using all of the words. Okay. I can do this. And because I'm an adult, and I'm Zen as fuck, I can totally, *totally* handle it. "I'm good. How are you?" See? Piece of cake. *Liar.*

"I'm good." He smiles, glancing down at the floor.

I duck down just a bit and catch his eyes. "You still smile the same way," I say softly. That was such a stupid, vulnerable thing to say. But I'll own it. Because he does. And I've missed that smile. So much more than I've allowed myself to believe.

He rubs the back of his neck, eyes intense. "Shit, Jess. It's so damn good to see you," he ends on an exhale. He's looking at me as if he's been searching for me every single day of the past eight years we've spent apart. Missing me as much as I've missed him.

And I'm sure that's what I'll be telling our kids someday, when I tell them the story of how we found each other again after all these years and fell madly in love—for the second time in a lifetime.

But that thought strikes me down as if I've been hit by a bolt of lightning, because: *What if he already has kids?*

In reality, I know next to nothing about this man standing in front of me. Not anymore. For all I know, he could already have a wife and kids. And a nanny and a dog and a white picket fence, and a big, giant house and a who the hell knows what else, but I can't stick around and find out. And his hands are in his pockets, so I can't see if he's wearing a wedding band on his finger. And I should have dug deeper when I saw him online, except that I couldn't bear to do it then either.

But that's okay. I take a deep breath. *It's okay.* Because I don't want to know. I don't want to know how much happier he is with his life without me in it.

My god, this was such a mistake. Standing here with him, soaking in every little detail and difference between the Greyson I used to know and this stranger in front of me, who doesn't feel anything like a stranger at all. Seeing his smile and letting it wash over me. Hearing his voice. The way it's changed and deepened after all of these years.

It's too much. It's all too much, and I can't do this.

I fumble with a hasty goodbye and make a quick exit, running the entire two blocks back to my house, iced mocha long forgotten. Tears stream down my face, my neck, my arms.

Such a mistake. A lapse in judgment that twists and churns inside my stomach with the pain of regret, with all of the mistakes I made back then, too.

Because that's the thing about mistakes. Some of them you learn from, and some of them you grow from, and some of them even make you a better human being in the end. But sometimes we spend our entire lives running from the ones we can never escape.

Nine *Before*

"HEY, YOU." GREYSON sat down beside me.

I'd been finishing up a drawing on the stairs outside of school, long after most people had already headed home for the day. I slid my pencil into my sketchbook and the book into my bag.

"Hey, Greyson." I forced my lips into a half-smile, pushing away everything that made me feel so heavy.

He thought something over for a few seconds and then turned to me, casually resting his hand over my knee. I say *casually*, because he didn't seem to have a second thought about it, but me? His touch seared straight through my black jeans, branding me. *MINE, MINE, MINE,* I wanted it to say.

"So, tell me what you think about this," he started confidently, squeezing my knee. "Lame, or totally badass pickup line?"

"O…kay," I replied, narrowing my eyes at him as I tried not to smile. What *was* it with him and making me smile? And how was I supposed to hear anything he was saying when his fingers had found the rip in my jeans at my knee? He was touching me, skin on skin, hand on leg, completely unaffected.

He cleared his throat, turning to me fully. "Are you a library book? Because I can't stop checking you out."

I shook my head, smiling. "Totally lame."

"Was that an earthquake? Or you did you just rock my world?" he continued.

"That one is even worse."

"You're like a Sharpie, super fine."

I scoffed in disapproval, even though that one was kind of funny. "No. *No.* Those are terrible!" I laughed, but the truth was, any one of those lines would've worked on me had he been seriously directing them my way. Because words, and his mouth, were a great match. It really didn't matter what he was saying, they just looked so good coming out.

And then I realized that he'd actually gotten me to laugh, despite the exceptionally crappy mood I had been in. Had he done that on purpose? The look on his face told me I might've been right. Like he'd achieved some kind of goal in making me smile. *God, he was perfect.* Too perfect.

"Alright, give me your phone number and we can try to come up with a great pickup line together," he said, completely serious even though there was a twinkle of mischief in his eyes.

"Ha! Smooth."

He bit his lip, holding his phone out to me.

I looked down at it and back up at him. Wait, he was serious? "You're serious?"

"Holy shit, man! Greyson!" Jaymes yelled as he walked right up to us.

No. *No, no, no.*

Not Jaymes. Not *now*.

Jaymes was…a friend of mine. To put it loosely. His eyes quickly darted between Greyson and me, questioning.

Greyson stood up, and he and Jaymes embraced in some sort of a man-hug-handshake thing. They both wore shit-eating grins, too. All while I flailed around inside my brain, trying to figure out exactly what the hell was happening.

"I heard you might be coming back! How the hell are you?" *Jaymes.*

"Good; I'm good, man." *Greyson.*

"Hell yeah. What are you up to tonight?" *Jaymes.*

A shrug. "Nothing much, still settling in." *Greyson.*

So, they knew each other, that much was obvious.

"No way; you're coming over tonight. Party at my place. We're celebrating. You down?"

Greyson's eyes darted to mine briefly. "Yeah, sure. Sounds good."

"Awesome! And I see you've already met my girl!" Jaymes curled his arm around my shoulders possessively.

Greyson's eyes fell on mine again, all traces of that perfect smile gone. I'd only known him a short time, but I knew the look of disappointment when I saw it.

I palmed Jaymes' face, gently shoving him away from me. "Not his girl," I clarified.

"Not yet." Jaymes smirked. "Still working on her; she's playing hard to get."

Greyson's eyes narrowed in confusion.

I rolled mine, desperately trying to bring humor to the situation where there was none. "Give it up, Jaymes. It's not happening, and you know it."

But the truth was, we kind of *were* more than friends, or less than friends—I didn't know. It was complicated. I'd never had to explain it before, or never *cared* to explain it before, but when I'd first moved here, Jaymes and his crazy group of friends had given me a distraction I needed from life. The drinking, the parties, the chaos, it all drew me in. I spent more nights at Jaymes' than I didn't. It helped me forget, for at least a little while, who I was, and all of the fucked-up bullshit that came along with it.

And while he could be an epic a-hole, and most nights I could hardly stand him, other nights he was my closest friend.

It's just the way it was with us.

When he was finished with his random hook-up of the night, he'd slip into his bed with me and we'd both fall asleep. And that was it. I never crossed that line with him. Not once. But I guess that's where the lines had blurred, because I knew he wanted more even though I didn't.

I didn't have it in me to want someone like that.

Not until Greyson came along, anyway.

Ten *Before*

"**YOU WERE SO** right about that one," Sara said as she pointed at Greyson from across Jaymes' living room. "He. Is... *Yum!*"

I slapped her arm down. "Don't point at him!" I whisper-yelled.

She laughed. "So, since you can't have him, can I?"

She was joking, but I still felt a pile of bricks drop into the pit of my stomach. "Don't even think about it," I grumbled.

She laughed louder. "Down, girl. I'm kidding. But what are you going to do about Jaymes? You know he probably already gave Greyson the whole 'don't even think about touching my girl' speech, right?"

I threw myself back into the seat cushion, groaning. Yes, I didn't doubt that he did. I swung my feet into her lap, pulling at the strands of her hair with my fingertips, and started braiding them. Her hair was bleached so blond it was almost white, the complete opposite of mine.

But we were opposites in a lot of ways. Our hair, our eyes, our height, our body types, the way we dressed, our general outlook on life. As soon as I turned eighteen, I was getting the hell away from this place, and this life, and never looking back, but she had more of the: *if you can't beat them, join them* attitude.

"I know we don't do the whole 'girl gossip, sharing feelings' thing," she said, "so I've never asked, but aren't you and Jaymes…?"

I scoffed. "What do you think? You're here every night too," I stated the obvious. If Jaymes and I were actually hooking up she would know it. *Wouldn't she?* But I guess I'd never really denied it before either, and the look on her face said that *no*, she didn't know. "We're just friends—"

"Who sleep together," she interrupted.

"Keyword being *sleep*, nothing more. Open your eyes. You see Jaymes, he screws around with everyone."

"Yeah, keyword being *screws.*"

I laughed halfheartedly. "Exactly. If I actually meant anything to him, he wouldn't be sleeping with a different girl every other night, so he's full of shit. We're just friends."

"Just friends," she repeated skeptically.

"Just. Friends," I reiterated.

"Fine." She sighed. "You know I believe you, but will Greyson?"

"Ugh. I don't know, but I need a drink."

"Yes! Brilliant idea." She hopped up, grabbed my hand, and pulled me off the couch and into her arms. "Operation Jessie and Greyson commences," she whispered in my ear, giggling. I guess she'd already started drinking without me, because Sara only giggled when she was drunk. She left the room and returned with an empty tequila bottle. "Who wants to play spin the bottle?!" she yelled, and people slowly began forming a circle in the middle of the living room.

But me? No thanks. She might've loved the attention—or lived for it, really—but I was much happier in my corner of: *if you don't smile or make eye contact with people, maybe they won't realize you exist.* And besides, if Greyson was ever going to kiss me, it was going to be because he wanted to. That much I was sure of. And I didn't want to stick around and watch everybody kissing each other, *especially* if it involved Greyson, so I went outside for some fresh air instead, grabbing a half-empty bottle of Jack on my way out.

I hit my favorite patch of grass in Jaymes' front yard, laid back against the uphill slope, and looked up at the sky. At all of the stars, and the full, bright moon.

There was something about the moon. The way it reminded me of the hope I sometimes clung to. A sliver of light in all that darkness.

Real deep, Jess.

I pressed the bottle of whiskey to my lips, swallowing back the burning amber liquid.

"Hey, Jess," Greyson's voice seeped into my skin, mixing itself with the whiskey. "Mind if I join you? Spin the bottle isn't really my thing."

"Is it anybody's thing?" I laughed.

He chuckled. "I honestly didn't think people still played it."

"Sara just likes to…make things interesting." I patted the grass, and he sat down beside me. His face came into view, and *damn*, but he looked even better in the moonlight. I held the bottle out to him.

"Nah, thanks. I don't drink."

"Like, ever?" I took another sip.

He shrugged. "Not really."

I wondered if he cared that I was drinking, if it was something that turned him off or not.

"So, I'm just gonna go ahead and ask…why didn't you tell me you had a boyfriend?" he asked.

I looked back up at the sky, sucking in a deep breath. "Because I don't."

"Jaymes says differently."

"Of course he does." I huffed. "Would it matter to you if I did have a boyfriend?" *Thank you, whiskey.*

He hesitated, taking a moment with whatever words were swirling through that pretty head of his. "I'm not sure."

"What's that supposed to mean?" I immediately replied, narrowing my eyes at him.

He took a deep breath, blowing it out slowly, and then shrugged again. "It means that it's pretty obvious I'm into you, but Jaymes already threatened to cut off my legs if I so much as thought about it." He laughed, but it wasn't funny. I wanted to run inside and punch Jaymes in the face. "There's something between you two I clearly know nothing about, and Jaymes is a really good friend of mine, so…" he left the words hanging, leaving me to fill in the blanks: *So, I can't have you. You can't be mine. I can't touch you. Whatever this could've been between us, ends here.*

And as much as I wanted to *kill* Jaymes, I couldn't help it…through the weight that had settled in my stomach, I smiled. "You're into me?" I asked.

Yep. That's what I had taken from all that. Because the more I thought about it, the more I wasn't too worried about the rest of it. I wanted one thing and one thing only, and there was no way in hell I was going to let Jaymes keep me from getting it.

Eleven *Before*

"HOLY MOTHER OF all things holy," Sara whispered, sighing dramatically. "Remind me again why we've never done this before?"

"I don't..." were the only words that got past my lips before I swallowed the rest of them whole, because there he was. Joining his teammates out on the football field. In full gear. Big, bulky, padded jersey, and those pants. Those pants that didn't hide much of anything. Not those muscled calves, or those toned thighs, or up higher, to his tight...

I swallowed thickly.

Arms. I was totally talking about his arms. I swear.

So...that's what Greyson looked like in uniform.

Okay. I could handle it. I could totally handle it.

I turned and buried my face into Sara's side. "*Oh. My. God*," I groaned. Whined. Maybe cried a little.

"Singing to the choir, girl. Singing to the choir!" She stood up, pulling me with her. "This is going to be so much fun! Let's go. Hurry up. Hurry!"

We nearly tripped over ourselves getting down the empty bleachers, cameras in hand. We were working on a photography project: *"Life in Action,"* and Sara had called dibs on the football team. I didn't think I'd ever been more thankful for something in my life.

Okay, okay. Get it together, I told myself as we reached the sideline. Sara crouched down and immediately started taking some photos. It took me a little longer to snap into action, my eyes still glued to the team—okay, on Greyson—lining up on the thirty-yard line. Because seriously? How the hell was I supposed to take a decent photo when Greyson was standing in front of me dressed like that?

But somehow, eventually—by some miracle—I managed.

I focused on the team, the way they moved out on the field, practiced and synchronized like a dance routine. I focused on my camera, on the snap of the shutter and on timing a shot just right.

A player leaped into the air to complete a catch. *Snap.* Tumbled to the ground. *Snap.* Fumbled the ball. *Snap.*

His hand reached out for it, straining, his fingers finally grasping the ball in a desperate grip. *Snap.*

It was easy to lose myself this way. In the quiet and stillness that came with watching life through the lens. I'm not even sure how much time must have passed by, but before I knew it Coach Anderson had blown the whistle, players halting in their tracks.

Greyson slid his helmet off. *Snap.*

Shook out his hair. *Snap.*

Squeezed water into his mouth. *Snap.*

Water spilled from his mouth and trailed all the way down his chin and neck. *Snap, snap, snap.*

He looked over at me then, a slow smile forming on his lips.

The way I saw it, I had one of two options: One, I could pretend I hadn't had my camera zeroed in on him for the past few minutes and completely ignore that knowing smirk of his. Or two, I could keep my camera steady, and capture everything about him that made my insides feel like a swarm of butterflies had just come to life and were fluttering their giddy wings against every cell of my body.

So, I did what I had to do; I went with option two, taking pictures of him the entire time he was walking toward me.

"Hey, Jess. What are you guys doing out here?" He was out of breath, his voice raspy and strained. It forced a hundred different images through my mind, a hundred alternate scenarios for why his voice would sound that way.

And then I was blushing. *Great. Awesome. You don't* do *blushing, Jess. Try to remember that!* I mashed my lips together, twisting around in search of Sara. She was sitting on the bleachers, already scrolling through her camera roll.

I turned back toward Greyson, held my camera up. "Just taking pictures," I answered. *Good one, Captain Dumbass.*

He laughed. "I can see that. But what for?"

"Photography project."

"Ah, that's right." He nodded. "Get any good ones?"

"Yep." I smiled; we both smiled, skirting the obvious. The fact that he'd just caught me taking at least a dozen pictures of him. I guess he wasn't going to call me on it, and I think I might've fallen for him a little harder then.

"Well, I have to head into locker now," he said, gripping the back of his neck in one hand and his helmet in the other. "See ya around, Jess."

"See ya, Grey." My eyes didn't leave him as he walked away. Not until his tall, lean, muscled form disappeared around the corner of the locker building.

I sighed.

Sara bumped into the back of me, snickering. "Could you be any more obvious?"

"Shut up."

"Well! What did he say?"

"Nothing really." I shrugged.

"Oh, come on! I saw the way you two were looking at each other. If he said something juicy, you better spill."

"Something juicy?" I laughed. "I wish." Only in my dreams. Only when the thoughts that had been running through my mind just before falling asleep bled into my unconsciousness. Only *then* did Greyson say things like *"I want you,"* and *"I'm yours,"* and *"I'm going to kiss you now."* "He was just asking what we were doing taking pictures out here, and…that's pretty much the gist of it," I finished.

"Lame." She scoffed, rolling her eyes.

"Totally lame."

And it hit me then, with the subtlety of a freaking freight train, that something had been noticeably different between Greyson and me just before—when we'd been talking. Something was off, skewed. Unlike our usual interactions.

The way he hadn't touched me, not once. The way his smiles had been genuine, but hesitant, if not a little distant. The way he hadn't flirted at all, aside from that single knowing smirk he'd thrown my way. And the way he'd just casually said, *"See ya around, Jess,"* like he could wait a day, a week, a month before seeing me again. Like it didn't matter to him at all when that would ever actually happen.

Was I being dramatic? Probably. But the absence of all these things made me feel inexplicably hollow inside. Because I realized then, that those silent words that had filled the space between Greyson and me the night of the party…he'd obviously meant them.

Twelve *Before*

AND THAT'S HOW the next few weeks went.
Me: desperately flirting.
Him: brushing it off like it was nothing.
And maybe that's because I totally sucked at flirting. At best, he probably had no clue I was attempting to at all. At worst…he probably thought I'd been incubated all sixteen years of my life and had only just discovered what the outside world was like: *Ooh. Boy. Me like.*

Whatever the case, he was too good at appearing oblivious. Or actually *being* oblivious. But I refused to believe that was the truth.

We'd worked on our poetry assignment over those few weeks, too. Last we left off, we were trying to figure out how to combine our interpretations of it into one cohesive presentation because our takes on it were night and day. Mine was one of loss and turmoil; his was one of devotion and remembrance. It made sense, though. That he'd be able to find the positive in it. He was light—a happy, glass-half-full kind of person. And I was…well, I was me.

I spent a lot more time with Greyson than I'd expected to, though, outside of our assignment. In first period, at lunch, in the hallways between classes, at Jaymes' parties. We always seemed to find each other on that same slope of grass, talking under those stars for what felt like forever. I wasn't just infatuated with him anymore—no, I actually *liked* him. Like, as a human. His personality, his likes and dislikes, his positivity, his humor. I really, *really* liked him.

But again…he seemed oblivious. Everything between us was completely platonic. Utterly and tragically and disgustingly platonic.

Ugh.

Except for those soul-reaching smiles of his. He couldn't help those.

But tonight was going to be different. We'd talked so much by this point that I was pretty damn sure I could finally make a move without being entirely rejected. Because Greyson's actions might've said one thing, but I swear the way he sometimes looked at me spelled out something completely different.

He wanted me too, I was sure of it.

Wasn't I?

Yes. Yes, I was.

Right? Right. *Right?* Hell, I didn't know, but I knew I had to go for it. I knew I would forever regret it if I didn't. And what was the worst that could happen?

A lot. A whole fucking lot.

I was pulled from my thoughts when my dad walked into the kitchen. One thing that had definitely changed since that first night with Greyson at Jaymes' party was that I was now sleeping in my own bed, at my own house. The closest thing to it, anyway. I didn't want to keep giving Jaymes the wrong idea—or, if I was being totally honest with myself, I didn't want to keep giving Greyson another reason to stay away from me.

My dad and I didn't say anything to each other as he strode across the open space, quietly pouring himself a mug of coffee. It wasn't unusual, the silence. After my first few days of living here, and the complete lack of communication on my end, he and his wife seemed to be content in leaving me be. I couldn't tell if they were just super observant and giving me the space I needed, or if they actually just didn't give a shit. Either way was fine by me.

His wife swept into the room then. A tornado of chaos. Two screaming babies strapped to her body like a suit of armor, a diaper-bag of weapons haphazardly slung over her shoulder, a bottle in one hand and a shoe in another as she hobbled across the kitchen trying to get it on her foot.

Dad held her steady. I kept eating my cereal, more intrigued by their interaction than normal. I didn't know why, but I had the sudden urge to grab my camera and snap a shot of it.

So, I did.

All eyes in the room landed on mine. All eight of them if I was counting. I quickly stuffed the camera into my bag, barely catching the sad smile on my dad's wife's face before she smoothed it away. It wasn't the first time I'd noticed her holding something back. So maybe she did care.

And maybe I was the asshole.

She wasn't the one who'd done anything wrong, after all. Wasn't the one who'd abandoned me before I was even born and wasn't the one who hadn't cared to ever call or write or visit. She wasn't the one forced to play dad with her own child when my mom died.

But I'd been down one road with one mother. I didn't want to go down this one with another. *One year.* Thirteen months, and I'd be eighteen and out of here. They'd forget all about me and go back to life as usual. I couldn't wait, and I was sure they couldn't either.

My dad turned toward her, planting a kiss square on her mouth, brushing off the whole strange encounter. "Super-mom, ready for battle," he said, chuckling, and it immediately irritated me. He and I were nothing alike; we weren't supposed to share the same thoughts.

I stood from my stool at the bar-top, quickly sliding my backpack over my shoulder.

"School?" he asked, as if it weren't where I was obviously headed. I didn't answer him. "Why don't you take your car, sweetie?" he added quietly.

My whole body tensed, clenching with unreleased anger. I'd spoken an entire five sentences to him in the past few months, and he was calling me *sweetie?* I wanted to scream, but I answered with a *"No thanks,"* through gritted teeth instead. I didn't want anything more from him than I needed. A bed to sleep in, clothes on my back, food in my stomach. I'd figure the rest out on my own. And he sure as hell didn't care before, when I'd been living with a deadbeat, drug addict of a mother, so why the hell did he care now?

I slammed the front door closed behind me, wishing I could fast forward time. To tonight. Next year. Ten years from now. But I'd settle for the next few hours. *Just get me to that party.*

Instead, the day seemed to go by in slow-mo, mocking me with a middle finger raised to my face. But eventually, after for-*fudging*-ever, I landed myself on that same couch, with my same best friend, drooling over the pictures we'd taken over the last few weeks. I'd brought my favorite one for Greyson. The one of him chugging down his water at football practice. The one where half of it was sliding down his chin and neck. The same one that I may or may not have had hanging in my room since the day after I took it.

I wasn't a complete psycho, though. It was only one of a few dozen other black and whites that were pinned to my wall. That were *not* of Greyson, thank you very much.

Sara noticed me finger-petting the image of him in my lap. "He's still playing hard to get, huh?" she asked.

I made some sort of indecipherable noise. A snort, a grunt; I didn't know. It only made her laugh, before saying under her breath, "Speak of the devil."

I looked up, only to find Greyson sauntering into the room like a *goddamn* model straight out of GQ. Honestly, it wasn't fair for someone to look that good. He was wearing some new black chucks, dark jeans, and a plain white shirt, so really, it didn't even make sense, the effect he had on me. *How the hell was I supposed to make a move when he looked like that?* But I had to face it, he kind of always looked like that. Without even trying. I wasn't sure he even knew how good-looking he was.

Our eyes met from across the room, and he threw one of those tilted smiles my way before heading into the kitchen with Jaymes and the guys.

And that was my cue. I was going to go outside and wait for him on the grass, and when he met me out there like he always seemed to, I was going to suck it up and make my move. No matter how scared shitless I kind-of-sort-of felt about it.

I was outside for maybe five minutes before I felt him sitting down beside me. My eyes were closed, my back pressed against the grass. Two shots in and the devil on my shoulder was screaming at me to not back out, while the angel on the other was reminding me of the thousand and one ways we were about to embarrass ourselves.

"Hey, Jess," Greyson said, the smoothness of his voice slipping beneath the surface of my skin the way it always did.

I could feel the weight of his gaze on me. It settled over me like a warm blanket, and I lingered there, in that moment, believing that maybe he did want me as much as I wanted him.

"Hey, Grey," I eventually said. I opened my eyes to him, and I was right. His eyes were already on mine. Communicating something that definitely didn't equal just friendship.

So, I went for it. "Listen, Greyson. I can't keep pretending I don't like you. Like, *really, stupidly* like you, so...are you actually oblivious to my ridiculous attempts at flirting with you, or have you really not noticed me making an ass out of myself?"

The corner of his mouth hitched up the tiniest bit. So, he hadn't been oblivious, that much was obvious. "Listen, Jess," he turned the tables on me. "I've already told you I'm into you, but I can't give you anything more than friendship right now."

"*Right now*?" I latched onto those words mischievously.

"Jess," he warned, a little exasperated. But if his smile had anything to say about it, he was also kind of amused. "Friends. That's all we can be."

"But *why*," I whined.

"Because Jaymes—"

"When are you going to get that Jaymes and I aren't together?" I interrupted. I was so sick of Jaymes and his stupid claim on me.

"He says he loves you," he offered.

"Ha!" I laughed. "Is that a joke?" But his face said that it wasn't. "Okay. Wow. That's ridiculous. You see that, right? What he does every night? With all those girls? I don't know much about love, but that...that is *not* it."

His eyes lingered on mine, hanging on my last words. I could see the way he was turning them over in his mind, deciding what they meant. To him. To me.

"And what about me? What about how I feel?" I pushed.

He took a deep breath, quickly releasing it. There were words on the tip of his tongue. Words I could tell he was holding back. "I still can't do that to him, Jess," he said instead, forcing an alternate set of them forward. "And like I said before—Jaymes is a really good friend of mine, and I owe him a hell of a lot better than that. I couldn't do that to him, genuine feelings for you or not. So again, friends are all we can be. Take it or leave it, I guess."

I'd be lying if I said his offer didn't crush me. Just a little. "That's not fair," I said quietly.

"Life isn't fair." He shrugged.

And touché. Because didn't I know a thing or two about that.

Thirteen *After*

THE THING WAS, I had felt so numb for so long, that Greyson was the first person to come into my life and make me feel something. To make me feel anything at all. And only five minutes into seeing him, after all of these years, it feels like he's done it all over again.

The aftermath is still lingering days later. I can't shake it. Can't shake seeing him again.

What was he doing here?

Does he live here?

Is he here on press tour? Does he have a show in town? Will I run into him time and time again, or was it a single, fleeting moment I'll never get back?

Did seeing me affect him as much as it affected me?

The need to know all of these answers has become borderline obsessive. Along with the need to self-analyze those last few moments I spent face to face with him—over, and over, and over again.

Why did I have to run off like a total spaz? Why couldn't I have kept it together long enough to hear the answers I needed and go home and completely lose my shit in my own space, on my own time?

I hate that I had fooled myself into thinking I was okay. That I thought I had accepted the course my life had taken. A personal sacrifice made and experienced for the sake of self-growth and art.

I was wrong. Because these feelings, these long-forgotten *fucking feelings* he managed to dig up in a matter of minutes, won't go away. *They won't. Go. Away.*

But if I'm being completely honest with myself, I'm not sure they ever have. I've just gotten used to spilling them onto the canvas. To twisting every memory, and experience, and regret into my craft so I don't have to deal with them on any level beyond that. Because if I avoid the thoughts, and pour them into pictures and paint instead, they can't haunt me, right?

I had honestly thought so. For a long time, I had really, *really* thought so. *God, I'm such an idiot.*

I take a deep breath and shake off the burning thoughts, focusing instead on the paper in front of me. Because if there's one positive in all of this, a yin to the yang, it's that I now know exactly what was missing—from the painting.

The heart. That's the part that needs to be real. It is the bleeding, feeling, life-pounding epicenter of it all, isn't it? The beginning and ending of everything.

As soon as the idea clicked, hours post-Greyson run-in, I ordered one of those anatomically correct hearts online, along with a packet of fake blood—because apparently, you can order fucking anything online now—and receive them in less than forty-eight hours.

I heard that package hit the floor of my front porch this afternoon and was up faster than a teenager on prom night.

Pretty sure I scared the living shit out of my mailman.

I pull the image of a bloody heart from the tray in front of me and plunge it into the rinse tub, clipping it on the line above me to dry when I'm finished. I step back and observe it, inexplicably relieved at the perfection of it. But it is perfect, and it'll fit into the painting effortlessly.

It's what sets me apart, I think. These snippets of reality pieced into my paintings. A mash-up of reality and fiction. A portrayal of what I know to be real and what feels like never was.

This one will be the last piece for an art opening I have this weekend—in the heart of the city. It won't be my first art show, but that doesn't make me any less nervous. If anything, I think I become more and more anxious with each one. In part, I think, because I put a little more of myself into these pieces each time. Ripping away a chunk of the darkness and leaving it behind on every painting until it was almost gone.

At least that's what I had thought. Until I saw Greyson again. And now I don't know anything. Up from down, left from right, day from night. Because call me crazy, but I just can't shake this feeling that seeing him again has changed everything. That my life—my hopes, my dreams, my fate—has all been turned upside down. Like all of it has been picked up and flipped on its motherfucking axis, and I'm not sure how to cope.

Fourteen *Before*

SOMETHING I HAD noticed about Greyson pretty quickly, was that he made me laugh. A hell of a lot more than I was used to. And it was the real kind of laughter, too. The kind that plants a tiny seed of light inside your soul and lingers there for a while. It was just so easy for him, so effortless, to dig through the muck and climb right up and over my walls and casually take a seat next to my heart as if it were no big deal.

And the funny thing is, I didn't even notice it at first—how happy I was around him. I just knew that I was drawn to him, that there was nothing in this world I'd ever liked more than the way I felt when I was with him.

It's how I'd managed to keep my attraction to him to myself since the night he'd drawn the friendship line in the theoretical sand between us. Because surprisingly enough, whatever it was that we did have, it wasn't worth losing because of how badly I wanted him.

I kept reminding myself of this as I watched him worrying his lip between his teeth.

He sat across from me, leaning forward with his elbows on his knees, his eyes glued to the notebook sitting on the table between us. We were in the library working on our poetry assignment, and I was having the hardest time keeping my eyes off of his—well, everything. But especially his mouth. *A mouth I was going to draw the shit out of later.* I could've filled an entire sketchbook with those lips alone, really.

He had no clue, though, seeing as how he was the only one of us two actually focused on the assignment in front of us.

"This is shit, isn't it?" he asked suddenly, looking up from his notebook.

I shrugged. "I mean, yeah, sort of. But like, unicorn shit. All pretty and glittery on the outside, but when you get down to it...it's still shit."

He laughed, and *my god,* the way he laughed. Deep, and throaty, and genuine. I wanted to swallow it up and keep it as my own.

It kind of felt like mine, though. Because he had laughed at *me*, at what I'd said, and he hadn't once taken his eyes off of me the entire time. He still hadn't. And as his green eyes penetrated mine, I couldn't think of a single reason why I shouldn't try to kiss him.

His laugh drifted into a sigh as he leaned back in his chair, running his hand through his hair, effectively pulling me away from that thought. "We're never going to finish this," he said.

I didn't tell him I was totally okay with that, that I liked the time it forced us to spend together—alone. I shrugged instead, saying, "Our views on it don't exactly mesh well, but we'll figure it out. Eventually."

We both smiled at that, our eyes drawn to each other's as we waded into a comfortable silence, and I saw something brewing in his stare that I didn't recognize. That familiar fluttering began making its way through my body, starting at the core of my stomach. These looks of his were going to kill me. Everyone had a breaking point, and I was way too close to mine.

As if he sensed it, he broke the contact, looking down at his things. "Can I take you somewhere?" he asked, tossing his stuff into his backpack.

Fucking duh, I almost said, but managed a slightly saner, "Sure."

"Cool. I just need to stop by my house to grab something really quick."

"Sounds good." I was pretty sure I'd made a decent enough attempt at seeming calm and collected on the outside, but on the inside? I was screaming in excitement while simultaneously waving sparklers and doing cartwheels through the neighborhood of my mind.

Because...*Greyson's house!*

I was going to see where Greyson lived. Maybe see where he slept. Maybe steal something of his that smelled like him to cuddle with at night.

Nope. Rewind. That was creepy, Jess.

We gathered our things, walked out to the parking lot, and hopped inside his car. Excuse me, hopped inside of *Lady*.

Was it weird to be jealous of a car? Probably. But I wasn't jealous because I wanted to drive a car like her, even though that was a thought, too. I was jealous because I wanted to hold the spot in Greyson's life that Lady did. The slot of *his girl,* which it was clear Lady was.

We peeled out of the parking lot, and Greyson threw his arm up to rest on the center console, pressing it fully against the length of mine. I was sure he'd move it, but he never did, only sliding away for brief intervals to shift gears before bringing it back.

When I finally managed to look up at him, there was a sly smirk on his face. So, he was doing it on purpose. If he wasn't careful, I was going to fling myself across his car and kiss that smirk right off his mouth. He seemed to register that thought as soon as it drifted through my mind and moved away, but not without shaking his head and smiling while doing so.

It was only then that I realized the direction we were heading in. And the farther we drove, the more I was sure Greyson was playing some sort of joke on me. We were getting closer and closer to my dad's house on the opposite side of town. Had he figured out where I lived, and this was some twisted way of throwing it in my face?

I was well aware of the difference between mine and my friends' living situations. But I didn't consider any of it mine. I was like them. Used to the barely scraping by, welfare check to welfare check kind of life. It was why I'd never told any of my friends the truth. But I was starting to think I'd been found out, until Greyson pulled into a long driveway five estates down from my dad's.

Turned out, Greyson lived right down the street from me.

Turned out, his family was just as rich as mine.

Fifteen *Before*

"**NOBODY'S HOME, IF** you want to come in for a sec."

I stared at him like an idiot. But was it just me, or did that sentence have layered meaning? Clearly, I wanted it to have layered meaning, but the sincerity of his expression told me it was all in my head.

I cleared my throat. "Um, sure, yeah, sounds good."

And then he got the door for me. It shouldn't have been a big deal, but he hadn't done that since I'd stupidly become "off-limits" in his mind. And I was probably reading too much into every little thing he was doing, but it sort of felt like things were shifting. Sliding back to the way they were before.

It was confusing; he was confusing.

Or maybe it was just me and my hormones desperately wanting to make something out of nothing.

We quietly made our way up the long pathway and few short sets of stairs that led to his front doors. I didn't know why my heart was pounding so hard. But I could feel it in my throat, and in the tips of my fingers. *This doesn't mean anything. We're just grabbing something from his house real quick. Get it together.*

But when we stepped inside his house, I just sort of…froze.

Because his house was insane.

Black and white on white and black; and marbled floors; and sparkling, ornate glass fixtures; and all these smooth, sharp, geometric lines; and a huge, open space that directed my attention straight to the floor to ceiling windows lining the entire back wall of his house, showcasing a gigantic pool as big as a freaking lake—that overlooked green hills and an actual lake down below.

I'd thought my dad had money. This was on a whole other level.

"Jess?" Greyson was stopped halfway up his dramatically curved staircase.

"Sorry." I moved my feet, belatedly following him. "Your house is stupid beautiful," I admitted.

"Thanks," he replied with a forced smile, seemingly out of habit—an automatic response. *Interesting.* I took note and quickly filed it away.

As I made my way up the stairs, my eyes were drawn to the picture frames that lined the walls of his staircase. Professionally taken black and whites of France, Italy, Greece, Morocco, Brazil…

"Does Jaymes know you live here?" I wondered out loud. I was surprised Jaymes wouldn't have given him shit for it—or have said anything about it at all. The fact that he even liked Greyson in spite of it was kind of a shock in itself.

He laughed. "Yeah, he knows." And I could tell he knew exactly why I'd asked.

We reached the top of the stairs, and my heart was still pounding away. I couldn't help it. But weirder than that, I felt kind of hollow all of a sudden. A dark, heavy pit sitting at the bottom of my stomach. Because I was here, in Greyson's house, and it felt like it should mean something, except that it didn't. It didn't mean anything at all.

There was no buzz of anticipation. He wasn't holding my hand and sharing secret looks with me. I wasn't here because his parents weren't home and he wanted to sneak me into his room and have his way with me. He wasn't going to lead me into his bedroom and push me onto his bed, and he wasn't going to climb on top of me and kiss me speechless.

But I wanted that. I wanted it desperately. And it killed me that he didn't.

Because it was clear to me then, that these desperate feelings of mine were completely one-sided.

I hated it. Hated the constant underlying feeling that I was all alone in this world. Stranded on an island with my SOS drawn in the sand and no one there to rescue me.

I was still working on that part: rescuing myself.

Sixteen *Before*

WHEN WE WALKED into his bedroom, it took about one-point-two seconds for my attention to be completely diverted elsewhere, because on his wall, up above his bed, was an original black and white painting—by the *freaking Ace*.

"Shut. Up!" Excitement had effectively flowed into all the melancholy spaces of my heart.

"I didn't say anything," Greyson chuckled, drawing out his words in confusion.

I'm not sure I even registered what he said before barreling on. "No. Way. No way!" I spun around on him.

Again, with the confusion on his end.

I pointed at the painting. "You have *an Ace Painting?!*"

"A who?" he quietly laughed again. If I wasn't so excited, I might've stopped to admire the way his eyes were shining with amusement—at me. But again, the painting!

"Aramis Clair-Edouard? I love him—love his pieces. Like, obsessed, and now I'm secretly contemplating knocking you over the head with something so I can steal it and run far, far away. Would totally be worth the jail time," I finished that last sentence under my breath, which only made him smile wider.

"You really love art, don't you?" he asked sincerely, his eyes contemplative, maybe even finding these little bits and pieces of me interesting.

"I do." I sighed, sitting down on the edge of his bed. I really did. I loved the way art said different things to everyone. Loved the way a hundred different people could look at one painting, or photograph, or drawing and see completely different things, could walk away from it with a hundred different emotions, and feelings, and ideas.

I loved the way there was an infinite amount of ways you could express yourself through it.

I told him all of this, and he seemed to really take it in, visibly sifting through all of my words. Time sort of stood still then, with me on his bed and him standing in front of the painting, both of us simply staring at it for a long while. My eyes swept over the chaos of lines, and squiggles, and pictures within pictures that formed the whole painting before us.

"I guess I never thought of it like that before," he eventually said, turning to face me. "I assumed a painting was a painting and we all saw what was obviously there. But you're absolutely right." He sat down next to me, the bed dipping down with his weight, forcing me closer. "It's like music. There are lyrics, and everyone hears the same ones, but it doesn't mean they hear them the same way, you know?"

He turned to face me, and I instantly got lost, trapped in his gaze. I was such an idiot. We'd gotten way too close. It wasn't safe here. Where I was so close, I could see every little speck of green that made up Greyson's perfect pair of eyes. Close enough that I could accurately imagine the way the scratch of his cheek would feel against my palm, and so close that I could reach up and fist his black shirt in my hand and pull him in a few inches and press my lips to his.

I forced a breath in and out of my lungs. And another. "Totally," I said, mildly breathless. It was a decent enough attempt.

He smiled, his tongue sliding out momentarily to wet his lips.

"I think all art is like that," I continued, eyes glued to his mouth. "In all its forms."

When I looked back up at Greyson's eyes, I found that his gaze had been drawn to *my* mouth, but he quickly cleared his throat, standing from the bed and gripping the back of his neck with both hands. "Couldn't agree more," he said, his voice rough.

It was like an arrow shot straight to my core. *Kiss him, kiss him, kiss him!* it screamed.

No. No way, I shook off the thought. He'd have to make that move. If we kissed, I wanted to know with one-hundred percent certainty it was exactly what he wanted. He already knew I liked him; I didn't need to make a bigger ass out of myself.

So even though he was doing it again, looking at me with unspoken words that said anything but friendship, nothing happened. He didn't pull me into him, and he didn't kiss me.

Instead, he pulled a guitar to his chest.

"So..." he started. "There's an open mic tonight."

It took a few beats for it to click. "And you're going to play?" I said, treading cautiously. *Was this really happening?*

"I was thinking I might have enough balls to go up and sing this time." He looked down at his guitar, taking a single pass over the strings with his thumb.

Breath in. Breath out. *Totally calm.* "And I get to come watch?"

"Well, yeah." He chuckled, amused. "That was the plan."

"And um, will anyone else be there?" I feigned nonchalance.

"Next time, maybe." He set his guitar back down in its case, sliding his hands into his pockets. "But I think it'll be too much pressure to have everyone there tonight. So I'm hoping that one friend—that's you," he flashed his tilted smile at me, "will be enough pressure to force me up there. And once I know I'm not a complete chickenshit, I'll invite the guys.

"...And I might also be putting off the fact that I work at pub, because then I'll never hear the end of, *'Steal the booze!'* And *'Get us free food, Greyce!'*"

I laughed at that. "Oh, for sure." Totally made sense. Jaymes and the guys would hop on that train so quick. Sara, too. But wait... "So, you've never done this before? Singing in front of people?"

"Nah." He said it like it didn't mean anything, but this was a huge, HUGE fucking deal. "So you cool with coming?"

I smiled at him, biting down on my bottom lip, almost speechless. *Almost.* "Am I okay with it?" I asked, floored. "Hell yes, I'm okay with it! This is badass, Greyson!" I couldn't contain my excitement any longer, because *holy shit!* I was going to hear Greyson sing.

And he wanted me to hear him sing.

In a room full of people.

For the first time. Ever.

Holy. Freaking.

Shit.

Seventeen *Before*

IT WAS A small place. Dark. Simple. Dirty wooden floors, and a long, sticky bar. But it was filled with people—drinking and laughing and having the time of their lives. At least that's what the alcohol was clearly telling them.

Greyson and I were sitting at a small table in the back corner. We'd been there for at least thirty minutes at this point, and his knee was still bouncing relentlessly. I couldn't help but smile. It was fascinating, this side of Greyson: Nervous, vulnerable.

He was tapping a beat against the table with his hands when I slid one of mine over one of his, stilling it. "You're going to do great, you know."

He chuckled, looking down at me. "You have no way of knowing that, but thank you."

I went to pull my hand away, but he flipped his over, wrapping his fingers firmly around mine, holding my hand hostage in his. Except I was a willing participant, and his hand felt more like the warmth and comfort of a womb than a prison with the way it soothed me.

And maybe it comforted him too, because his knee wasn't bouncing as much, and his chest seemed to be expanding and contracting a little easier than it had been before.

My eyes trailed up his chest, up his throat and over his mouth he was biting down on, and landed on his eyes. He smirked, somehow knowing I'd been staring at him even though he was looking straight ahead at the woman on stage reciting a poem she'd written.

What was he thinking about right now? This very second? With his hand wrapped around mine?

Probably nothing like what was going through my mind: That I could go the rest of my life without ever letting go.

I looked back down at our hands just as his thumb made a quick pass over my knuckles. Quick enough to draw zero conclusions from, but that's exactly what I was doing. Drawing conclusions. *Why was he still holding my hand?* Because he *did* want me. He'd probably turn toward me in about two seconds and pull my face into his hands and then *finally. Freaking. Kiss* me, and then he'd most likely put all of his babies inside of me, right here in the middle of this bar.

I laughed at myself, and then proceeded to purposely bang my forehead down onto the table, effectively smacking some sense back in there while I was at it.

Greyson's grip on my hand tightened, and I peeked up at him to see that he was laughing too, his eyes still on the stage. And then he pulled my hand closer to himself. Caging it against his chest.

I swallowed thickly, my pulse quickening. It was a little hard to breathe, there against the table. But I didn't want to move. Didn't want to break whatever spell I'd managed to cast on Greyson, because this wasn't like him. This wasn't like anything, *anything,* I'd ever felt before.

Like I mattered. Like I was important to someone. Because for at least that small sliver of time, my presence calmed him like his calmed me. There was no question about it; I could feel it deep down in my bones.

Another few minutes passed before he tore his gaze away from the stage and looked down at me. "Wish me luck," he said, squeezing my hand once before standing up and grabbing his guitar.

"Good luck!" I shouted at his retreating back, shaking off the weight of the last few minutes. I threw in a few shouts of encouragement for good measure. I was definitely the loudest and most obnoxious person in the room, but I didn't care. I couldn't hold my excitement back; I didn't want to.

He climbed on stage with a smile and an excited glint in his eyes, sat on the stool front and center, and pulled his guitar into his lap.

I hadn't realized I was holding my breath until his fingers made those first few passes over his guitar strings, the sound of it weaving through the room. My breath came out in a relieved rush. He was going to rock this shit so hard it wasn't even funny. But the very next breath I took got stuck in my throat, because he'd started singing into the microphone.

I might've died then. Before coming back to life and falling for him all over again.

His voice was soft yet gruff. Gravelly, yet smooth. A complete contradiction of highs and lows and strength and subtlety that reached inside my chest and wrapped its claws around my heart, squeezing with a level of desperation I'd never felt before.

He looked down at his guitar most of the time, but every once in a while, he'd search for me in the dark and smile through his words when he found me. I'd like to say that I remembered every single word he sung that night, locking them safely inside a little treasure box buried within my brain, but I was so lost in his voice, so lost in the moments his eyes would seek mine, that I only really caught half of them.

I'd build a house out of stars, a past full of scars.
Rewrite my name, take all of the blame.
If you'd come back again, back again, back again.

He finished his song, and the crowd went crazy. Clapping, and hollering, and drunken, slurred words of approval. I, on the other hand, was in complete and total awe. My mouth might've been hanging open. Just a little. He smiled shyly—the first of its kind I'd ever witnessed from him—and made his way off stage. When his eyes found mine, that shy smile grew bigger, brighter, more at ease. He strode straight toward me and didn't stop until he was right in front of me. Not nearly enough time to process any of this before he picked me up in a tight hug, squeezing every ounce of air from my lungs.

His arms.

Around me.

Firm, and strong, and unwavering.

His face was buried in my neck, and I felt him inhale a deep breath. He didn't say anything, not a single word. And he didn't let me go. My heart was pounding out of my chest, echoing throughout my entire body. I closed my eyes and relaxed into his embrace.

"That was..." he said, trailing off, inhaling and exhaling into my hair again.

"Fucking amazing," I finished for him. There were no other words for it. He was absolutely amazing.

"Yes, that." He laughed, slowly sliding me down his body to land on my feet. Except he didn't pull away, and I didn't step away either. So there we stood. Toe to toe, chest to chest. I looked up at him, and we both seemed to be forcing air into our lungs at the same time.

"Thank you," he said quietly, the breath of his words falling over my face.

"For what? I should be the one thanking you. I just witnessed the first-ever performance of the one-day, mega-famous *Greyson Hayes*... Will you sign my face?"

He burst out in laughter. We were so close that I could feel the vibration of it tickling my skin. But I was selfish. I wanted more than that. I wanted to feel the weight of it against my body when he held me close. I wanted to feel the breath of it against my lips as he kissed me. There were an infinite amount of reasons and ways for him to laugh, and I wanted to own them all.

We were still standing only inches away, and not for the first time that night. But this time he was definitely looking at me like he wanted to kiss me. And I know for a fact that the way I *needed* him to kiss me was written clear across my face.

For a second there, I was absolutely sure he would.

Until he didn't.

He cleared his throat and stepped away. "I can get you a free dessert," he said, eyebrow raised. "Chocolate lava cake?"

I forced a smile. "Sure."

I guess if I was being honest with myself, chocolate *would* come second to a kiss from Greyson. If Greyson were the waves of an ocean and chocolate was the deepest, darkest depths of it.

Eighteen *Before*

HIS EYES. HIS eyes, his eyes, his eyes. It was those damn green anchors of Greyson's that were going to be the eventual death of me. They kept landing on mine from across Jaymes' living room.

We were playing a phenomenal game of pretend.

Pretending we didn't share something that special earlier.

Pretending I wasn't the first person he'd ever wanted to hear him sing on stage.

Pretending we hadn't been *that* close to kissing.

Pretending, pretending, pretending.

I was great at pretending. But I felt like I was going to burst.

Did he like me, or didn't he? No, strike that. I wasn't an idiot. He liked me, at least a little bit. It was just that *a little bit* wasn't enough for him to risk burning his bridges with Jaymes over. And for that, I was at a total loss. Because if he felt even a fraction of what I felt, it would be worth burning down the whole damn house.

Yet here we were. Pretending.

I knew exactly what would make pretending easier: whiskey.

I lifted Sara's legs from my lap and stood from the couch, making my way into Jaymes' kitchen. He had a nice house. Nicer than any of our friends, anyway, and nicer than anything I'd ever grown up dwelling in. And his mom was never home, always either working or staying the night at her boyfriend's house a few hours away—hence the parties Jaymes constantly threw.

I reached into the back of his mom's liquor cabinet for the good stuff when I felt a body press into the back of mine.

"What do you think you're doing?" Jaymes said, his lips touching my ear for a brief second before pulling away.

I fell back down onto my heels in defeat and spun around, forcing him a few steps back with two hands on his chest. It wasn't that I didn't like Jaymes. It was just that...sometimes I really didn't like him.

He was pushy. And pushy got old, quick.

"You leave my bed empty for weeks and then come in here and try to sneak my top-shelf? Tsk, tsk," he said, stepping back into my space.

I scoffed, mildly amused. "If you think I'm going to feel sorry for you, you're delusional. I'm sure you've had no trouble at all finding a new bedtime companion."

He smirked. "But you're still my favorite."

"God, you're such a douche," I said through an unwitting smile.

Honestly, I didn't know why I liked him. Probably because he made me laugh with his stupid and blunt honesty. There weren't enough wholly honest people in this world, so sometimes the rare ones who were came off as complete assholes. Prime example: Jaymes. Could I really fault him for that?

Absolutely. I absolutely could. But I also respected him for it.

He placed his hand on my shoulder, running it down the length of my arm before taking my hand in his and pulling me to the side. He reached up and grabbed the bottle I'd had my eye on and poured us each a shot. I held my glass up to him, and he clinked his against mine, his dark eyes boring into mine.

Something I hadn't mentioned about Jaymes before? He was far from unattractive. Tall, toned. Mischievous eyes and a dimpled smirk to match. Sometimes I didn't understand why I couldn't let myself like someone who made it so blatantly clear that he wanted me.

"To getting you back into my bed, and hopefully under me, real soon," he toasted, biting my chin before tossing back his shot.

Ah, there it was. The understanding I was missing two seconds ago.

I swallowed my shot in one gulp, wiped his slobber from my chin, and started making my way back to the living room.

He pulled me back by my hand, forcing me to turn around and face him again. "In all seriousness, I miss you." He wrapped his arms around me, pulling me in for an aggressive, arms-squished-to-my-sides hug before releasing me. "I miss our sleepovers. I miss the way you crazy-talk when you're dreaming, and most of all," he paused for dramatic effect, "I miss accidentally copping a feel in my sleep." He winked, and I shoved him away with a sarcastic laugh.

"Always a pig. Tell me again—why are we friends?"

He clutched his heart as if my words hurt him, mocking me. "That's cold, Jess. It really is."

I shook my head at his stupidity, biting back a smile. Why did I like him? Why did I hate him? Once again, it wasn't lost on me that Jaymes plus Jess equaled complicated.

When I turned back around to leave the kitchen, Sara was standing there eyeing me suspiciously. I shrugged my shoulders and rolled my eyes, relaying a silent: *Typical Jaymes,* and left for the living room, plopping down onto the couch. Two seconds later, Jaymes followed, sitting down right next to me. He threw his arm around my shoulders, giving me zero space.

I saw the way Greyson's jaw clenched from clear across the room. His eyes were burning holes into the side of Jaymes' unsuspecting face.

And yeah, this whole scenario was not good for my case.

"You know what," I said, tossing Jaymes' arm up and off of me. "I think it's time for me to go. I'm tired." I yawned.

He quickly nudged my head toward his crotch. "Aww, babe. Right here, in front of everyone? Okay!"

I smacked his hand out of my hair and sat back up. "In your dreams," I groaned. Jaymes had the lovely habit of shoving my head toward his manhood every time I yawned, saying I was already halfway toward a blowjob, so I might as well make that last stretch.

"Every night," he responded, making a crude gesture with his fist.

Yep. He never failed to remind me of the many reasons I also couldn't stand him.

Greyson stood suddenly. "I'm heading out, too. You need a ride home, Jess?" He was simply asking. At least that's what it must have looked like to everyone else, but I felt the way his eyes reached into me, pleading, demanding. It made my stomach flip.

"Um, sure. Yeah, that'd be great. Thanks," I managed to reply. I stood from the couch and gave everyone in the room a small wave before following Greyson outside; he hadn't acknowledged any of them.

We made it halfway to his car before he spun around on me. "Does he always talk to you like that?" he asked.

It took me off guard. The anger behind his words more than anything. "Who, Jaymes? Have you met the guy?" I laughed. "Of course he does. It's *Jaymes*."

"Doesn't it bother you?"

Yes. No. Of course. I shrugged. "Not really."

He bit his lip, slowly nodding, his obvious irritation betraying his silence. He opened Lady's door for me but didn't wait around long enough to close it. And then he started the engine, wordlessly pulling away from Jaymes' house. He remained quiet, driving, even though he had no idea where I lived.

So, it appeared he was giving me the silent treatment. *Awesome.*

I let the silence linger, watching him. I didn't know what thoughts were running through his mind, but I saw the way he jumped from one to another, each one somehow making him grow more and more irritated.

"Does it bother *you*?" I finally felt the need to ask him.

He laughed under his breath, his fingers tightening around the steering wheel. It was a while before he finally answered—with only a half-assed shrug thrown my way.

Okay...

How in the hell had we gone from two hours ago to now? From holding hands in the corner of a dark pub, and watching him perform for the first time ever, and him running straight to me and pulling me up and into his arms in his excitement...to *this?*

I started quietly giving him directions even though he hadn't asked for them. A right here, a left there, and so on and so on. My mood was shifting, too. Growing darker. Irritated.

Because really? What the hell was his problem? I hadn't done anything to deserve his cold shoulder. I let that thought simmer, growing angrier.

He must've caught on that we were heading toward his house, but he still didn't say anything.

He didn't say anything the entire way there. Not even when we pulled up to the curb out front. Only his eyes gave away his surprise, widening just a fraction.

My knee was bouncing, agitated. Did I just walk away without a word, or confront whatever...*this* was?

I went with the latter. "So, you're not going to say anything to me? This is how our day ends?" I asked him.

He ran his hand through his bleached-blond hair, half of it falling back into his face, and sighed. "No," he said quietly. "No. I'm sorry, Jess. I just…"

I felt all of my irritation melt away with his words. At the amount of sincerity and remorse I felt in them. "You just…?"

He shrugged, refusing to say whatever words were on the tip of his tongue, and the wave of frustration rolled its way back in. I bit back an irritated growl, blowing out an audible breath instead.

"You just…maybe like me more than you'll admit. And maybe, it does bother you. The way Jaymes is with me."

He finally looked over at me, his green eyes pinning mine. "I'd say that's pretty obvious."

"But you won't do anything about it?"

He leaned his head back on his headrest, closing his eyes, taking in a deep breath. He was still facing me, but I would've missed the way he barely shook his head *no* if I hadn't been watching him so intently.

I nodded even though he couldn't see it. "Honestly, I feel like I'm missing something. Because Jaymes doesn't give two shits about anyone but himself, so I can't, for the life of me, figure out why someone like you would be so loyal to someone like him."

He clenched his jaw. Once, twice. Before laughing. If you could even call it that. It was short, dark, unamused. "Jaymes is a prick," he said, shrugging. "Doesn't change the fact that he's one of my only true friends. Or the fact that I owe him more than I can ever repay."

It wasn't the first time he'd mentioned this. I couldn't imagine *why*, or for what, he'd ever owe him for. But I could see the way that, for whatever reason, it weighed on him.

"Will you ever tell me why?" I swallowed thickly.

He shook his head again, shutting me out, and I wanted to scream. I wanted to cry. I wanted to punch something. I knew it wasn't justified, but it felt like I was constantly losing something that was never even mine to begin with.

Maybe the way I felt about him was a lost cause after all.

I opened the car door, stepping out. "Goodnight, Greyson."

"It *should* bother you," he quickly said, quiet, his voice rough.

I knew he was talking about Jaymes, about the question he'd asked me earlier. But what did it matter?

"Yeah, it should," I simply said, shutting his car door. I walked away from him without another word, knowing we'd somehow move on from this and keep on pretending.

Pretending Jaymes' opinion meant anything to either one of us.

Pretending we weren't drawn to each other.

Pretending that any time we were in a room together, it didn't feel like all of the oxygen had been sucked out of it.

Pretending, pretending, pretending.

We were so good at pretending.

Nineteen *After*

"SHE'S GOT DEMONS in Her Throat and Dreams in Her Eyes."

It's my favorite piece for this collection. A woman clutching her chest, looking off into the distance. A graveyard of war and wings and ruin at her feet; a vast, beautiful sky of stars and wonder beyond her. That's what she's focused on, the beauty beyond the devastation.

My phone chimes from across the room. I wrap the painting up and slide it into the slim cardboard box for transport tomorrow before walking over and picking up my cell. *Seventeen* messages. Five missed calls. Two voicemails.

I listen to the voicemails first—both from my agent—updating me on the details of this weekend's showing, and then I scroll through my messages. Almost all of them are from a single group-text thread. I shake my head, smiling. My friends are nuts.

Sita: *Bitch! Where are you?!*

Maggie: *We're at the bar when you get here!*

Like they'd be anywhere else, I think to myself and bite back another smile. I've been so wrapped up in work that they've forced me into a night out now that I'm done, before the showing. Not that I would have fought them on it. And these messages are a huge reminder of how much I miss them.

Maggie: *Prime Sam ogling vantage point, BTW.*

Kat: *Rest assured, I've managed to get Sita to slow her roll with a few Moscow Mules. But seriously, where are you?*

Maggie: *OMG Sam just reached up for top-shelf liquor. Eight pack abs. Yes, I counted them. Yes, it was worth the $27.*

and children and promotions, and successes and failures. It doesn't matter how different we are, or where our lives take us, we always find our way back to each other.

Maggie is a single mom. A homebody who loves reading a good book and spending time with her babe more than anything else. She's super healthy, super vegan—much to Kat's dismay—and just a pure-hearted person and an amazing friend.

Sita is definitely the wild one of our group, adventurous to her core. A work at day, party at night kind of soul. A science professor at our own WSU who still manages to get out of bed at the crack of dawn and go hiking at six-a.m. when she fell into bed drunk at one—*two, three*—in the morning.

And then there's Kat. Our newly married police officer who does so much good for our community through charities and fundraisers it's ridiculous. She's incredible, and she inspires all of us to do better.

And there you have it. The artist, the bartender, the scientist, and the police officer. It's like the beginning of a terrible bar joke. But in reality, we're kind of the best ever.

We kick back a few more drinks and quickly fall into our usual rounds: something new, something positive, and something to expel. In no particular order.

Maggie tells us about her daughter, Charlee, losing her first tooth this week and the adorable toothless smile she's got going on now, and something about the insane price inflation of tooth fairy costs. We all gush over Charlee for a long while before Sita starts in.

"Something new, I met a deliciously handsome and incredibly intelligent man the other day. Something positive, I'm *positive* I can get him under me. But something to expel?" she half-groans, half-whines. "He's my student!"

I nearly spit out my drink in a burst of laughter. "Sita!"

Kat and Maggie echo much of the same.

Sita holds her hands out in defense. "I know! I know. I would never. But *Christ,* he's only six years younger than me. Anywhere else and I'd be all over it, but because I'm his professor and he's my *student,*" she spits the word, "it makes me a total fucking creeper."

We all crack up at her expense.

"I'm sorry," I say, trying to tamp down my amusement.

Kat chimes in with a, "Yeah, sorry babe, but that would *so* make you a creep."

"Maybe hit him up once he's out of your class?" Maggie adds helpfully with a shrug.

Sita makes some sort of noncommittal noise, chugging down the rest of her recently delivered martini.

"Okay, I'm just going to say it," Kat begins, diving into her Three S's. "Husband and wife sex is the best. Pretty sure I got pregnant last night."

"You can't possibly know that yet," Sita sasses, always the scientist.

Maggie scoots closer to Kat. "Wait. You guys are trying?"

"I mean, not officially," Kat answers. "But yesterday was a damn good effort in the name of."

I smile, shaking my head at her. "Nice."

"Oh, it was so much more than nice," she hums the words, and we all roll into another fit of laughter.

"And your something to expel?" Sita asks.

"Oh, yes. That." Kat diverts her attention to our bartender. "Sam! Another!" And then she turns back to us. "Hand to God, the next person to meow or purr at me in the middle of a traffic violation, is going to get a billy-club shoved up their ass."

I do spit my drink out at that one. Back into my cup, luckily.

We're all laughing, beyond tipsy, and it's been at least two whole hours since I've thought about Greyson. But it's my turn now, and I know I have to tell them about seeing him.

I go all in. "I ran into Greyson last week."

All heads swivel toward me.

"*The* Greyson?" Maggie treads softly.

I nod into my Jameson and Coke.

"What?! Where?!" Sita blurts.

"The coffee shop. *My* coffee shop," I say, swallowing back the sudden overflow of emotion. *Ugh, get it together.*

But they home in on this immediately, the mood of our conversation drastically turning from loud and rambunctious to quiet and concerning. And *this,* this is everything.

These girls are my everything. Loving every manic piece of me.

I tell them every detail. The way it felt to see him again. The way I'm terrified he has this whole new life I could never fit into—not that I'm supposed to fit into it or anything, but still. The way I ran off and cried into my pillow for two hours straight before putting on my big girl pants and transmuting that shit into something productive. The way I've been secretly hoping to run into him again, because I refuse to believe that it ends here. *It can't end here.*

They already know about our past. The way we collided in high school and left each other with two different versions of who we used to be. They know he's a musician. A musician who unexpectedly became famous two years ago when a video of him singing in uniform overseas went viral. Now there are dozens of viral videos. I haven't watched them, though. Couldn't bear to after that first one.

Rumor has it there was a slew of record labels waiting for the very minute he was honorably discharged from the military. That not days later, he was signed, working on his first studio album. And now he's on a country-wide tour.

He is legitimately, bona fide famous, yet somewhere in the depths of my soul, he still feels like mine. The Greyson that changed my life with one look, one word, one touch, one kiss.

Not the world's Greyson. But *my Greyson.*

Twenty *Before*

IT WAS ONE of those mornings. The ones where I woke up and rolled over in bed and forgot where I was. Disoriented. Displaced.

I felt outside of myself. Like my body was lying there in bed, but my consciousness was lurking in the corner, watching the lump of a human inhaling and exhaling under her covers, wondering why she bothered to get up at all sometimes.

It didn't have anything to do with Greyson. Not really.

It was true he provided a distraction. Something to look forward to. Someone whose light seemed to wash out my darkness when I was with him.

But the darkness catches up. It always does.

It didn't matter what I did, what false distractions I latched myself onto, it was always there. Waiting. So damn *eager* to pounce.

And when it did, it came without warning. Like swimming in an ocean and being completely blindsided by a wave. The way it crashes down on you and pulls at you, dragging you under, shoving you so far beneath the surface that for a moment, you're sure you won't survive it. That you'll drown and completely succumb. That was what my darkness felt like. No rhyme, no reason. It just came for me, over and over and over again, trying desperately to take me out.

I buried myself deeper into my bed and blankets. Shutting out the world. It would be there for me when I woke up again.

That was how it worked, right? It kept turning. Kept moving.

There wasn't a single human on this planet that could stop it. Life went on with or without you. And that morning, I didn't care to be a part of it. I was weighted to my bed. At least a hundred pounds heavier. It would feel like carrying two people out of my sheets instead of just the one of me with the effort it would require. So I didn't bother to try.

I just laid there, unmoving, drifting in and out of sleep.

It was late afternoon by the time my body refused to let me keep lingering in bed. My stomach churned with hunger, and my mouth was dry. I had to get up soon...

I reached over and opened my nightstand drawer, digging into the far back until I could feel the familiar worn edges of the picture.

It was the only one I kept of her. Of my mom.

I was in it, too. We were in a parking lot somewhere, her arms wrapped around me from behind. I was maybe three. Young enough to still think the world of her. My cheek was smudged with dirt. I was barefoot, drowning in one of her shirts that she'd rolled the sleeves up on. I looked so happy—in my oblivion.

I didn't know why, but I'd always kept that picture with me. Maybe it was because it was the only proof I had, that at some point, in some way—in her way—my mom loved me.

Twenty-One *Before*

BY THE TIME I finally rolled out of bed, the sun was already starting to set. I stood up—too quick—and my vision went black before fading out and leaving me with the sight of my bare feet on the wooden floor of my room.

I walked over to the pictures on my wall. There were twice as many now—and more of Greyson than I would've cared to admit. But looking at them made me smile. Especially the one of Sara with bugged eyes and a mouthful of marshmallows. We'd been playing "Chubby Bunny," a game where we stuffed ourselves full of marshmallows until we couldn't say "Chubby Bunny" anymore, and I'd taken that picture of her just before she spat them all out into Jaymes' sink.

I ran my fingers over the other pictures, stopping on one of Greyson. *The* one of Greyson. My favorite one. There were two of them now. Because after he officially shut me down that night, I never gave it to him. It would've been exceptionally awkward. To hand over the physical proof that I was obsessed with him after he basically told me it was never going to happen. So, yeah, no. I didn't give it to him. But maybe I'd have the guts to give it to him some other time.

I walked back over to my bed, grabbed the picture of my mom and me I'd shoved under my pillow, and added it to the collage on my wall. Right next to the one I took of some wildflowers growing through the rocks on the hills behind my school. They kind of reminded me of each other, those two pictures, gave me the same feel. That it was possible for something beautiful to grow from such a dark and desolate place.

My stomach growled, effectively pulling me away from the weight of that thought. I didn't want to go downstairs, but I had to. I was starving, my stomach twisting with hunger. I looked down at my loose shirt and shorts and shrugged. It was decent enough. Not that they'd pay much attention to me anyway—my dad and his new family. I bet I could go down there and shatter every glass against the wall and they'd barely bat an eye.

But *oh*, how wrong I was. As soon as I stepped foot in the kitchen, I could feel their eyes trailing my every move. Elizabeth—my dad's wife—pulled the twins from their highchairs and kissed my dad on the cheek, saying something too low for me to hear before leaving the room.

After another awkward minute or so, my dad cleared his throat. "Could I speak with you for a moment, Jessica? Please."

I turned to him with a granola bar halfway to my mouth and leaned back against the counter, giving him a silent yet reluctant go ahead.

He slid some pamphlets out in front of him, spreading them out on the table. I couldn't see what they were. Probably for some boarding school he planned on sending me off to so he wouldn't have to see my face anymore.

"Liz and I have been talking, and..." He swallowed, clearing his throat again. "I know you're not very open to talking with us, and you have every reason to be closed off and angry, but we think...we think it would be good if you could talk to someone. Someone you might feel comfortable enough opening up to."

What the hell was he going on about?

"We thought it best to give you some time, but it's been months now, Jessica, and you still walk through this house with your shields up."

My fingers tightened around the counter behind me. *I* was the one with a problem?

"You need to talk to someone about your mother."

My heart was racing, pumping blood through my veins in overdrive. What the hell would he know about what I needed?

"I—we had no idea things had gotten so bad for the both of you. Your mom, she never—"

Fuck that, and *fuck* him. I threw my granola bar onto the counter, taking an anger-fueled step toward him. "How in the hell *would* you know?" I cut him off. "Did you ever call? Did you ever even *try* to come and see me? No! You didn't! You don't know shit about how bad it got! And you know what? That's *fine*. But you don't get to act like you give a shit now!" I yelled the last sentence so loud my voice went hoarse by the end of it.

Because seriously, *this was bullshit!*

"Jessica," he pleaded. "I want nothing more than to explain to you—"

"Fuck your explanations!"

He didn't even flinch at my words, at how loud they'd come flying out of my mouth. "We have to make the best of this situation," he continued in vain. I wasn't hearing any of it. I didn't think it was possible to be that angry, yet there I was, ready to break everything in that goddamn house of his.

I rubbed at the ache in my chest. What had he said? Make the best of this *situation?*

"That's not what I meant," he cut in, somehow reading my mind.

"I don't care what you meant," I said through clenched teeth, walking straight out of that kitchen and through the front door, slamming it as hard as I could behind me.

I only made it to the curb out front before I almost lost my shit. I was pissed, livid. At myself more than anything. Because I felt like I might cry, but screw that, and screw them, and *screw everything!*

I sat down on the curb, taking deep breaths, squeezing my knees against my chest, rocking back and forth.

I got it. My mom was fucked up. She loved drugs more than she loved anything or anyone else. She didn't give a shit about life. She didn't give a shit about herself. And she sure as hell didn't give a shit about me.

That was it. End of story. I didn't need a therapist to tell me that.

I pulled my phone from my back pocket and held it in front of me, my finger lingering above the screen, quickly realizing that there was no one I could really call. No one I *wanted* to call.

I dialed Sara anyway. It rang and rang and rang. Then went to voicemail, twice.

I dialed Jaymes, and he picked up on the third ring, but I could barely hear him through the noise on his end of the line. "Jess?!" he yelled into the phone.

"Yeah," I said. "Hey, Jaymes, could you—"

"Hey, Jess! I can barely hear you! Let me call you later!" and the line went dead.

And there it was. My whole two friends.

I nudged the small rocks in the street around with my toes for all of three seconds before thinking, *screw it*, and dialing Greyson.

It rang once, twice.

"Jess?" he answered. His voice sounded almost as soothing over the phone as it did in person. *Almost.*

"Hey, Greyson. Can I...do you think I could come over for a little bit?"

I could hear him shuffling around, hear the rustling of fabric. Was he in bed? Was he changing? *Was he naked?*

"Jess?" Greyson asked, snapping me back to reality.

"What?" I replied. I hadn't heard anything he'd said.

"I said, 'Are you okay?' You sound off."

"Oh. Yeah. I'm okay, I just… I really need to get the hell out of my house," I told him honestly.

There was more shuffling around on his end of the line. "Just give me a couple of minutes, and I'll come get you. We can go for a drive or something."

At his offer, I felt half of the tension slip away from my body. "Okay. Thank you."

"Nah, don't worry about it," he said, genuine, like it really wasn't a big deal at all.

And it was ridiculous, the way I fell in love with the words that came out of his mouth.

Twenty-Two *Before*

GREYSON JUST DROVE. He drove and drove and drove, drawing out the silence, somehow knowing I needed it. He didn't say a word. Just played song after song and kept driving.

I had no idea where we were headed, but I didn't care. Because just being in his car with him relaxed me. It was as if the last time we'd been in his car together had never happened. It wasn't awkward, or tension-filled, or forced. It was simple.

Quiet. Comfortable.

It gave me time to process. Time to come to the conclusion that I was angrier than I realized. I was holding anger inside of myself like poison. Allowing it to fester and bleed into every part of me. The most frustrating part was that I didn't know *why*. Not really.

It just lingered. A steady, churning ball in the pit of my stomach, and I didn't have the first clue how to get rid of it, or at the very least, how to begin chipping away at it.

But I thought to myself, *at least I know it's there.* That had to be a start, right? I thought so; it was a good enough start for me.

I was pulled from my thoughts when I noticed the ocean peeking at us from in between the buildings and houses we were passing by. I looked down at my phone, checking the time, and realized it had been over an hour since we'd left. The sun had almost fully set. *Had it actually been that long already?*

We still hadn't said anything to each other, and I couldn't help but start to think that while things didn't feel awkward or strained on my end, that maybe they did on his.

I looked over at him, for the first time since we'd left. He was in dark swim trunks and a white tee, a slow smile curving his lips as he quickly glanced over at me and then focused his attention back on the road again.

So, no. Not awkward. And I guess he'd known where we were headed all along, too.

He rolled his window down, the wind forcing his hair to dance around his face. I rolled my window down, too. The salt-thickened air blew into the car, coating my skin, whipping my dark hair all over the place. I could already smell the sand and waves from where we were.

I closed my eyes and soaked it in. The salty air, the smell and feel of it caressing my skin, the sound of waves crashing as we got closer.

When we were as close to the beach as we could get, he pulled into a spot along the street. He didn't open my door for me, but that might have been because I hadn't really given him the chance to. I'd hopped out of his car so quickly he barely had his door shut before I'd shut mine too.

I watched him, purposefully, as he slid some coins into the parking meter. He was always so calm, so sure of himself. In a completely non-arrogant way. I found that I admired that about him. A lot.

We both started walking down the sidewalk and toward the darkened shore without a word, but still, it didn't feel uncomfortable.

We made our way down the steep stairs that led to the beach, and Greyson hopped down the last three-foot drop into the sand and turned around, holding his hands out for me. I grabbed them and jumped down in front of him, looking up into his eyes with a small smile.

That smile felt weird on my lips. Out of place. A contrast to the way I'd felt since waking up that morning.

He turned away and led me toward the water by my hand, stopping right where the sand shifted from dry to wet, and sat down, releasing his hold on me. I sat down next to him, sinking my toes into the soft sand. I didn't know how it had escaped my attention until that very moment that I'd never put any shoes on, but it had.

I took a deep breath, pulling my knees to my chest, and rested my head on Greyson's shoulder as we looked out at the black and white-tipped water colliding with the shore. He leaned his head down on mine, and we just sat there for a long while, in perfect silence.

How had he known exactly where to take me? Exactly what I needed to help calm my soul?

"Do you miss home?" were the first words he said to me that night. They took me off guard.

Did I miss home? That was a loaded question. I swallowed down my conflicting emotions. I barely had a grasp on what they were.

"Sometimes," I told him honestly. "It just...it wasn't all good, you know? So it's hard to miss sometimes, too."

I felt him nodding his head against mine. "You want to talk about it?" he asked.

I shrugged. I sort of did. More than I'd ever wanted to. But it still wasn't enough to get me talking.

He let the question drift away, picking up some sand between his fingers and sprinkling it down onto the top of my foot. He did it again, and again and again. Granules of sand piled onto my foot until it was buried, and then he started in on my other foot.

"You missing your mom?" he asked after a while, after both of my feet had disappeared under the sand.

I swallowed thickly. Let a minute pass, and then another.

"Yeah, I do," I finally whispered at the ground, afraid to say it out loud. Afraid that if the Universe heard me say it, it would force me to unlock that space in my heart that so desperately wanted to cry for her. And for me. The child me, and the sixteen-year-old me, and for everything we'd lost. Because despite it all, despite *everything*, I did miss her. So much.

Was that sick? Did it make me sick? It felt like it. Because how could I miss someone who was hardly there in the first place? Someone who didn't care about me. Someone who, at the very least, didn't even care about my well-being? It made my stomach turn.

And there it was again, that darkness. Instantaneous. Fogging everything. I didn't want to think about my mom. I didn't want to think about how much I missed the ghost of someone who was never even real to begin with. It felt like my heart was making someone up, someone different, someone I *should* be missing who never actually existed, and it was confusing as hell.

"I'm not sure what to say other than *that really fucking sucks.* And I'm sorry…

"…I wish you weren't sad," he said, and I felt how much he meant it. Or maybe I was just feeling how much I wished I weren't sad, too.

I turned to him, feeling his arm slip from my shoulders. *How had I not realized his arm was around me?* "Then let's do something else—anything else—but talk about her right now," I said. "I…I don't really want to think about it anymore today."

"Yeah, of course," he replied right away. "Here." He dumped a pile of sand into my lap.

"What the…?" I looked down at the sand on my legs and then over at him with narrowed eyes, genuinely confused.

He shrugged, biting his lip as he smiled, before shaking his head. "I don't know," he laughed, "It was the first thing I thought of."

"Seriously?" I couldn't help but smile. He was really good at that. Making me smile. Even when I didn't think I wanted to.

He looked at me then, eyebrows raised, silently challenging me, and began scooping an even bigger pile of sand into his hands.

I pushed him down before he could dump it on me, throwing my leg over him and trapping his arms against his sides with my knees—*and no*, it didn't escape my attention that I was straddling him, but there were more important things to be worried about. Like the way he'd somehow managed to flip me over onto my back in the next second without the use of his hands, for one.

I reached down at my sides and grabbed two fistfuls of sand, but he was quick. He threw himself on top of me, effectively stilling my arms. Even if he hadn't wrapped his hands around them, I didn't think I could've moved.

I was breathing heavily, my chest expanding and contracting faster with the adrenaline that was coursing through me.

He released one of my arms and trailed his finger along the collar of my shirt. *What was he doing?* I swallowed thickly, watching as his eyes followed the movement of his hand. Watching as he slowly licked his lips. Still watching as he brought his other hand up…

…and shoved a handful of wet sand down the front of my shirt.

"Oh my god! What is wrong with you?!" I screeched.

I grabbed my own handful of sand and slapped it onto the top of his head. It didn't faze him. He shook it off like a dog, splattering it all over me.

"What are you doing?!" I yelled with my hands out in front of me, blocking the rainstorm of sand falling from his hair.

He laughed, shrugging. "Keeping your mind elsewhere." It was a simple enough answer. So why did it make me feel so many things? Why did it make me feel seen?

I sat up and attempted to wipe off the sand that was all over me, but it was useless. It was *everywhere*.

Greyson stood up and held his hand out for me. "Come on."

I reached out to him, and he pulled me up. And then he walked straight down to the shore and dove into the water, expecting me to follow, I assumed, but he was crazy. The water was just hitting me at my ankles from where I stood, and it was *freezing*. No way in hell was I getting in there with him.

His head popped up above the surface a few yards out. "Get in!" he yelled over the crashing waves.

"No way! Not happening!" I yelled back.

It was then that he proceeded to make his way out of the water, head straight toward me, and throw me over his shoulder—*Good job, Jess! You really should've seen that one coming!*—and walked us right back into the ocean, with no small amount of struggling on my end, or expletives thrown his way.

How the ocean wasn't frozen, I had absolutely no idea. Because the frigid water that was attacking every inch of my skin was *so. Mother. Effing. Cold!* I was going to die of hypothermia, I was sure of it. And my bones had to be turning into bone-shaped blocks of ice, too.

"You are such an *asshole!*" I screamed through my laughter.

He smirked in response, amused; we both knew he was the furthest thing from it.

It was only a few torturously cold seconds later that we ran out of the water, grabbed our things, and raced back to his car. He cranked the heat way up as we sat there, our teeth chattering.

"Okay, that might've been a terrible idea," he said through the sound of his teeth knocking together.

"Yeah," I replied, but that was a total lie. Because it was the *best* idea—that whole night. One of the best, ever.

And as I curled into the warmth of my bed later that night, I had the startling realization that I hadn't once thought about kissing him. I hadn't worried about the dynamics of our relationship, or what any of it meant. What a look or word from his mouth could be construed as. That night, we were just two friends. Mutually platonic.

And somewhere in the middle of all that platonic-ness, I guess I had found something in Greyson I'd never really had before:

A friend I could count on.

Twenty-Three *After*

HALF THE EVENING passes by in a blur. Flutes of bubbling champagne and small-bite appetizers have been passed around the room. Trays of them still float through the open space as guests mingle, discussing and studying the art around them. *My* art.

It never gets old. Never ceases to amaze me that people are still interested in what I have to say, expressed on each canvas that lines these stark white walls. I glance up at the exposed ceiling, at the piped lighting overhead that illuminates the room. At the steel beam supports that hold this building's structure together.

I'm hiding is what I'm doing. Behind the reception desk. Not avoiding anyone, per se. I just like to give the viewers some space, a little bit of time to take in the paintings without the pressure of the artist hovering. I like watching them from a small corner of the room, like studying the honesty in their expressions when their eyes land on a piece they connect with. It's my favorite part, hands down. Also, it doesn't hurt to sneak an extra flute or two of champagne in while I'm back here.

The receptionist, and my good friend, Ricky, swipes another off a passing server's tray and holds it down to me with a knowing smirk.

"Thank you, Ricky. Now, how about one of those cucumber sandwich thingies?" I throw him a ridiculous smile, taking the champagne from his offered hand.

"You're pushing it, baby girl," he says, and I laugh.

"Oh, please. You know you want one too."

He holds out for a few seconds, pretending to think about it, before admitting, "You know I do. Those microscopic sandwiches are delectable. Be right back, babe." He leaves me with a smile on my face and a flute of champagne in each hand.

Maggie rounds the corner of the reception desk in a haste. "Okay. Don't be mad."

"Mags, you can't just start a sentence like that," I say. "It immediately sets me up for failure. Why do you look so nervous? What happened? What's going on?" One sentence runs into the next.

She doesn't say anything, turning to the large doorway of the gallery instead. Greyson steps through with enough grace to be a member of the royal family. Dressed top to bottom in a dark, perfectly fitted suit.

My pulse immediately picks up speed. "What the hell did you do?" I whisper, as loudly as can be deemed appropriate for a whisper. So pretty much, I whisper-yell the question loud enough that Greyson looks straight over at me. Thankfully, the rest of the crowd seems to be oblivious to my outburst. I set one of the two champagne flutes down on the counter and tug my friend into my personal space. "Seriously, Maggie, explain yourself right now, because Greyson is walking this way and you only have about three seconds to tell me all about how you've lost your damn mind!" I finish through a set of very clenched teeth.

Is it hot in here? It's definitely hot in here.

And her time is up.

"Hi, Jess. I hope you don't mind that I'm here," Greyson says as he steps before us, all calm and confidence.

"No, of course not." I laugh nervously. "Thank you for coming." I reach my hand out to shake his. Like a lunatic. Except that this *is* my art showing, and I tend to shake hands and thank everyone who walks through those doors, so it's completely normal and not awkward at all. *Keep telling yourself that, Jess.*

"Great. That's great." He smiles and slides his hand into mine, and it nearly kills me. Everything just kind of stops moving and pumping and circulating inside my body, ceasing to keep me alive. For at least a few stuttering seconds, I'm sure of it. "I'm going to go take a look around. Hopefully we can catch up later?" he asks.

"Sure," I say before really thinking too much about it. I seem to have lost the ability to string more than two coherent thoughts together at once. That, and I've got a friend or three to grill at the moment.

He steps away and submerges himself in the crowd, and I feel a small pang of loss at his disappearance. I'd give anything to see his face when he takes in that first painting. So many of them are of him, or about him, in one shape or another. The broken pieces of myself I pieced back together after he left.

Will he see it? Will he recognize that? I guess I'll soon find out.

I spin around on Maggie. "Explain. Now."

She's all wide eyes and guilt. Guilty, guilty, guilty. "Please don't be mad. I just...I saw how sad you were at dinner the other night, and I couldn't help myself. I figured passing the information along about the opening wouldn't be such a big deal. Either he'd come, or he wouldn't. I mean, you're glad he's here, right?"

I take a deep, calming breath. "I think so," I admit.

"Okay, good," she says with a nod.

Sita rests her elbows down on the counter opposite of us. "Why so serious?" she asks with a mock pout.

"Greyson's here," Maggie and I answer at the same time. Her, with a level of calm I'm obviously still lacking.

"What?! Where?" Sita asks.

Maggie guides her attention to an unsuspecting Greyson.

"What in the actual fuck, Jess?" Sita exclaims under her breath. "I see you failed to mention the extreme level of *hot* your ex was."

"Oh my god, shut your mouth. That is not what's important here. What do I do?" I try not to whine, but I fail miserably by the end of that sentence.

"You stand tall, is what you do," she says, all bossy and business and the Sita that I know and love. "This is your art showing. Go out there and enjoy it. Mingle; have fun! This is your night. And you deserve it, because these pieces are *wow,* Jess. They're amazing. So go out there and own it. Let the rest fall into place, okay?"

Her words instantly help me reach a level of calm I can be comfortable enough in. Because she's right. She's absolutely right. "Okay, yeah," I say, feeling more myself than I did before her speech. "That's exactly what I'm going to do. Thank you." I give her a tight hug and slip off into the crowd.

Twenty-Four *Before*

OKAY. SO. YES, I hadn't once thought about kissing him the other night. But—and that was a *huge* but—just because I hadn't thought about kissing him that night, did *not* mean that the urge to went away. If anything, it came back with a raging vengeance. Because the need to kiss him tonight felt like a living, breathing thing inside my chest, aggressively attempting to claw its way out. It was all I could think about.

My lips, on his.

His, on mine.

The way his mouth was moving right now, saying… *something.*

Wait. What was he saying?

"…romanticized heartache, but a soul-deep devotion to Lenore. He can't forget, because the raven—or his own subconscious—won't let him, because what they had was strong enough to stay with him even after she was gone. So even if he tells himself he wants to forget, he'll never actually allow himself to—the raven's presence won't allow him to—and the raven is of his own making. We can agree on that much, right?"

Holy shit I wanted to kiss those smart and pensive words right from his mouth. But I forced myself to skim through them instead, thinking them over. He was right, dammit.

"I guess," I relented. "But it's still not *admirable*, and I don't think he's *choosing* any of it. It's dark, and ugly, and flat-out heartbreak to the point of insanity. I mean, he knows Lenore is dead but still thinks it could be her at his door, and he's talking to a *bird.* Real or imagined, it's crazy…having loved someone to the point that your entire reality and sanity have been altered because of it. It's not romantic, it's *sad*."

"And that's why we're not putting any of that in here," he said, laughing under his breath as he typed some words onto the slide we were currently working on, before moving on to the next one, typing a simple: *The End.*

"We're done?!" I jumped up and clapped my hands in excitement.

"We're done," he echoed, and I did a little victory dance of celebration.

He shook his head, smiling with one side of his mouth hitched up higher than the other, and closed his laptop, setting it onto the lounge chair beside him. Then he pulled his arms above his head, stretching as he stood. I swallowed thickly, all rational thought fleeing from my mind as I watched him—watched the muscles in his arms flexing above him.

The dimly lit water of his pool shifted and shimmered in the darkness behind him, a thin veil of steam rising from it, providing the perfect backdrop for a picture I would've easily punched someone in the face for. If only I'd had my damn camera.

But then? He pulled his shirt off. Walked straight to the edge of his pool, and gracefully dove in. My heart stopped beating for at least three full beats, I was sure of it.

I stockpiled a million mental snapshots of that whole experience. Shirtless Greyson. The muscles in his back contracting as he raised his arms above his head and dove in. His abs disappearing beneath the surface of his pool, one by one in slow motion—at least that's how it would forever remain in my memory, anyway. And him, swimming back toward me, droplets of water falling down his eyelashes and cheekbones. Down his nose, and lips, and chin.

And then I wanted to punch *myself* in the face, for not having the foresight to always have my camera with me if there was even a slight possibility Greyson would be in the vicinity. In fact, I was pretty damn sure it would go down in history as one of the biggest missed opportunities of my life. *Way to go, Jess!*

I dragged my eyes away from him and pulled my socks and shoes off, tossing and kicking them to the side as I made my way over to the edge of his pool and sat down, slipping my feet into the warm water.

"Uh-uh," he said, shaking his head as he moved closer. "Get in with me."

I blinked. Once, twice. "What?"

"Get in the pool with me."

"Um…" I forced myself away from the many thoughts a shirtless Greyson approaching me conjured in my mind, but all I could really manage was a, "Yeah, no, I'm good."

He moved even closer, forcing water to splash up onto my knees. He stopped right in front of me, gripping the edges of the pool on both sides of my legs as his green eyes shined with mischief. "Am I going to have to pull you in?" he asked.

I forced a laugh through a shaky breath. "I have nothing to change into," was the only reply I could come up with.

He looked at me pointedly in response. *You live right down the street*, his look clearly said, so his next words surprised me. "You can wear something of mine," he offered easily, shrugging.

I'm not ashamed to admit that those words, from his mouth, had me immediately ready to do a swan dive straight into his pool. But I managed to keep my cool, sitting firmly where I was, drawing tiny circles in the dark as night water with my legs.

"Come on. One victory lap to celebrate," he pouted, his bottom lip pushed out toward me, and *that. Is exactly. When it happened.*

I broke. Hit my limit.

Officially.

Twenty-Five *Before*

I MEAN, HE couldn't just *do* things like that!

He was practically begging me to do it. To go ahead and press my mouth right up against that protruding bottom lip of his. And what other choice did I have?

None. The answer is none.

Because I couldn't stand it any longer.

I liked him. So much. He was funny, and smart, and kind. He was flirty, but not pushy. Charming but not douchey. He wrote music, and played instruments, and sang like he was the *goddamn* lovechild of some pop icon and a legendary rock god, and somehow, *somehow,* he had easily become my favorite person.

But *freaking hell*, I was too damn stubborn. There was still a part of me—a part that could stick itself where the sun doesn't shine, for the record—that was holding onto my resolve, onto the determination that Greyson would make the first move.

And for whatever reason, it felt important. That I wait for that.

If it would ever even happen.

He cocked his head to the side as I watched him, his eyes narrowed, visibly assessing. I'm not sure what it was that he was trying to figure out because I knew my feelings were written clear across my face, laid bare for him to see, yet there he stood, less than a foot away, quiet. Simply studying me.

His eyes roamed the features of my face before landing on mine and pinning themselves there.

I sat there in defiance, my gaze never wavering from his.

And there was something about the way we looked at each other then. A push and a pull. A storm of *what-ifs* raging behind our eyelids.

I swallowed thickly, biting down on my lip to keep from saying the things that desperately wanted to break free: *Just do it, Greyson. Kiss me! I know you want to; I can see that you want to. Why won't you just do it?*

His gaze trailed a path from my eyes to my mouth, and then back again, and I knew it. I fucking knew it. *I know you so well, Greyson!* I wanted to scream and shake him until he understood.

It was killing me, the way he was looking at me like that. Like he intended for me to see exactly what it was that he wanted, even though he didn't have the guts to say it…or do anything about it.

I tore my gaze away from him, focusing on the ripples of water traveling methodically across his pool instead. It must have severed our connection for him, too, because he finally broke the silence. "You gonna get in or what?" he asked lightly, as if the past few minutes had never happened.

"Nope. I'm good here," I immediately replied, looking back at him with a forced smirk, attempting to will the tension away, too.

But then he slid his wet hands around my calves with a smirk of his own. "Guess I'll be pulling you in then," he said, his voice low.

And you know what? *Screw it,* I thought. This was bullshit.

I reached down into his pool and cupped a handful of water in my hands, and then proceeded to splash it right in his smug face.

He sputtered, wiping a hand down his dripping wet features. "What was that for?" His eyes were comically wide, but I had a point to make here. Whatever it was.

"Because *you*, Greyson!" I yelled a little louder than necessary, and he looked even more confused than he did a second ago. I didn't blame him. Even I had no idea where I was going until I got there. "If we're going to be *friends*," I continued, deciding to draw my own imaginary lines in the sand, "you can't just, like, casually touch my legs like that, and flirt with me, and look so *friggin'* attractive sometimes that it hurts, and you *definitely,* most certainly, cannot just rip off your shirt whenever you damn well feel like it and then proceed to dive into pools in slow motion!" There. I said it. And fuck! It felt good. I mean, where did he get off friend-zoning me while constantly doing all this shit, anyway?

"Rip off my shirt?" He smirked, more than a little amused. "And dive into pools in slow motion?"

I pointed my finger in his face, digging it into his cheek. "And that! No smirking. It's like you know how hot you are when you do it. So, knock it off!"

He burst out in laughter. I was sure he would've been doubled over if it didn't, you know, involve him drowning himself. "Oh my god," he said, catching his breath. "I fucking love you, Jess."

And…yeah.

Record. Scratched.

Heart. Stopped. Mind. Obliterated.

Stick a fork in me; I was *done.*

Twenty-Six *Before*

"**YOU KNOW WHAT** I mean," he quickly said, choking out a cough and clearing his throat. And holy shit, but was he *embarrassed?*

Oh my god, he *was* embarrassed.

That was a first.

And then I rolled my eyes. Because even pink-cheeked and wide-eyed, he was still way more attractive than it was fair for him to be.

Probably even more so, if I was being honest.

God, he sucked.

"Do I?" I eventually responded to his statement, because being a pain in the ass and giving him shit for it was a far better option than finding myself stuck, analyzing why he'd said those three words in the first place.

He raised his eyebrows at me, and I raised mine right back. *What are you going to say about it now?* I taunted him with a look.

He bit down on his bottom lip and smiled, and before I knew what the hell was happening, I was completely submerged in Greyson's pool.

He'd thrown me in. He'd *actually* thrown me in. *That shit!*

I broke the surface with a smile; I couldn't help it. "You're going to regret that," I said, and immediately dove for him. I threw both of my hands over the top of his head, attempting to shove him under, but it was a useless effort. He just laughed and simply grabbed my arms, placing them back down at my sides.

I met his gaze, watching his lips curve into a smug smile while already mentally plotting another attempt—*maybe I should try to shove him down by his shoulders instead*—when I noticed the small scar on the bottom of his chin. I'd never seen it before. *How had I never seen it before?*

I reached out and traced the short line of it with my finger. "Where'd the scar come from?" I asked.

His eyes immediately darted away. "Just some childhood accident," he said, shrugging. He was trying to remain unaffected, but I could see the way his breathing had picked up. And the way he was repeatedly squeezing his right hand into a tight fist beneath the surface of his pool.

He was lying. I wasn't sure what to make of that. But something inside of me urged me to dig deeper because I knew there was something there to find. I think I'd known that for a while now.

I turned my hand over for him to see, water dripping down my arm and back into the pool. "This scar here," I said, pointing at the faint line at the edge of my palm, swallowing down my fear and the magnitude of this moment I'd somehow found myself in. It wasn't lost on me that I was about to share something with Greyson I'd never told a soul. My heart was pounding, my hands subtly shaking. "I split it open on the corner of a wall once. When one of my mom's boyfriends shoved me into it."

He lowered his head slightly, his jaw clenching. He still wasn't looking at me.

"And this piece of lead," I continued with a deep breath, pointing at the tiny grey speck at the center of the same palm. "Is from when her drug dealer stabbed a pencil into my hand…" I swallowed again, forcing the unexpected—and unwelcome—onslaught of tears away this time. "To teach her a lesson when she was late on payment.

"Joke was on him, because she didn't care," I finished. I wasn't sure the last part was even audible, but the way Greyson looked at me then, his eyes pinned to mine with understanding, I knew he'd heard every word.

My heart was pounding even harder than before. *What did he think of me now?*

I slid my hand over my throat, feeling my pulse throbbing beneath my palm as time ticked by. As I watched him—thinking, breathing, swallowing, his Adam's apple dipping down and back up again and again.

Was I way off base here? Was he silently judging me behind those green eyes of his? Was he going to say something? Anything? I was starting to feel like I'd made a huge mistake. Like I'd overstepped a boundary that Greyson clearly wasn't ready to cross with me yet, until...

"It was always an '*accident*'," he said, and I swear I could feel the walls between us slowly crumbling. "'*I didn't see you there,' 'I didn't mean to push you that hard,' 'I was angry; I wasn't thinking straight.*' It was never about the fact that he was a drunk, or the fact that he was an asshole even when he wasn't drinking." He shrugged. "So, I got this..." he pointed at the scar on his chin, "the night everything changed and my dad finally dragged his sorry ass to rehab."

My stomach turned. I never would've guessed that any part of Greyson could match a part of me so closely, yet here it was. The hurt, and pain, and darkness that hid beneath our surfaces. "I'm sorry. That's shitty," I said quietly. It was the only thing I could think to say.

"Yeah, me too. About your mom. I had no idea." He looked down at me, meeting my gaze. "Guess that's something we have in common then, huh?" He laughed darkly, his mouth twisting sardonically.

"Yeah," I said, and my tone echoed his mood entirely. "Adults suck."

"Adults suck," he agreed as our backs hit the wall of his pool.

We stood there, side by side, letting everything we'd shared with each other slowly sink in. I guess we'd both learned that lesson early on…that adults were full of shit. That the preconceived notion that they have it all together and know what they're doing, was total bullshit. Most of the time they were more screwed up and confused than we were, they were just a hell of a lot better at pretending they weren't.

"Is that why you don't drink?" I asked him after a while.

He nodded. "Yeah. Doesn't really appeal, you know?"

"Yeah, I get that," I said, and he scooted a fraction closer, his arm bumping mine in the water. I wasn't even sure he was conscious of it—this physical need to be closer that he seemed to be unaware of.

But I knew it, because I felt that need, too. Every time I was with him. Like there was this invisible string tied around my heart that was attached to some unknown part of him—his eyes, his heart, his mind, I didn't know exactly. Maybe all of it. Probably all of it. But it pulled me in, closer, and closer, and closer every day.

Our silence stretched out in front of us as we stood there in the water, and I couldn't stop my mind from wandering. From worming through the last hour of conversation and analyzing what all of it meant. What he'd shared with me, what I'd confessed to him, the three words he'd accidentally said before we took a turn for the dark and ugly.

The *I* and the *love* and the *you*.

I fucking love you, Jess.

I turned those words over in my mind. The way he'd easily said them—with a smile on his face. The way they sounded as they fell from his lips, and the unfiltered honesty I saw in his eyes when they did.

And then the way he'd quickly taken them back in embarrassment, like maybe there was more truth in that moment than he wanted to let on.

I pushed my hands through the water, forward and back, again and again. At some point, Greyson turned to face me, and when I looked into his eyes, I saw that same raw honesty in them. Like maybe he'd been turning these things over in his mind, too.

And it should have been awkward, standing there, staring at each other for that long without saying a word, but somehow, it wasn't.

I think an entire conversation passed between our eyes.

Thank you for sharing that with me, Jess.

Yeah, you too. It means a lot to me. That you did.

It means a lot to me, too.

I took a deep breath. *I really like you, Greyson.*

I know. I really like you, too.

I know.

And I know I said I couldn't do this. But…I want to, Jess.

I know.

Badly.

I know. The hint of a smile curved my lips.

And what I said before, earlier?

Yeah?

I think I might've meant it.

I know. And Greyson?

Yeah?

I'm pretty sure I feel that way, too.

His lips tilted in a slow smile, the color of his eyes shifting with the light of his pool, brightening and dimming into a hundred different shades of green.

My heart was racing again—for a completely different reason. It was hard to breathe, hard to swallow. I wanted to reach out and touch him, hold him, kiss him, *feel* him. I wanted it more in that moment than in the million times that had come before it, and the look in his eyes told me that maybe he wanted the same thing.

But instead of closing that last foot of space between us, he closed his eyes. Took a deep breath. "I should go inside now," he finally said.

"Why?" I asked in a soft whisper.

He licked his lips and swallowed, and when he opened his eyes...there was a heat in them I'd never seen before. And then he stepped toward me, his body gliding through the water, and I think it was all the answer I needed.

His chest touched mine, expanding with deep breaths. I could feel the pounding of his heart beating a relentless rhythm against my own. And they warred with each other. Hammering, and pounding away, and waiting. Waiting for whatever it was that would happen next.

He pulled his hand up out of the water and slid it across my cheek, before sliding it into my hair. I stopped breathing. Nearly choked on the knotted ball of anticipation that was lodged in my throat, because the way he was looking at me...

Was he actually going to kiss me?

I sucked in a belated breath, closing my eyes. I was severely aware of everything happening around me. The warm, rhythmic splash of water hitting my arms. The cool breeze rushing past my shoulders. The five electric points of Greyson's fingers gently pressing into the back of my neck, the minty smell of his breaths falling over mine, and the darkening shadow of his head dipping closer, closer, closer.

I waited. I waited, and I waited, and I waited, but the press of his mouth on mine never came.

"I *have* to go inside now," he said instead, regret lacing his words.

The anticipation and excitement that had coiled itself inside my body fled for its life. *He wasn't going to kiss me.*

I swallowed thickly, clearing my throat and nodding as I opened my eyes. "Goodnight, Greyson," I said. I was disappointed. Of course I was disappointed.

But the *"Goodnight"* he whispered against my lips still stayed with me all night.

Twenty-Seven *After*

THE REST OF the night passes the same. In a blur.

Almost all of my paintings have been sold, and the food and champagne have dwindled along with the crowd. But while I should be wholly ecstatic and ready to celebrate the success of tonight, I can't help the disappointment I feel curling in my stomach and tightening in my chest. Because Greyson is gone.

I lost track of him hours ago. He said he wanted to catch up, but somewhere in the midst of everything he must've decided it was exactly what he didn't want to do.

Did I scare him off?

I try not to dwell on that thought as I thank and bid goodnight to each guest as the night continues to wind down.

It's only when the lingering crowd has thinned out to a straggling few that I spot him at the back of the gallery, eyes hooked on my favorite painting, rapt. He sits on the white bench across from it, closed off to the world. Leaning forward, elbows on his knees, fingers steepled beneath his chin. His shirt is taut across his broad shoulders, his jacket lying over the bench beside him.

I'm ashamed at the level of relief I feel at the sight of him. But it's there whether I like it or not, so I swallow it down and accept it for what it is.

I slowly make my way over to him, taking in his expression of deep concentration, watching as at least a dozen thoughts and emotions flit across his eyes.

To be a fly on that wall is exactly my thoughts right now. To be inside his mind and know precisely what he's thinking. To know why he's drawn to that painting in particular.

Does it remind him of being overseas?

Does it remind him of his own wars, both literal and figurative?

He tears his gaze away from the piece as I step closer, his eyes raking up and down my body before meeting my own. His Adam's apple slides up and down his throat with a slow swallow as he shifts his body toward me, just barely.

It didn't escape my attention that the last time I saw him, I was in ripped jeans and a loose, paint-streaked shirt, so his obvious appraisal and appreciation of my strappy heels and curve-hugging black dress makes my stomach flip, releasing a flurry of butterflies I haven't felt in so long.

I sit down next to him, running my hands down the short skirt of my dress, and look up at the painting. "You seem drawn to this one," I say.

He shifts his posture slightly, straightening a bit. "Yeah," he replies. "I'm not sure what it is about it, exactly...but I feel a definite favoritism toward it..."

"...Reminds me of a lot of things."

What things, Greyson? I want to ask, but I don't.

"You, mostly, if I'm being honest," he answers anyway.

I swallow thickly, taking in an unsteady breath.

"There was always..." he pauses a moment before continuing, "It always felt obvious to me, the undercurrent of sadness in you, even before..." He inhales and exhales a deep breath, gesturing toward the painting. "But I never imagined it felt like this."

And there it is.

Pegged.

Just like that.

By the only person in the world I imagine could do so.

And what is there to say to that, really? So I find myself simply nodding, silently agreeing with his words. I honestly don't think I even saw it myself back then—the weight of it. Felt it, absolutely. But understanding the depth of it, and the amount of therapy and art it would take to get me through it, not even close. I had no clue.

"It's my favorite, too," I eventually say. "I'm having a hard time letting go of it."

He turns to me fully, and I allow my eyes to sweep over his face without restraint. To linger on the curves of his full lips, and the small scar on his chin buried beneath the scruff of his five o'clock shadow. His nose, his cheekbones, his jawline—the strong definition of each of these features that make up his perfectly imperfect face.

When my eyes meet his once more, I realize he's been studying my face just as freely.

He smiles. Uneven, hesitant. "Maybe you'll come by my house sometime, then. See where I've hung it on my wall."

It takes a few lingering seconds for his words to sink in, but when they do, I suck in a quick breath. *He bought it?* "You—"

But Ricky walks over, interrupting me before I can finish that sentence, and the dozens of others running quickly behind it. "We're done, baby girl!" He sweeps me up and spins me around, and I can't help but laugh. "We're going out to celebrate!" When he spots Greyson, he has no shame in asking, "And just *who* is this delicious slice of man cake?" low enough that only I can hear.

Please don't show a reaction; please don't show a reaction.

"Ricky, this is Greyson, an old friend," I introduce. "Greyson, this is Ricky, my crazy and amazing newest friend."

I can see the way Ricky almost chokes on his next words. "Oh? So nice to meet you, *Greyson*."

Greyson stands with an amused curve to his lips, and they shake hands.

Ricky turns to me, bugged eyes. So much for not showing a reaction. I hide my smile and hold back a snort of laughter. He turns back to Greyson, smooth mask of feigned nonchalance in place. "The girls and I are going out to celebrate our lovely Jess, here. Would you like to come?"

It doesn't surprise me that he asks. Nothing with Ricky does at this point. I look to Greyson with a soft smile, waiting for his answer. Expertly hiding the fact that so much of me is hooked on his impending response, waiting on bated breath. I want him to come. Desperately.

"Of course, absolutely," he says, eyes glued to mine. "If Jess doesn't mind," he adds.

"No, of course not. I'd love for you to come," I easily admit. The relief I feel is palpable; hopefully it's not as evident to him.

But the deeper I sink into his gaze, the more obvious it is that he does know. He can see right through me. Can somehow look into my eyes and see straight down into my soul just like he always could.

But more than that, he willingly lays himself bare, too. Allowing me to see right through him as well.

And he's just as relieved as I am.

Twenty-Eight *Before*

SO, THE NEXT day, I was completely taken off guard. Because Greyson was ignoring me. I was sure of it. We hadn't talked all day. Not once.

In first period? He'd barely even glanced my way. In the hallways? He was mysteriously absent. First break? Still absent. And now, at lunch, he was so engrossed in that notebook of his that he wasn't paying any attention to anyone around him, let alone me. He was wrapped up in his own little world, sitting inside of an invisible bubble separating him from the rest of us. *From me.*

I tried to not let it get to me. I tried so hard. But it was impossible when I knew the reason he was being suddenly distant and quiet had to be because of me. Because of everything that had happened—or *almost* happened—between us the night before.

I was having such a hard time drawing the lines between then and now. Lines that should've been showing me exactly what had changed for him between *"Goodnight"* and the most genuine smile I think I'd ever seen anyone wear, to this morning. To this moment right here, with Greyson sitting as far away from me as he could while still appearing, for all intents and purposes, to be a part of our group.

And honestly, I was used to this kind of ebb and flow with us. The way he seemed to retreat every time he gave me too much of himself. But it was different this time; it *felt* different this time. Because I'd thought for sure this time it *would* be different…after everything.

The bell rang, sucking me back into the present. I sat there and waited for Greyson, my foot tapping nervously against the concrete step. I waited, because we always walked to the back of campus together for our next classes, but instead of looking up and finding me, he flipped his notebook shut, slid it into his bag, and walked across the quad to the front of school without once looking back at me.

It's not that I didn't expect it. It's just that it cut deeper than I thought it would. I dug my fingertips into my chest, pressing against my thundering heart and shaky breaths. Anger, and resentment, and a churning in the pit of my stomach battled for my attention, but I shoved them down—down along with my pride, because despite the way he clearly regretted handing those pieces of himself over to me last night, I still found myself standing up and following him.

He had to have known I was behind him, but he didn't stop. He didn't slow down or turn around or acknowledge me at all. If anything, his pace only picked up as he strode across the parking lot, almost too quick for me to keep up.

I think I'd decided right then and there, before we'd even had the conversation that followed, that I was over it—the back and forth, the give and take away, the uncertainty. I was better than that; I deserved better than that. I knew that, and yet it still hurt. I knew that, and yet my throat still tightened, and my heart still felt like it had been bruised.

"Greyson," I called out, just as he reached Lady's door.

The muscles in his arms tensed as he gripped the straps of his backpack and reluctantly turned around. He ran his hand through his hair, slid it down the back of his neck, returned it to the strap of his backpack—all while refusing to look me in the eyes. He was scanning the parking lot instead. The school, the trees, the sky, his shoes.

I'd spent a lot of time watching Greyson, studying him. But it was different this time. This time I wanted to shove him, and strangle him, and kiss him, and scream at him to never talk to me again.

Like that would be a problem for him. Clearly.

I hated the way he made me feel then. Vulnerable, exposed. A little broken. Enough for him to see my hurt through the cracks.

Then get on with it, Jess. End this once and for all and get the hell out of here.

"So, you regret it then," I dug the words out from where I desperately wanted to keep them buried. The almost kiss, the *I love you*, the opening himself up to me; I wasn't sure which one of these things I was talking about, but it didn't matter. It felt like he regretted them all.

He sighed and finally looked up at me, sliding his hands into his pockets. "I didn't say that," he said. His features were smoothed in a way that expertly hid whatever thoughts or emotions were lurking behind them.

I scoffed in response, crossing my arms in front of me. Anger simmered in my veins. "You haven't said *anything!*" I yelled, and I debated turning around and just walking away, because there was no way in hell I was going to let him see me cry. But I kept my feet planted where they were and managed to hold it all in—the tears, the chaos of screaming attempting to claw its way up my throat.

I bit the inside of my cheek, released it. Took a deep breath, and released it, too.

It was his eyes. His eyes were what said everything he clearly didn't want to: *Regret, regret, regret.*

"You don't have to say it. It's pretty obvious," I said with more calm than I would've thought possible.

He cleared his throat, and a sliver of that regret slipped through his mask. If I wasn't mistaken, it almost pained him just to look at me.

Awesome.

I pressed the heels of my hands into my eyes. They burned with unshed tears. Tears I wanted to set free. I wanted to sit down in a hidden pocket of the world and let a lifetime of them go, because I was exhausted, *so fucking exhausted*, from holding them all in.

"Shit," he exhaled. "*I'm sorry,* Jess. I am. But I've told you I can't do this. I'm not just saying it to be an asshole; I *can't* want you. I can't. I don't know how many times I can say it and still feel like I mean it." He stepped toward me, involuntarily, and ran his hand through his hair, his gaze searing into mine. "You know this isn't simply about Jaymes, right?" he pleaded. "It goes a lot deeper than that. I like you, Jess—a fucking lot—but if we did this?" He gestured between us with one hand. "I'd only end up hurting us both in the end. I got caught up in a moment that I shouldn't have, and I'm sorry. I thought we could be friends—that I could be your friend, but..." He took a deep breath and released it, a look of broken resignation settling on his features. It made my stomach drop. "I'm not sure that's a good idea anymore. I think we should distance ourselves," he finished.

His words felt like a punch to the gut. He was breaking up with me, *even though we were never even together to begin with.*

A bubble of insanity slid up my throat and spilled out of my mouth. "*Wow.*" I laughed, bitter and angry. "I mean, you must think so highly of yourself, *sparing us both.* How noble." I turned around to walk away but spun right back around again. "You know what? Fuck you, Greyson."

He actually looked hurt by my words. *Good.*

"Jess," he said, a last-ditch effort, before exhaling a "*Fuck,*" his fingers gripping his hair tightly. He let it fall with an audible sigh and turned around without another word, Lady's door slamming shut. Her motor thundered, tires squealing out of the parking lot.

I was good at that.

Pushing people further than they pushed me.

Twenty-Nine *Before*

AND THAT'S HOW Greyson and I had effectively screwed up our friendship. It had taken five weeks, less than four seconds of knowing him, three slightly embarrassing rejections, two almost kisses, and one too many nights under the stars to build one of the best friendships I'd ever had.

But it had only taken one conversation, two broken hearts, and three words to ruin it all.

Or maybe it was more than that. Maybe it had been simmering for a long time, waiting for the right second to boil over. Maybe it had been inevitable. But he wouldn't talk to me after that, would hardly even look at me. I didn't care, not really. At least that's what I kept telling myself. But I couldn't ignore my heart.

It was a little broken, or…a lot broken.

In reality, it felt like a part of my world came crashing down on me. Like an eclipse came in and stole back all of the light Greyson had given me.

I was alone in the dark now, a single, flickering flame faltering in the wind, but I was enough.

"Jessica?" Elizabeth asked, ripping me from my thoughts.

"Y—yeah?" I stumbled over the word. Dropping my spoon back into my bowl of cereal, I turned around to look at her, unintentionally narrowing my eyes.

"Could you keep an eye on the boys for me? For just a few minutes? I need to run into the restroom, and they just started eating.

"…I sure would appreciate it," she added hastily.

"Um..." I swallowed past the weirdness. But...*this was weird, right?* Yeah, it was totally weird, because she'd never, not once, asked me to help with the twins before. And what the hell did I know about keeping babies alive? Not just one, but two of them.

Nothing. The answer to that was nothing. But the only response that was willing to jump off the tip of my tongue was, "Sure."

I mean, how hard could watching two nine-month-olds eat their dry Cheerios be? And I was...intrigued, I guess.

"Thank you," she said with a smile, genuine—both the words and the pleased tilt of her lips.

I didn't know what else to say, so I didn't respond, turning to the twins instead. They were adorable, I could give them that much at least.

I stood up and walked across the kitchen, pulling a chair over to their highchairs and sitting back down in front of them. "So...Reagan and Ashton..." I started, and then laughed at myself. I'd never been around little kids before, but I'd been around these two enough times to know they couldn't talk yet. Not anything beyond the cute babbling and giggles and occasional *Mama* and *Dada* they were capable of.

They laughed, too, smacking their hands down onto their trays. Cheerios bounced into the air and back down, again and again. They thought it was hilarious. I stole one of their Cheerios and tossed it in the air, catching it with my mouth. Ashton giggled, and Reagan followed. So I did it again, and they burst out in laughter again, and I couldn't help but smile. My smile shifted into laughter the harder they giggled.

Who would've thought Cheerios could be so damn funny?

Reagan looked at me with wide, excited eyes, bumping his fists together, and Ashton squealed before doing the same fist-bumping motion.

I mimicked them with my own hands, not knowing what the hell I was doing, but their eyes grew even wider in excitement.

"They're signing '*more.*' They want you to do it again." I was slightly startled by my dad's voice, but I didn't show it.

"Oh," I said, standing and quickly sliding my chair back over to the table. "That's cool."

"They seem to really like you," he said. An icebreaker. One of many he'd attempted over the last few months, but like every other time, I wasn't sure what to say.

What I was startled by, though, was the way I was having a hard time grasping onto the anger I usually felt when he tried.

I think I was too tired to be angry. Or just…tired of being *angry*, period. So I answered him, with the nicest words I'd directed his way since moving in. "Yeah, I kind of like them too."

Maybe I'd given him all the anger I'd had left to give the last time we were in this room together.

He smiled in response, a slow, genuine tilt of the lips.

It immediately made me uncomfortable. Itchy, and weird, and…uncomfortable. So I walked away. But as I turned the corner and made my way up the stairs, I found that I was sort of smiling, too.

Just a little bit.

Because of Ashton and Reagan, I told myself.

Thirty *After*

THE AESTHETIC OF Toca Madera never ceases to fascinate me. But the way it provides a backdrop for Greyson is downright sinful.

Because there he stands—dark suit, dark hair, light eyes in the darkness of this room—surrounded by deep-red, velvet couches, black walls, and gothic chandeliers providing muted light to the room around him—and everything about it is just so damn *sexy*, and seductive, and *sinful*.

Sinful, sinful, sinful, because the thoughts running through my mind right now are anything but holy.

And *holy shit*, but adult Greyson is so fucking attractive it hurts. Literally—*physically*—aches inside my chest.

And obviously, I already knew this, having seen him twice in the past two weeks, but I wouldn't know it with the way my heart skips at least eight solid beats when he spots me at the bar and smiles, one corner of his mouth pulling up higher than the other in the way I've always loved.

There's something about the way he looks at me now that's different from earlier tonight, though, and different from the day we ran into each other at the coffee shop, too.

An intensity, a familiarity, in the way he strides toward me, eyes searching mine.

I could be crazy, but his are saying so many things.

Is there still something here? Do you feel this too?
I've missed you.
I've missed you; I've missed you; I've missed you.

And surely, if he was taken, he wouldn't be here right now, looking at me like *that*, right?

A throat clears beside me. "We're embarrassing ourselves here, ladies," Ricky says.

I force myself to look away from Greyson. It's no small feat. I have to peel my eyes away from his face and body, inch by agonizing inch, before I can turn in my seat and face Ricky.

And it's only now that I see the looks on my friend's faces, the way their mouths have all hit the floor. Every single one of them.

Except Ricky's. He's the one who invited him here, so he's not at all surprised, obviously.

"Really, guys? We're more civilized than this." I say.

Kat is the first to pull her attention away from Greyson and back to me. "*That's* Greyson?" she whispers.

Oh. So that's the surprise: *Surprise! Greyson is hot as fuck.*

If I could love them any more than I do in this moment, my heart would burst. They could've easily looked him up online, behind my back, but it's clear they never did. They kept their promise not to.

The surprise on Kat's face, and Sita's at the gallery, tells me that.

Maggie has seen him once before, though; she was there when I saw his viral video for the first time. But I'm starting to think I should've given them all permission to stalk him online because *holy hell,* but they really are over the top right now.

"Reign it in, bitches," Sita says as Greyson closes the last few feet of distance between him and our table, and I can't help but laugh.

"Guys, this is Greyson. Greyson this is Kat, Maggie, and Sita," I introduce, pointing down the line of them. "And you met Ricky earlier."

Greyson nods, smiling. "Nice to meet you all." He sits down in the seat beside me, the seat that Ricky has magically vacated with the speed of lightning, and I watch as my four best friends immediately dive in and start interrogating him.

They ask him about his music, and life on tour, and how long he's in Seattle for, and I really want to hear the answers to these questions but my ability to listen is being drowned out by the mosh-pit of thoughts churning in my mind.

This is surreal. Greyson sitting here, in conversation with Maggie, Kat, Sita, and Ricky. Past and present colliding. Two worlds fusing themselves together.

Somehow, I can physically feel it happening. Piece by piece, stitch by stitch, they're sewn together, and I'm left with the picture in front of me: Smiles and laughter on the faces of five of the most amazing people I've ever had the pleasure to know.

It squeezes at my heart, tightening in my chest. A snapshot of this moment could never capture the way it makes me feel. Like being welcomed back home with open arms after years of being gone.

Warm and inviting. Strange, yet entirely familiar.

Laughter erupts again at something I've missed, and I pull myself out of my own head and force myself to be present, to take this all in and enjoy it. For however long it lasts.

Greyson is telling them about the first time he ever played for a crowd—how nervous he was. I remember it with a soft smile, my eyes on his side profile as he tells his version of the story.

"Mostly, I was nervous because of this one," his knee nudges mine beneath the table as his eyes find mine, before focusing back on my friends again. "Of all the people I could've asked to come, I had to ask the one whose opinion mattered to me the most."

They all smile, eating up his words. But it's those same words that latch themselves onto my throat and constrict my airways with raw emotion. Because I didn't see it then, but I see it now—how much he means that.

"You didn't seem that nervous," I lie despite my thoughts, and the conversation easily moves on.

"So, the showing!" Ricky squeals. "Can you believe it?!"

My friends are the best at this—rerouting my attention. I shake my head, because I can't believe it. Any of this, really. But I've never had this many paintings sell so fast. "I can't," I say truthfully. It blows my mind.

Sita asks about a few of the sold paintings. If they mean what she thinks they mean. I give her some short, vague answers about some and a few in-depth ones about the others, feeling Greyson's eyes burning holes into the side of my face the entire time. He continues to watch me as I talk, but it doesn't deter me.

When I glance at him—mid-sentence—he's wearing a smile. A proud smile. An adoring smile. One that ignites a spark low in my stomach, and I have the sudden urge to climb out of my seat and into his and straddle him.

Ricky clears his throat purposefully. "You were saying?"

I choke back my laughter. *Wow. Get it together, girl.*

But Greyson's knee grazes mine again and again, until he gives up and lets it rest against me. And that spark I mentioned a few moments ago? It ignites, bursting into flames and rapidly blazing through my body. How does the touch of a knee feel like so much more?

"I was saying," I refocus my attention with a much-needed breath, "that *'Sign of His Time',*" the portrait painting of a man's face gazing—smoldering—at the viewer—*me*—through burning smoke, "was really just the channeling of my unhealthy obsession with Harry Styles."

Maggie and Kat burst into laughter, Sita with a, "Oh, god, not this again," and Ricky with an, "Mhmm. I totally understand, baby doll."

A funny look flits across Greyson's face as he smiles at me, subtly shaking his head.

And yep.

I still want to straddle him.

Thirty-One *Before*

I WAS STARTING to resent all things Greyson at this point. But at the top of my list? Was the way he perfectly filled out those stupid fucking football pants of his.

It was obnoxious. Obscene. *And irritating as hell.*

"Why are we here again?" I whined for the millionth time.

"Oh, shut up," Sara said. "I told you, a few more pictures and then we'll head over to Jaymes' place."

I groaned. "Isn't there something else we can do?"

"Like what?" She looked over her shoulder at me, genuinely perplexed.

"I don't know!" I threw my arms up. "*Anything* else. I'm bored of the same old same old."

"Okay," she said with a patience filled tone that immediately irritated me. Screw that tone. "What do you have in mind?" she added, only half invested now, too busy taking pictures of the crowd celebrating another touchdown. I didn't know which team was winning, because I refused to pay attention.

"I'm not sure yet…" I eventually said. "…but I'll figure it out."

So why was it that thirty minutes later, I found myself sitting on the couch of none other than…*who?* Yep. Friggin' Jaymes.

I was pouting like a child while Sara fed me shots of vodka every so often. Because let's face it, she was right. There was shit else to do in this town.

She was currently laughing at something Jaymes had just said, or maybe it was the private dance he was jokingly giving her from the coffee table that was just funny in general. I guess the dancing was meant for the both of us, but my mind was stuck elsewhere. Focused on something else entirely. Or *someone* else.

Someone who happened to be walking through Jaymes' front door at that very moment. Freshly showered and back in regular clothes. If you could even call them that. Because they shouldn't have looked that good if they were just regular jeans and a black tee, right?

His hair was still damp, tossed back in an effortless, perfect mess. His green eyes shined with the happiness of winning a perfect game—not that I'd been watching or anything.

I turned my back to the doorway, facing the TV instead. I knew I didn't want to be here for a reason. *Thanks for being the living, breathing reminder of all the things I can't have in life, Greyson.* But I realized a heartbeat too late that I'd be forced to watch the back of him disappear into the kitchen from this angle. From the top of his impeccably mussed up head to the bottom of his perfectly scuffed up shoes. And then watch as some random girl followed him through, wrapping her witchy fingers around his wrist and pulling him to a stop to say something in his ear. *Good one, Jess!*

He leaned down and listened to whatever stupid thing she was saying, her claws still grasping his arm. And then? He gave her one of his small, tilted smiles.

One of my *smiles.*

My stomach turned, jealously twisting my gut. *So this was how he was going to play it? Seriously?*

I tried to ignore it. Them, my jealousy, Greyson's successful attempt at being a total asshole by flirting with someone else right in front of my face. Because funny thing? I'd never once actually pegged him for one. Yet here he was. Smiling at another girl like an asshole straight from asshole-land where all the other assholes lived.

I downed the last of my most recent Sara-made concoction, not even flinching at how warm it was. I flipped the red cup over, set it down onto the coffee table, and spun it around mindlessly. Around, and around, and around. Ignoring everyone in the room, the house—the kitchen entryway—as best I could. Which was saying a lot. But then I heard it: her laughter. The girl Greyson was still with. *With? Ugh. Maybe I should point her out to Jaymes so he can piss on her, too.* Then Greyson would be alone at this party like I was.

Her laughter made my skin crawl. Like nails on a chalkboard. Or someone chewing with their mouth wide open. Or like some random girl clearly laying claim to *my* Greyson while I was forced to sit across the room and watch.

It pissed me off. Her fakeness more than anything, because I knew Greyson, I *knew* him, and he was funny, but he wasn't *that* fucking funny. I couldn't stand it any longer.

So, I turned around and did one of the stupidest things I'd ever done. I stood up, grabbed Jaymes' hand, and led him straight down the hallway and into his bedroom.

Like I said, stupid. But sometimes jealousy makes us do stupid, *stupid* things.

Thirty-Two *Before*

I'D LIKE TO say I pulled Jaymes into his room and brushed the whole thing off, or told him the truth, or did anything but what had happened next, but I was hurt, and angry, and I'd felt all alone. And I'd finally concluded that if Greyson didn't want me, there was someone else standing right in front of me who did. Someone who'd never once not made it clear to me that he did. In whatever twisted, backward way that was.

"Jess, babe?" Jaymes asked, clearly amused. I'd never dragged him into his room like this before. My hand was still clenched around his. He raised his eyebrows, a wicked smile curving his lips.

*Green eyes, and full lips, and a tilted smile...*those are the things I imagined in place of the features in front of me as I shoved all rational thought to the side and pulled Jaymes in for a kiss.

As soon as my lips touched his, he immediately took control, growling against my mouth and thrusting his hands into my hair and pressing my body right up against his. His mouth was aggressive, punishing. There was skill, and fire, and passion in his kiss. It lacked for nothing except for the most vital thing: my actually wanting to be there, with *his* lips pressed against mine.

But it still felt nice. Nice to be kissed; nice to be wanted. Nice enough that I kept our kiss going, opening my mouth to his, letting him slide his tongue over mine.

I'm not proud to admit that I made out with him for a while. A long while. Long enough for my lips to feel numb from the assault of his talented mouth. Long enough for us to have ended up on the bed with his shirt thrown on the floor. Long enough that he was starting to push for other things to happen.

Things I knew I didn't want. Not with James, anyway.

I sat up, pushing him a few inches away, breathing heavily.

"*Holy shit*, babe. Best fucking kiss of my life," his breathy words fell over my lips. "I knew it would be like that with us," he added, dropping onto his side on the bed beside me.

Regret immediately rolled through my stomach, making me sick. *What the hell did I just do?*

He ran his hand through my hair, and I closed my eyes.

What you clearly wanted to do, you idiot, I answered my own question, trying not to think about the way I'd felt Greyson's eyes burning holes into my retreating back as I'd led Jaymes down the hallway and into his room. Or the way Jaymes was currently pressing small kisses up and down my neck, staking his claim.

Nail, meet coffin. *You can't take it back now.*

"You good?" Jaymes asked, pulling me away from those thoughts, and pulling himself away from my throat to look into my eyes.

I smiled halfheartedly. "Yeah, I'm good."

"Then what's that raincloud of thought behind those sexy eyes of yours about?"

I had to physically hold myself back from rolling said eyes. I shrugged instead. "I'm thinking about how much of a child you are. 'Give an inch, take a mile' ring a bell? I don't go around kissing just anyone, you know."

He laughed. "Believe me, I know. *God, do I know.* You give hard-to-get a whole new meaning, Jess."

"Shut up." I shoved him.

"Why is that, though?

"Why is what?"

"That you don't hook up?"

I shrugged again. "Doesn't really appeal when you've had men twice your age trying to grope you since you can remember," I answered without thought.

"The fuck?" He reared back, dark eyes boring into mine. *"Who?"* he questioned, looking ready to beat someone down in my honor. I wasn't going to lie and say that it didn't make me feel good inside, that someone cared that much.

"My mom's boyfriends," I answered. "Her sugar-daddies, her drug-dealers—you name it. She didn't care that they hit on me; they did it right in front of her face, and she didn't do anything about it." Out of all the people I would've thought I'd be comfortable enough telling this to, Jaymes would've been dead last. I guess there was a first time for everything.

Proven by that stupid, stupid kiss, my subconscious reminded me.

Go to hell, subconscious.

"That ever happens again, you tell me. I'll beat the shit out of whoever tries to touch my girl," he said.

I snorted. "Sure thing." I didn't correct him, because he always called me his girl. Way before tonight ever happened.

"Jess, baby." He smiled mischievously, tapping my forehead. "You finally let me inside you." ADD, this guy. No. Really. And it showed. "It all makes sense now. But it was only a matter of time before you fell prey to my charm...

"So, you want to let me inside you in other ways?" He moved his lower half against me suggestively.

"Ha! No. Go to bed." I hit his shoulder, forcing him to lie down again. I turned off the light and pulled the covers up, and he wrapped his arm around me, breathing in contentment against my spine as we slowly drifted to sleep.

And I still remember those last thoughts I'd had before completely succumbing. How sometimes it felt like I'd been handed this life with full control, with nothing out of reach if I wanted it badly enough. But how other times it felt like I'd been strategically placed exactly where I was. Like a piece on a game board, destined to go down certain paths, where the only control I actually had was over the small fragments of time in between all the places I was predestined to land.

Like there, in Jaymes' bed.

Because no matter how badly I hadn't wanted things to end up that way, and no matter how hard I'd tried to fight it, it felt like God had other plans for me all along, and the joke was on me. The joke had always been on me.

Thirty-Three *Before*

WE WERE AT lunch the next day, sitting at a small table in the middle of the quad. *We,* as in Sara and Jaymes, and a few of his other friends. But also "we" as in whatever it was that Jaymes and I were supposed to be to each other now. He'd shown up at school that morning with a donut and iced coffee in hand—for me—kissed me on the cheek, wrapped his arm around my waist, and walked me to class, officially staking his claim for everyone to see.

But he'd also slapped Sara on the ass as we'd dropped her by her class first, had bought another girl lunch ten minutes ago, and had slipped a note from a different one into his pocket. So, we weren't *together,* together. Which, honestly, was a huge relief. But also, he definitely felt like our kiss gave him permission to touch me a whole lot more than either one of us was used to—which was saying a lot. I wasn't sure how I felt about that.

His fingers were currently hanging from my back pocket as he talked with the guys. I focused on my sketchbook in front of me, drawing Sara's profile. She was quiet today. Withdrawn. I chalked it up to her a-hole of a father, because she always got like that after he'd been in town for the weekend. But it felt like something bigger must have gone down, because she was even quieter than usual. Even more pissed off at the world than she usually was, too.

I didn't blame her. Our parental situations were night and day, but it didn't make either one of them any less shitty. Her mom worked some nine-to-five, barely scraping by, and her dad—I didn't know what the hell her dad did, but what I did know, was that he only came home every other weekend, and when he did, the energy in their house completely shifted. He was rough with her mom, beat on her brother, and ignored Sara for weeks at a time, literally giving her the silent treatment because of the type of clothes she wore, or because of the guys she hung out with, or because of something as stupid as her cracking open his two-liter bottle of soda without his permission.

I'd learned all of this based on observations alone, but even worse than that, I'd also heard him call her a whore and a slut more times than I could count, when he actually *was* talking to her. She shrugged it off like it didn't matter, but I could tell that it hurt her. I mean, of course it did. We couldn't be abused and neglected by the only people in this world we should've been able to count on to love us and not be scarred by it in some way.

Sara bit down on her bottom lip, lost in thought.

I drew her that way, shading around the space where her teeth dug into her lip. Shading underneath her chin and around her sad, somber eyes.

I vaguely heard one of the guys ask Jaymes a question that involved me before he wrapped his arm around me and pulled me into his side, his other hand coming up to grasp my chin as he placed a kiss square on my mouth. My eyes went wide as I pulled back.

"Jess is mine now," he said with a stupid grin, eyes locked on mine. "She finally let me inside her last night," he added, a pride-filled tone that slipped past his smirk.

I shook my head at him, holding back a mouthful of curse words, and, if I was being totally honest, an exasperated laugh, too. Because we both knew exactly how it sounded. We both knew the truth behind those words. But for whatever reason, we both kept our mouths shut. I guess I didn't really care what anyone thought about what did or didn't happen between us. It was none of their damn business.

But when I finally looked away, I saw the back of Greyson's head moving in the opposite direction from our table.

I tried my best to ignore the way my heart climbed up into my throat. *Had he been standing here the whole time, and I hadn't noticed? Or did he just happen to be walking by?*

Either way...*Did he hear what Jaymes had said?*

I had no clue. Maybe he had, or maybe he hadn't.

I wasn't sure which one of these I hoped it was more.

Thirty-Four *After*

SITTING HERE NEXT to Greyson, in a private little bubble of friends and laughter and a past momentarily forgotten, has filled me with a buzz even alcohol can't compete with.

I should be exhausted after tonight. After these past few weeks of battling with the sunrise, painting until its glow crept through my studio windows. But I'm filled with so much energy right now I could run a marathon.

"Alright, ladies and gents, I'm out." Kat is the first to throw in the towel and call it a night, backing her chair away from the table.

"Yeah, me too. Sitter's waiting." Maggie boards the leaving train.

But I'm not ready to go, I want to whine like a five-year-old. *Just five more minutes.*

But everyone begins to stand and pull themselves—and their belongings—together, getting ready to head out. Everyone except for me. And Greyson. I'm glued to my seat, and he's glued to his, and we sit here, in this mildly uncomfortable state of limbo.

I have no idea what's running through his mind right now. Why he's still sitting there, eyes drawn to mine.

Maybe there's a tiny toddler dictator in his mind, too, screaming that he doesn't want to go home yet either.

I laugh at myself beneath my breath, and eventually, embarrassment wins over. I give in to the pressure building between us, the pressure to say or do something—*anything*—and come to a stand.

"It was really good to see you again," I say at the same time that he asks, "Can I drive you home?" His lips softly say the words, but his eyes beg the question, and my heart starts beating a little faster, a shaky nervousness spreading through my limbs.

"Ricky is supposed to drive me." I don't know why I say it. Who *cares* who's supposed to drive me, we all know who I *want* to drive me. And God knows I don't want to play another round of Twenty Questions with Ricky. He certainly didn't hide his excitement over this turn of events on our way over here, so I can only imagine what the ride home will be like.

"Can I talk to you for a sec?" Sita interrupts my thoughts.

"Yeah, of course," I say. I already know she's going to be my calm force, the grounding words I need to settle these thoughts running haywire in my brain.

She guides me away from the table, far enough to keep our conversation private but close enough that I'm still distracted by Greyson standing from his seat and sliding his jacket over his muscled arms and wide shoulders.

"Holy *shit,* that man is attractive," Sita whisper-shouts instead of the calm I expected, making me laugh. "And not just here," her palms hover around her face and body, "but in here, too," she taps her forehead.

I meet her eyes. And laugh. Again. Because I know. *I know.* He's kind of amazing. Maybe a little more than I've let on.

That sunshine that used to radiate from him shines even brighter now, somehow illuminating the space around him.

He's light, and he's warmth, and he's drawn me into his orbit all night with his smile alone.

"My face is right here, drooly-pants," Sita says, and her fingers gently grasp my chin, dragging my attention away from him and back to her.

"Sorry," I say, and I mean it. "What did you want to talk about?"

"Yes. That." She takes a deep breath, reigning herself—and the dozens of other comments I can see playing behind her eyes—in. "Okay. Now, listen to me," she says. "You are not going home with Ricky."

"I'm not?" I ask, amused.

"No! You're not. This is Greyson we're talking about." Her entire demeanor shifts with that statement, going from lighthearted and playful to concerned and sincere. "*Your Greyson*. And he's offered to drive you home. How often do these kinds of opportunities present themselves to us, Jess?

"You have your questions; I know you do. You've had them for a long time, and the answer to all of them is standing right there. Do not let this opportunity go."

I know she's right. I do. It's just that I think I'm still too scared to hear the answers. *Terrified* of what some of them might be, really.

We've done an excellent job of keeping conversation light tonight, barely skimming along the surface. I'm not ready to dive deeper yet.

"The fact that he showed up at the gallery—and waited *hours* for it to be over just to talk to you, says it all," her words cut through my thoughts. "He's clearly still into you, too."

"I never said I was—"

"Oh, put a lid on it, would you? The sexual chemistry between you two is so palpable that even *I* need to go home and take a shower." She shifts right back into her smart-ass self. Crazy, this one. In the best way.

"Right." I hold back my smile.

"Let the man take you home, Jess," she orders.

"Yes, ma'am," I give in. Because I know I don't want to go home with anyone else—regardless of what's to come.

I wrap my arms around her and hold on for a while longer than I'd planned, taking in a deep, calming breath. "Thank you," I say.

"Of course, babe. Good luck," she whispers, and I swallow her parting words down like a shot of tequila, hoping they give me the courage I need.

Thirty-Five *Before*

I STEPPED FOOT in my bedroom after school that day, and something immediately felt off. There was an easel and a line of paints, charcoals, and pencils in front of me that hadn't been there before. And when I took a few more steps into my room, there was a person that had never been in there before either. At least not when I'd been in the room with her. Because this was her house, so obviously, she had been in this room before, at some point.

Elizabeth, my...*stepmom?* No. My dad's wife. She stood there, staring at the pictures I'd pinned to her wall.

I dropped my backpack onto the floor by the dresser.

"Oh—hi," she said the words through a startled breath, jumping a little at my intrusion. "I was just leaving some things..." she gestured toward the easel and art supplies, "I've seen you drawing in your sketchbook, and I..." She took a step closer to the photos. "You did this?" she asked, neglecting to finish her previous sentence.

I swallowed back a rude response. It was like instinct, to throw fire at the people who stood in front of me before they could burn me first. "Um...yeah," I eventually found it in me to answer her.

I was sure she hated it, that she wanted me to take them all down immediately. To patch and paint her pristine wall until it looked like I had never marred it in the first place.

"They're beautiful," she said, in a soft, awe-filled way that took me completely by surprise. "The way you've arranged them, but...the pictures themselves. *You took these?*"

I cleared my throat, feeling more uncomfortable than I wanted to admit. My hands were starting to sweat. I wiped them down the sides of my jeans. "Yeah...I did."

She smiled tentatively. "You're good. *Really good.* You should seriously think about art schools—if you haven't already."

The urge to talk to her came out of nowhere. Words bubbled up my throat, ready to be set free, but I clenched my teeth down around them. I'd never told anyone my hopeless dreams of places I would never see and colleges I could never afford. I wasn't going to start now.

But of course I'd thought about them. Nearly every day for the past decade of my life. Since the very first time I'd put pencil to paper and drew castles in the sky I desperately wished I could live inside of.

"That's not really in the cards for me," I finally answered instead.

Her face scrunched up in that way it does when people feel sorry for you. I hated that look. "How so?" she asked. "There are scholarships and awards, and I know your father would—"

"No," I shook my head, cutting her off. We weren't going there either. Not now, not ever. I didn't know what my future looked like, but I knew it would be painted without his help. I could do it on my own, like I'd done almost everything else on my own since the first day I could remember.

Our lingering silence turned awkward and uncomfortable. On my end, anyway. I didn't know why she kept standing there, staring at my pictures when there was nothing left for either of us to say.

She released a breath. "I'll leave you be then." But she paused by the doorway, adding a, "Happy Birthday," with a sad smile.

And, oh. *Oh.* It all made a little more sense now—the easel, the art supplies. I swallowed. "Thank you," I said quietly, and I meant it.

"You're welcome." She hesitated, stalling another step. "You know…I'm a firm believer that if you believe in yourself hard enough, you can make any of your dreams come true…

"But no one has ever made it to the top without accepting a little help along the way," she finished, and walked out the door.

And I think that to a lot of people in my situation, her words would've sounded like total bullshit. But I knew, somewhere deep down, that what she'd said was true. It was just that the world had taught me I couldn't rely on anyone but myself if I wanted to make it through this life in one piece.

Thirty-Six *Before*

IT WAS THE first time I'd ever attempted to put paint on a canvas in a way that made sense to me, the day Elizabeth had left all those supplies in my bedroom for me to use.

But it wasn't the first time I'd tried to channel the darkness I felt stirring inside of me into something else—into something outside of myself, attempting to turn that churning ball of pain and confusion into a thing of beauty instead of allowing it to fester and drag me under.

There was something about the brushstrokes of paint, though, that felt entirely new. That felt even more calming than the sound of pencil scratching against paper. I wouldn't have believed it was possible until that day.

I got lost in it.

I must've sat in front of that easel for hours. Until the sun had fully set, and the sky had shifted from bright blue and orange to magenta and indigo, and then dark. Dark, and sprinkled with stars.

When I finally pulled away from the painting, I found myself staring into my own eyes. A simple self-portrait of a girl. Only…her hands were wrapped around her neck, fingertips digging into her own flesh. But looking into her eyes, you wouldn't know it—that she was strangling herself. She looked oblivious—sad, but entirely oblivious—of her own self-destruction.

And as I sat there, studying the features of my own face staring back at me, I could feel something slowly happening. A click; a shift. Something of magnitude rearranging itself inside of me, connecting thoughts of my past to the emotions of my present in a way I hadn't understood before.

I spent the next two weeks holed up in my room like that. Painting, or constantly looking forward to the next chunk of hours I'd be able to spend in there, learning the differences between brush and pencil, paper and canvas. Learning to process my feelings in a way that made sense to me.

It also happened to be far better than the alternative…allowing myself to linger on thoughts of Greyson. On the betrayal I'd seen in his eyes the day after Jaymes had made his stupid announcement, or the way we hadn't said a single word to each other since our fight in that parking lot. And it was better than focusing on the way I'd been feeling more and more resigned with letting people believe Jaymes and I were a thing—with letting *Jaymes* believe him and I were a thing, too—with allowing *myself* to believe him and I were a thing.

Because I guess that's what we were now. What we had been for a while: *Boyfriend* and *Girlfriend.*

But more than any of that, more than all of it, those hours of solitude helped me chisel away at the walls I'd constructed around my heart. Walls I hadn't even realized I'd long been standing outside of.

Thirty-Seven *Before*

ANOTHER WEEK PASSED by.

Sara was still distant. More than ever before, really. But I had no choice but to leave her be. There was this unspoken rule between us, that we wouldn't talk about the shit that haunted us and dragged us down. And she'd quickly shut down all my offers to try and do something—*anything*—that would pull her out of her funk.

So, I had no other option than to wait it out, wait for her to come around when she was ready.

It was a little lonely, though, if I was being honest, without her usual, over-the-top personality in my face as an easy and welcome distraction.

But I was busy, too. Between painting, and homework, and school, and hanging out with Jaymes—more than I would've thought I'd want to, by the way—there wasn't time for much else anyway. But it had been nice, his company. I'd learned that while he was annoyingly pushy verbally, he actually wasn't all that pushy physically. And the fact that he'd been content with infrequent, small kisses and simply hanging out, watching movies, and not doing much of anything at all, kind of surprised me. Or *a-hell-of-a-lot* surprised me, if I was being completely honest.

That's not to say he was a perfect gentleman, though. *No*, that idea was laughable. His dirty mouth, and flirtatious nature, and wandering eye far more than made up for it. He was still the same old Jaymes, just without a new notch or two in his belt every night. One that I proudly had not put in there either, or ever planned to.

So, I made it through that week with minimal human contact. With Sara, my dad and Elizabeth, *Greyson*. I was good with it, I guess.

But our poetry presentation was due in a couple of weeks, and to say I wasn't looking forward to it would've been a massive understatement. Standing up there next to him, pretending the past few months had never happened, sounded like pure torture.

But I'd deal with that when the time came.

For now, I was going to turn in my *"Life in Action"* shots to Ms. Greenburg, my photography teacher, keep painting, and keep hanging out with…Jaymes.

…*Maybe.*

Thirty-Eight *After*

"NO WAY," I say under my breath as Greyson rounds the front of his car and pulls the passenger door open for me. It's Lady.

Lady.

I feel almost as nostalgic for her as I do for this man in front of me. *Almost.*

"Thank you," I say, smiling as I slip into the warmth of her embrace. She's exactly like I remember her—clean leather, sharp lines, and smooth class. "I can't believe you still have her," I tell Greyson as he slides into his seat, his eyes immediately finding mine—a sea of green, warm and inviting. Addicting. The way it makes me feel to look into them more than anything.

And he seems to take up more space than he used to, sucking the air from the car like it gravitates toward him, because I'm left with a minimal amount of oxygen left to breathe.

"Of course I still have her," he says, jokingly offended as he turns the engine over, and I finally find my breaths. I fidget with my purse, opening and closing the clasp on the front. "Lady and I are in it for the long haul." He grins, pulling away from the restaurant, away from the safety of surface questions and surface answers.

"Of course." I smile back, trying not to dwell on that fact. "I didn't mean to insult your one true love." I laugh, but the wounded look that passes over his features quickly robs the sound from my lips. I'm honestly not sure I even saw it. It was fleeting, there and gone too quick to be sure, but my heart still continues to beat faster.

He clears his throat. "How've you been, Jess?" His demeanor grows serious, his voice a little rough, hinting at the emotion I thought I saw in his eyes just a second ago.

"I've been good," I tell him honestly, even though here, in this moment, it kind of feels like a lie. But my life *has* been good. Better than I could've imagined for myself at sixteen-years-old, and I'm incredibly grateful for every beautiful piece of it. It's just that the reminder of the one thing that's been missing from my life all these years is now sitting right here next to me.

"How about you? How have you been?" I ask for the second time in as many weeks, avoiding the weight of my previous thoughts. I direct him onto the freeway, and he takes his time merging over the three lanes before answering.

"I've been good too, Jess," he says, but his eyes betray his smile. They mirror my thoughts, of years missed and lost, and it's too much to handle at once.

I turn and look out the window, watching the city lights disappear behind us. *What are we doing here?*

What are his expectations?

What are mine?

I have no clue. I have no fucking clue.

But why does it feel like my chest wants to cave in?

No matter how much I sit here and try to fight it, the pressure behind my eyelids surges forward, along with everything unspoken wanting to settle between us. Eight years' worth of questions waiting to be asked and answered.

My heart climbs its way up into my throat, and I force in a steadying breath of air, blinking tears away from my eyes.

In the very next breath, Greyson takes my hand in his. "I know...*I know*," he says with a resigned sigh, and I shift in my seat to look up at him. His green eyes are dark and intense, sinking into the depths of mine. "How about we save this conversation for another day—*soon*—but not right now. I say we take things slow. We've got time because I'm not going anywhere." He swallows, and I watch the movement in his throat. "And something tells me that this time, you're not either."

I wipe the tips of my fingers beneath my eyes, catching my tears before they fall, and nod. I can't say anything past this lump in my throat. Wouldn't even know where to begin if I could. Except, maybe: *You're right. You're absolutely right. There's no way in hell I'm ever running from you again.*

His fingers tighten around my hand, and I find comfort in his grip—*firm*, like he doesn't want to let go yet, either.

Fifteen minutes later, we pull up to the curb in front of my house—thoughts, feelings swirling. I unbuckle quietly, and we turn to face each other. Watching, not saying a word.

It's amazing, after all this time, to be this close to him again. Less than a foot of space separating us, his contemplative gaze sinking into mine.

My fingers ache to touch him. My heart screams out for his.

I feel empty. Empty of his touch, and empty of his kiss. And I'm pretty certain these feelings are written clear across my face, because at the same exact moment, both of our lips twitch and slowly pull up into two matching smiles. Smiles that connect between our eyes. Between his heart and mine, gently tugging them back together.

"I've missed you," I finally admit, and I can breathe a little easier now that I've ripped it off my chest and thrown it out there.

"I've missed you, too," he replies easily, his hand wrapped around mine again, thumb grazing my palm, and I'm still smiling. I can't help it. I never could when I was with him.

And I want to heed his advice and take things slow, however they may come, but I also feel the intense need to throw myself over this center console between us and land myself in his lap. To kiss him stupid after eight long years and never come up for air. I can hardly breathe, anyway, with the way his tongue has slipped out of his mouth to graze his lips for a brief moment as he continues to watch me.

Focus. Say something, Jess.

"I'm pretty busy the next few days, unfortunately," he says first, his hand slipping behind his neck in a firm grip. "But do you think I could come by sometime this week?"

"Yeah, of course." I nod, relieved. "Here." I pull my phone from my purse and unlock it, opening up my contacts list. "What's your number?"

The nine digits slide off his tongue with ease, and I shoot him a quick text: *Jess here.*

He smiles as he lifts his phone, screen lit up from my message. If I'm not mistaken, the tilt of his lips holds the same affection for me that mine do for him, and hope blooms inside my chest, sprouting from the seed of *him and I* he planted all those years ago—hope for us, and some kind of future where I'll get to see his face far more often.

But in the very next moment, my hope suddenly catches fire, bursting into flames and falling to the ground in a fiery mess. Because right there, on his left hand, I finally see it. Different from the other decorative rings that adorn his fingers.

A slim, smooth, slap in the face.

A wedding band.

Thirty-Nine *Before*

JAYMES LAUGHED AND bellowed in the middle of Maddie's Diner. He could hardly catch his breath.

"When I finally sleep with Jess, you'll damn well know it! It'll be plastered across my face like a fucking tattoo of bliss and happiness, because I'm pretty sure her p—"

I slapped my hand over his mouth, mildly mortified. I looked at him pointedly, *shut up, shut up, shut up!* written plain across my face. When I was sure he would, I peeled my fingers from his lips.

"—would be like holy water, cleansing me of all my sins," he finished anyway.

The guys laughed, and Sara's eyes brightened in a way I hadn't seen in a while. In a few weeks, at least.

But I didn't care about any of that right then. Not really.

Not when my heart was beating a mile a minute. Not when Greyson was sitting at the end of our long table, searing two identical, matching holes into the side of my face.

I had let him believe I'd slept with Jaymes—willingly. But now that it was out there, that I hadn't? I could feel the tension crackling between us like an atomic bomb getting ready to explode. Thick enough to strangle every person sitting between us.

I scooted my chair away from the table and stood up, quickly making my way to the bathrooms, avoiding the inevitable confrontation of Greyson's knowing eyes. I felt like such an idiot, far beyond embarrassed and straight into humiliated.

But he was faster than me, already two steps ahead.

Shit. *Shit, shit, shit.*

What did he want?

He pulled me around the corner, fingers gently biting into my arm, forcing my back against the wall with the amount of space he was giving me.

I sucked in a strained breath. I could barely breathe. Could hardly muster up the words I knew I needed to say because of the way he was staring at me, like he was staring straight into me. It threw me off-kilter.

He'd never looked at me like this before. Had never seemed this angry before, either…or this close to breaking.

"What do you want?" I finally managed. But the words lacked their intended weight, coming out as a soft breath instead of the angry growl I'd felt churning inside.

"Why would you lie about sleeping with Jaymes, Jess?" he asked. There was a layer of hurt and betrayal beneath the anger in his tone, his eyes matching the sentiment.

"Screw you," I said. It didn't matter why. It was too late, and it was none of his damn business, anyway. He didn't get to care *now*. Not when he'd practically forced me into Jaymes' bed in the first place.

He moved closer, his mouth inches away from mine, and I choked back the desperate need for him to close the distance between us. The last two, maybe three inches between his lips and mine.

"*Why*, Jess?" he asked—almost desperate.

I swallowed thickly, refusing to answer. My breaths had picked up, and I focused all my energy on trying to hide that fact.

He tilted his head to the side and lowered it, whispering into my ear. "Were you trying to make me jealous?" He laughed darkly.

My heart sunk, dropping into the pit of my stomach. *He thinks this is funny? This is a joke to him?* I was one second from pushing him the hell away from me when he pressed his body flush against mine, from our chests all the way down to our toes.

My heart climbed its way back up into my chest and started pounding—*racing*—my breaths coming and going in short bursts. I couldn't hide the way he affected me even if I wanted to.

"It worked, Jess," he growled. "It worked, and I'm pissed at you for lying, but I'm also *so fucking relieved*, and I don't know what to do with that."

"Go to hell?" I breathed, my last-ditch effort at pushing him away, because I knew—*I knew*—what was coming next. I could feel it with every bone in my body. With every heartbeat that thrashed against my ribcage. With every breath that rushed in and out of my lungs.

He pressed himself against me harder. "Been there. Done that," he replied, and finally—*finally, finally, finally*—after all this time of waiting, his lips slammed down on mine. Hard, relentless, *angry*.

I moaned against his lips, and his tongue pushed into my mouth—teasing, consuming, igniting. Every cell, every nerve ending, raged with a fire that burned through my veins.

I grasped his shirt and pulled him closer, tangling my tongue with his. He tasted like mint, and chocolate, and Greyson; he tasted like pure bliss.

And I had no idea how it had happened, exactly. How one second our eyes were glued to each other's, and in the very next, our lips were touching, *crashing*, pushed together with the force and intensity of weeks, and weeks, and a *lifetime* of waiting. But I didn't care; I didn't need to know how it had happened.

Because in those moments, I could feel just how much he'd wanted this, all this time, too—how much he'd wanted *me*—in the way his mouth moved against mine, slow and devouring. In the way his hands were hurried, and impatient, and smoothing over the curves of my body. In the way he was pressed right up against me, pushing the evidence of it into my hip bone.

Relief, like the weight of a thousand pounds being lifted from me, warred with the desperate need for more—like the strength of that weight being shoved right back down my throat.

I slid my hands around his neck and pulled him closer, kissing him harder, deeper, pulling his hair between my fingers. He made some small, deep sound that slid over my tongue—a grunt of approval, maybe; it set my soul on fire.

His tongue caressing mine; his teeth grazing my lips.

Our mouths pushed and pulled, and fought and danced, and nipped and soothed, and this kiss—*this kiss*—felt like the only thing I'd need for the rest of my life, and yet the single thing I couldn't go on living without. I wanted more, and more, and *more*.

And I was ready for more. I was ready to go as far as we could—*all the way*. Right then and there if he'd asked me to. I would've given him everything. Every piece of me. He could've taken every last broken one of them and never given them back, and I wouldn't have cared. I didn't care anymore.

But he pulled away abruptly. "Fuck. *Fuck, fuck, fuck!*" He slammed his hand against the wall beside me.

The look of regret on his face shattered my heart into so many pieces I wouldn't have known where to begin putting them back together again.

So I shoved him, as hard as I could, and choked back my tears. "Don't you *ever* fucking talk to me again," I nearly screamed.

I hated him. In that moment, *I truly fucking hated him.*

Forty *Before*

I RUSHED DOWN the hallway, tore through the restaurant, and pushed my way outside. I couldn't help the tears that broke free as soon as I burst through those doors.

And it immediately hit me, what I had just done: Cheated. On Jaymes. *Technically.* Or not technically, but just flat-out, blatantly, and clearly cheated. It honestly hadn't even been a thought in my mind when it was happening.

Why? Why am I such an idiot?

I shook my hands out and kept walking. I kept walking, and I had no plans to stop. I would walk all night if I had to, all the way across town.

Because I could still feel the whisper of Greyson's lips on mine, could still feel the ghost of his fingertips pressing into my skin—on my waist, and my ribs, and my hips, and my thighs.

I rubbed my hand across my mouth, angrily wiping away the traces of himself he'd left behind. I swiped away at my tears, too, at the steady stream of them spilling down my face.

Why did I let this happen?

Why was I so desperate that I ignored the flashing red *"Do Not Enter"* sign plastered across his forehead time and time and time again?

Why did I want him so badly that I was willing to take any piece of him I could get, no matter how much it broke my heart?

Because that's how I felt: Broken. Split wide open.

My mind was spinning, reeling. I couldn't latch on to a single thought or emotion I was feeling; there were too many.

But every single one of them was cradled by a hurt I couldn't ignore, no matter how badly I wanted to. It crept over my skin and reached inside my chest, seizing my breaths.

Was it so much to ask, that someone simply love me?

No ulterior motives, no hidden agendas, no secret list of all the reasons for why they shouldn't. For someone to love me, not because they were high or lust-filled or guilty or trying to take advantage, but because they simply…loved me, for everything and all that I was. Every scared, and scarred, and hurting piece of me.

A new wave of tears rolled in, and I couldn't stop them from falling. They were determined to spill, and spill, and spill and never let up. I could barely see two feet in front of me. I gave up and sat down on the curb, taking a deep, shuddering breath, squeezing my arms around my middle—my desperate attempt to suffocate the pain.

It wasn't coming in waves anymore; I was drowning in it.

Greyson's feet stepped into my blurry line of vision. I hid my face in my hands and shook even harder, crying even deeper than before.

It felt pathetic, this broken version of myself. But I guess that's what I'd been hiding from all this time. The abandoned little girl inside of me who was crying for her dead mother, who was desperately waiting for someone to come and pick her up and hold her and tell her that everything was going to be okay. That the world was not as cruel, or as dark, or as damaged as it felt. That I was not broken, I'd just been through the wringer and was pieced back together a little differently.

Greyson sat down beside me, his arm bumping mine. "I'm so sorry," he said—quiet, honest, full of remorse.

"Go away," I barely managed to reply, squeezing my knees tighter.

"I can't do that, Jess." He took a deep breath and released it. "I have to make sure you're okay. And I need to explain some things to you. I need you to understand that I never meant to hurt you, and I never meant to be such an asshole. I want to tell you everything—I *need* to tell you everything, if you're willing to listen. If you'll just hear me out…

"Will you please let me explain, Jess?" he asked, and the desperation in his words gave me pause. But I didn't think there was anything he could say that would change any of this. That space in my mind where I'd dreamt of him and I was now a big, black void. An endless expanse of darkness. No end, and no beginning, and nothing in-between. We never were, and we never would be. I got that now. I understood it in the way my heart ached at the idea that this *something* between us never was. It had all been in my head.

It took me a long time to respond, to nod my head and hear him out, but he waited patiently until I did. And I didn't do it for him, but for me. I wanted to hear whatever words he had to say so I could walk away from him once and for all with a clean break.

But his next words obliterated every thought, every feeling, I thought I knew when it came to Greyson.

"I tried to kill my dad once," he said, and the world around me stopped spinning.

Forty-One *After*

I KNEW I was in for a world of interrogation the next time the girls and I got together—*okay*, yeah. Let's be real; I was expecting no fewer than fifty messages in our group chat by the time I got home. And that's exactly what I got.

I fall into bed with a bone-deep sigh and open up our text thread.

Distraction.

Distraction is just what I need right now.

Sita: *It's like...you think you know someone and all of their truths, and then you watch a man eye-fuck her like she's his last meal, and HAVE WE MET BEFORE?! Hi, I'm Sita. It's so nice to finally meet you, Lady Enchantress, Mistress of the Temple of Cock-Tease, Seduction, and Debauchery.*

Maggie: *Oh my god. Ignore her. Seriously, though... You two were kind of intense.*

Kat: *Haha! Shit was definitely intense. I mean, damn, Jess. I didn't know you had it in you.*

Kat: *Literally. <<< see what I did there?*

Sita: *Except we did.*

Sita: *...Know that she's had it in her.*

Maggie: *OMG, you two!*

Sita: *Oh, please! If we didn't know it before, we'd know it after tonight.*

Kat: *This is true.*

Sita: *The question is, what was it like? Where does he rank among your handful of lucky captors?*

Kat: *Hahahahaha*

Maggie: *"Lady Enchantress" "handful of lucky captors"??? How much did you have to drink tonight, Sita?*

Sita: *Not nearly enough.*

Maggie: *Agree to disagree when you start sounding like a Tudor from the sixteenth century.*

Kat: *Bahahaha! Seriously gonna pee my pants right now.*

Sita: *In all seriousness, though...*

Sita: *Is he big? <insert eggplant emoji> too drunk to find.*

Kat: *How have I never realized until now that Sita TOTALLY goes sixteenth century when she's drunk?*

Sita: *You lie, peasants.*

Maggie: *Okay, but remember that time you asked the guy at the karaoke bar to show you his wicked ways, and I quote, "MY LORD"?*

Kat: *(A GIF of someone falling onto the floor in laughter.)*

I crack a smile.

If I've said it once, I've said it a million times, but I'll say it again: My girls are nuts.

Their messages go on and on like this, shifting into an entire conversation of GIF's alone, before:

Sita: *Jess, are you home yet?*

Sita: *Jeeeeeeesssss.*

Maggie: *Leave her alone. She's had a long night.*

Kat: *Or maybe her night's just getting started.*

Kat: *If you know what I mean. Wink, wink. Nudge, nudge.*

Sita: *We know what you mean. *eye-roll**

Kat: *You know there's actually an eye-roll emoji, right?*

Sita: *Still too drunk to find.*

Maggie: *LOL*

I decide to finally insert myself into their ridiculous conversation with a: *You three are too much. But I love you anyway.*

Sita: *Ah! You're here! There* Here... You know what I mean.*

Kat: *How did it go?!*

Sita: *Is he still there?*

Maggie: *Tell us everything!!!*

Sita: *Calm down, Mags. She's had a long night.*

Maggie: *Ha. Ha. Point taken.*

Kat: *Ignore them, Jess. Now tell us!*

I snort a laugh, because they're insane, and I love them so fucking much, but my laugh runs straight into an ugly cry without my permission, and they collide in a tragic mess. Tears stream down my face while I'm still laughing like an idiot, and then my laughter quickly turns into some form of a strangled sob.

Clearly, alcohol and exes and devastating revelations don't mix.

I may have had a shot or four more as soon as I walked through my front door, too, and it's hard to keep my emotions at bay when tequila has willingly opened the floodgates.

I thought we figured this shit out, God. I flop back onto my mattress and sink into my blankets with another bone-deep sigh, burying myself in my safe haven—another magical space of my own making. My comforter that feels like what I imagine lying a bed of clouds must be like, and enough pillows to build my own fortress.

I would know. Charlee and I have built enough of them.

I wipe my tears from my face and focus on my breaths and the comfort of my marshmallow kingdom enveloping me.

Inhale. Exhale.

And inhale. And exhale.

And I decide, just now, that I'm sort of pissed. It's an emotion I've long since been acquainted with, this deep-rooted anger born from somewhere I can't quite pinpoint, but I welcome it with open arms.

I have every right to be pissed, though, don't I?

Because shouldn't the first thing out of someone's mouth when there's obvious interest between you be: "*Hi, so nice to see you again. I'M MARRIED! I'm married, I'm married, I'm married.*"

"*In your face, motherfucker.* I'M MARRIED."

Especially given our history?

How did I not see the ring sooner? *How did* none *of us see the damn ring sooner?* Before hope and memories and feelings sunk their claws back into me?

And *fuck*, but it hurts. My chest aches, and my throat tightens, and *it fucking hurts.* Just like I knew it would when I found out he was taken. Because of course he's taken. He's *Greyson.*

What idiot would let that go?

This idiot, I remind myself, and then I reluctantly throw on my big girl pants and tell my friends what happened in one short, three-worded text. The zinger that still makes me want to throw up two hours later.

Me: *So, he's married.*

Forty-Two *Before*

"WHAT?" I ASKED. There was no way I'd heard him correctly.

"Last year," he swallowed, "after one his benders. After my mom had caught him cheating, and I'd found her…" he paused, clearing his throat. I swallowed my fear, and my feelings, and looked him in the eyes. They were full of pain. A pain I'd known my entire life. But he wasn't trying to hide it from me. He sat there, looking at me, imploring me to understand. "I found her on the bathroom floor in a pool of her own blood…"

I sucked in a breath, held it. *Oh my god…* I understood so much more than he knew. Images of my own mother flashed before my eyes, images I'd tried so hard to bury and forget. "I am so sorry," I whispered, releasing the weight of the world in four words.

He shook his head, shrugged. "She's okay now. But that night…she tried to kill herself." He was still shaking his head, lost in the memory. "My dad—this *selfish* piece of shit who called himself a man—had reduced this amazing woman, *my mother,* to someone who felt so fucking low that she wanted to leave it all behind—leave *me* behind. And I just…I lost it."

He swallowed, his hands gripping his knees tightly. "I hardly remember it—going through the motions. Dialing nine-one-one, holding her until the ambulances came, praying to any god who would listen that she'd be okay. I sat in the hospital with her all night…didn't leave her side the entire time.

"At some point, Jaymes picked me up and brought me home to grab some things from my house, but when we got there, my dad—*my fucking dad*—was shit-faced and had no clue what had happened. He was too busy bitching about dirty dishes in the sink and, *'Why wasn't there any damn dinner on the table?'*

"I'd planned on getting in and out, on running upstairs and grabbing my shit and getting the hell out of there. But then I heard him dragging himself up the steps, screaming for my mom to get her ass downstairs and make him something to eat or he'd pull her down into the kitchen himself."

Greyson slowly folded forward, elbows on his knees, head in his hands.

"I snapped," he said quietly. "I don't remember walking into his room; I don't remember pulling the gun from his safe and loading it. But I remember the look on his face when he attempted to take that last step up the stairs and his forehead met the metal barrel of the gun in my hand instead."

Holy shit. I took a deep breath, pulled my knees in closer to my chest. I was at a loss for words. This shit was...*fuck*. This shit was insane. But I didn't feel myself judging him for it. Call me crazy, but I...I didn't blame him. Not for one second did I blame him for what he'd done.

"My finger was on the trigger," he continued, "and I swear to God, I was going to do it, Jess. I was going to shoot him; I'd never been so sure of anything in my life. In that moment, I was only thinking...he didn't deserve to keep living this privileged life when he'd spent half of it pushing my mom to take hers, you know?"

The haunted look in his eyes made me want to reach over and touch him. To run my hand through his hair and brush my fingers over his cheek and tell him it was okay. That I got it. That I completely understood, and had I been in the same situation...I probably would've done the same exact thing.

"But Jaymes stopped me." Greyson's words cut through my thoughts, and puzzle pieces finally began clicking themselves into place. "I can still hear the words he drilled into me like it was yesterday. *'This piece of shit isn't worth your life, man. Think of your mom. Think of your future.'* It gave me enough pause that he was able to rip the gun from my hands, and that's when my dad gave me this," he ran a finger across the scar on his chin.

"I regret it every day, allowing myself to sink that low...

"...I don't want to be like him," he finished, his words soft and low. He looked up at me, his green eyes holding me in place.

And I saw myself in him then. In his vulnerability. In the way he'd opened himself up to me but was still fighting to protect himself, too. I think it was ingrained in us, in the people who had been through hell and back, to always be on guard and expect the worst in others.

I reached out and grabbed his hand without a second thought, sliding my fingers through his. I wanted him to know I was here, that he didn't need to be afraid of what I thought of him, because after everything he'd told me, after he'd let me in and placed his darkest secrets in the palms of my hands like this, he'd honestly never looked more beautiful—real, and flawed, and breathtakingly beautiful in the broken way he looked at me.

He squeezed his fingers around mine, tightly hanging on, and our eyes locked together, a deep and irrevocable understanding passing between us. A recognition and acceptance of what we hid from the rest of the world. It connected us, our familiarity with the kind of darkness most people couldn't comprehend.

"Jaymes saved me from a life wasted in jail and a future I could've never gotten back," he said after a while. "I'll never be able to repay him for that."

I nodded, understanding him completely. It all made sense now. And while I couldn't believe that Jaymes, *douchebag* Jaymes, had done something that amazing, that heroic and selfless, it finally all made sense now. Why Greyson was so loyal to him. Why he felt indebted to him. Why he wasn't willing to take something from him when he had essentially handed him back his life that day.

After what felt like a lifetime, I finally found my voice. "For the record, I don't think you're anything like him—like your father. And I know it sounds insane, but…I don't blame you, for what you did.

"I can't tell you how many times I expected to walk into our apartment and find my mom on the floor, OD'd and not breathing…Or how many times I must've thought about how it would probably make everything easier." *On her. On me.*

He squeezed my hand again, pulling it into his lap, his thumb skimming over my knuckles.

"But then it actually happened," I said, the words broken and quiet. Tears fell down my cheeks, and I wiped them away. I forced myself to finish even though I could hardly find my breaths. "But the worst part," I swallowed past the knot in my throat, a sob begging to break free. *The worst fucking part,* "is that I was right."

Forty-Three *Before*

"**THAT DOESN'T MAKE** you a bad person," he immediately responded. *But didn't it?* Didn't it make me a *terrible* person for ever thinking, or wishing, or feeling something so ugly?

"Sometimes people are too far gone," he continued. "That it feels like they already are."

I nodded, wiping away more tears. That's exactly what it felt like. Like she'd been there without ever actually being there. A shell of a person, of a mom, who'd flipped on the vacancy sign and had long given up on life.

"You haven't said much about your mom, but from the sound of it…she was in pretty deep?"

I nodded again, because again, he was right. Besides the obvious fact that drugs had taken her away from me, I'd never really known a sober mother. There were only three versions of her I'd seen, and sober had never been one of them. There was the euphoric, blissfully high version of her. The mom that blasted music from her *"good old days,"* and constantly burned food in the kitchen while begging me in vain to *"live a little,"* and *"dance with me,"* and *"just try it; one hit won't kill you, Jess."*

And then there was the version of her I sometimes, albeit reluctantly, found myself feeling sorry for, even though she was in a hell of her own making. The mom who'd lay in darkness for days at a time, sleeping and drifting in and out of deep depression. The mom I heard hurling her guts out at three-a.m. because she was coming down and hadn't been able to get her next fix. The mom who cried, and prayed, and promised that *this time* she would get sober, that *this time* she would be better.

But the version of her I got the most, especially in the end, was the side of her I hated the most. The fiend. The angry, and screaming, and willing to do whatever she had to do—to hurt and manipulate and steal from whoever she had to—to get her next fix, version of a drug-addicted mother.

That, or she wasn't there at all.

"She was," I finally answered Greyson's question, releasing a deep and shaky breath. "I don't think she could've stopped even if she wanted to. I mean, I *know* she couldn't. I knew...I knew she would go out like that...that it would end like that...

"So, yeah." I swallowed. "She was in deep. Way too deep for way too long." I blew out another breath and clenched my hands into two tight fists against my forehead, fighting off the rainstorm of tears I felt flooding forward.

I wasn't even sure how I felt anymore. About any of it. But I knew that the anger I'd felt about it all—*about her*—for so long, had somehow disappeared between one conversation with Greyson and the next. Like it had been taken away by the tide and washed out to sea. But somewhere in its wake, I felt a sadness and a loss I hadn't allowed myself to feel for her before.

And that locked space in my heart where the few good memories of her remained hidden and buried, filled with it.

The loss of my mom, the pain of it, lanced through me for the first time since the day I found her on our bathroom floor. As if it had lain waiting, building and multiplying in force and intensity for the past year, it slammed into me. I curled over on myself, a lifetime's worth of tears breaking through with a loud sob.

In the end, it didn't matter what my story looked like, how ugly or broken or damaged it was, *I was still just a girl who had lost her mom, far too early.*

Greyson's hands slipped around me, pulling me into the comfort of his arms, and I gripped his shirt in my fists and cried. I cried, and I cried, and I cried, and I didn't try to stop my tears from falling.

I cried for the girl who'd sat at the end of her mom's bed at six years old and didn't understand why she never wanted to get up and play with her. I cried for the girl who'd hid in dark closets when her mom's boyfriends raged and screamed and threw things against the walls. I cried for the girl who'd had to protect herself from the world when there was no one else around willing to save her.

And I cried for the girl who'd begged God, every night, to make things better but whose prayers were never answered.

There was a lifetime lost in those fifteen years. I'd been forced to learn how to love with a heart that was riddled with scars.

I was still learning. How to love myself, even though I'd never been taught how. How to love others. How to let them in without being afraid of getting burned.

I didn't know how long I sat there, crying, with Greyson's arms wrapped around me, but he never moved away. He just sat there and held me, the entire time. One hand running up and down my back, soothing, as the loss of my mother and a childhood abandoned washed through me again and again.

We'd hardly known each other, I realized. My mom and me. We'd never been *Mother* and *Daughter*. Instead, we'd spent all of our time in darkness, learning how to resent each other. And it hurt, beyond what I could fathom, that we'd never be able to change that. We'd never get that time back. Her addiction stole it all away from us.

But somewhere in the middle of that thought, in the middle of a world of pain and heartbreak, I remembered her smile. The glimmer of hope in her eyes when she told me she'd make it out alive this time. The laughter on her lips when she'd hand me a burnt chocolate chip cookie, or brownie, or piece of pie. The rare, soft passes of her hands through my hair when she'd thought I was sleeping.

I promised myself then, that I would try to remember these things more. That I would try to let these memories of her eclipse the hurt she'd caused, because in order to spread that much misery, she must have been waging one hell of a war inside of herself, too. All on her own. I couldn't pretend to fully understand it, but I knew I could learn to accept it.

Eventually, my flood of tears ran dry. I sat up and wiped away the evidence of it. I was sure it was useless; I could feel how puffy my eyes were, how red and raw my cheeks felt from wiping, and wiping, and wiping away at the steady stream that had poured down my face.

Greyson reached over and tucked my hair behind my ears, the corner of his mouth hitching up in a small, sad smile. And in the same way that I'd accepted all of his demons, I could feel the way that he wholly accepted mine, too. In the way his green eyes held mine with understanding. In the way he was still holding me, our arms and legs entangled between us. In the way he quietly whispered *"I'm so sorry"* more times than I could count.

"I know my situation is different," he said after a long while. "And I don't know the first thing about what you've been through," he added. But it felt like he did. It felt like he knew *exactly* what I'd been through.

"My dad made it out alive," he continued, "but it still feels like I lost him. I'll never respect him, and I'll never be able to stand being around him long enough to have a relationship with him." He shook his head. "Not after everything he's done. I can't.

"I can't stand that my mom took him back, or how they've swept everything under the rug like it never happened. And I think…I think that *you*, more than anyone, can understand why the first chance I get, I have to get the hell away from them."

I looked into his eyes again, and I didn't know how, but I knew what he was going to say before he said it.

He ran his hand through his hair, shifting away from me the slightest bit. "I have just over a month left before I leave. One month, and I'll be eighteen and graduated and officially enlisted. I want to start over, start a new life apart from all of this, you know? A life where I'll never have to look my father in the face again while pretending to respect him or having to rely on him for anything."

It was selfish of me, entirely selfish, but I hated the words that came out of his mouth then. Hated the idea of him leaving, of never seeing him again. But I understood. Of course I understood. I *had* to understand because I'd planned on doing the same exact thing for as long as I could remember.

Getting away. Starting over. Forgetting everything I left behind.

It's just that I didn't want to forget Greyson. And I didn't want him to forget me, either.

Forty-Four *Before*

WE LEFT THAT conversation as two different people. I could feel it, the pieces of each other we'd helped heal. And maybe that's why fate had brought us together in the first place. Maybe that's why I'd been drawn to him from the start.

I think I was okay with that. With walking away from him knowing we'd at least given each other that invaluable gift.

Because I'd never felt more at peace. With everything. With myself. With the road laid out before me.

I knew I still had a long way to go; I knew there was still a lot of darkness I would have to work through, but I could also see that small, beautiful sliver of light at the end of the tunnel now. I could feel the hope I sometimes clung to settle into my chest and make its home there.

It was going to be okay.

I was going to be okay.

Forty-Five *After*

SCREW IT. I'M buying a lottery ticket, and if I'm not a multi-millionaire by tomorrow, I'll be shocked.

Because what are the odds?

When Charlee and I turn around from the concessions stand a week later, arms full to the brim with popcorn and drinks and candy, there he is.

Greyson.

Looking as good as ever and as married as I never hoped he'd be.

"Jess, hey!" His face lights up when he finally sees me, and I smile, genuine, even though I feel as if I'm slightly dying inside.

Because he's not alone. A beautiful brunette stands beside him, toned body peeking through the shorts and adorable crop-top she's wearing beneath her oversized coat.

Greyson's coat, from the looks of it.

I hate her. I hate her immediately. I can't help it.

And isn't it amazing, how I've reverted back to a sixteen-year-old version of myself in a matter of seconds? *Get it together, Jess.*

"Jess, this is," Greyson turns toward her as I prepare for the blow, my body stiff. *My wife, my wife, my wife,* he's going to say, and it's going to crush me. "Brienne, my drummer's wife."

Wife. There it is. *Ouch.*

My heart drops, landing somewhere in the pit of my stomach—but, wait. *What?* "Your drummer's wife?" I ask on a breath.

"Yeah." He smiles. "And speak of the devil," a tall, tattooed man walks over, sliding his arm around her, "This is Matt, my best friend and bandmate. Matt, this is Jess," Greyson says, and I can tell from the surprised look on Matt's face that he knows exactly who I am. Yet his eyes are warm and inviting, friendly. I'm not sure what to make of that.

"It's nice to finally meet you," he says and holds out his hand for me to shake.

I shift my and Charlee's snacks around in my arms and reach out to slide my hand into his. "You, too." I smile, slightly nervous if I'm being honest, but I think I'm hiding it pretty well. At least I hope I am.

"Same here." Brienne grins widely. "And my god, she's *so* much prettier than you let on, G."

I retract my previous statement. I think I kind of love her. Immediately. "Thank you," I say, and shake her hand, too. "It's nice to meet you both."

Greyson hides a smile behind his fist at Brienne's words before clearing his throat and focusing his attention on me. "The rest of the band is in the theater already," he says after a moment. "If you'd like to join us. I know they're dying to meet you as well."

And what is that supposed to mean, exactly? They want to meet *me*? Why? *What would your wife think about that?* I want to say, but I hold my tongue and swallow back the words.

"Oh, no, that's okay," I say instead. "Another time, though? I've got my Charlee here, and we're already running late for our movie."

Greyson looks down at her, seemingly seeing her for the first time as his eyes widen just a fraction. He clears his throat. "I'd love to join you, then. If you two wouldn't mind?" He glances at Charlee again, adorably vulnerable in the way he waits for her permission.

"To see the Smurfs?" I laugh, breaking his stare and attempting to break the tension currently stirring between us. "Honestly, it's okay. You don't have to do that," I say, even though I want him to. But again...*he might have a wife,* my subconscious reminds me. The single word echoes in my brain, bouncing off the walls of my mind:

Wife, wife, wife.

His sharp features shift in disappointment despite his obvious effort to shield it, and I feel bad even though I know I shouldn't.

You could invite him over for dinner, Jess. Have that talk you two desperately need to have.

And we do need to have that talk. Now more than ever. That, and I can't find it in me to let him go. *Not yet.* Maybe not ever.

"Would you like to come over?" I give in to this churning need to not let him walk away even though it feels wrong. *He's not mine. He belongs to someone else now.*

But does he? I shove back against those thoughts, and ask, "After your movie? For dinner?"

"Yeah," he says, letting out a breath. Relief rolls off of him in waves. "That would be great. Thank you."

"Okay." I nod, more confused than I was prepared to be when I saw him again. My thoughts are a mess. So my mouth speaks for me, "See you soon, then. Enjoy your movie."

"You too." He smiles.

Maybe he's divorced? I wonder, while I absolutely do not just stand here and watch him walk away. Because that would be wrong, wouldn't it?

Broad back, sculpted arms, his ass in those dark jeans.

Nope. No way.

I don't notice any of it.

Forty-Six *After*

THE DOORBELL RINGS, and my heart soars straight into my throat. "Okay, Charlee. You ready?" I ask her the question I should be directing at myself.

And then I answer it for the both of us. "Yes, yes we are," I say with a deep breath as she nods sweetly.

"Do you think your friend will want to play Mario Brothers with us?" she asks.

"You know...I think he probably would." I answer her with a nod. And just like that, she's sold, grin wide and eyes excited. It's our tradition—making pizzas from scratch and playing Super Nintendo when she comes over. I got the Nintendo at a yard sale down the street a few years back. As soon as I saw it, I had to have it. I mean, who would get rid of such a classic gaming system? It's a relic, really. That thing.

And okay, yes, I'm nervous. And stalling. Clearly.

Deep breath in. Deep breath out. And I open the front door to a smiling Greyson holding a bouquet of daisies in one hand and a chocolate cake in the other.

"For the little Miss," he says, holding the flowers out toward Charlee, and she doesn't even bat an eye as she takes them from his hand and bounds away.

"I approve!" she yells from the kitchen, and I laugh.

"And for you." He hands me the chocolate cake. "If my memory serves me correctly, dessert is your one true kryptonite."

Dessert, yes. *And you.* No big. My heart beats faster, and I will it to calm.

I take the cake from his hands, biting back a smile. "Thank you," I say. "But where's the cake for you and Charlee?"

"You know," he laughs, "I seriously considered bringing two."

And then I laugh, too. "Kidding. I can share. I suppose." I jokingly shrug and set the cake down on my entryway table, holding my front door open wider for him. "Come on in."

He steps through the threshold and into my house, and somehow steals my oxygen in that one quick, seemingly ordinary move. But Greyson in my home, in my space, standing two feet away from me, is clearly not something I sufficiently prepared myself for.

I swallow thickly, clasping my fingers together to keep my hands from shaking. *Why am I so damn nervous?*

He looks around the room, slowly taking in my living room. Turquoise suede couches, vibrant Persian rug, macramé curtains...

I watch him the entire time, heart thundering.

When his eyes land back on mine, I can immediately recognize that this moment is surreal for him, too. Heavy. A little overwhelming.

It selfishly helps ease my nerves a bit.

But I'd still like to slide my hand across his chest and feel how hard his heart is beating. See if it matches the quick pace of my own.

"We're making pizza! Come on!" Charlee slices through our connection, refocusing our attention entirely.

"Mmm, I love pizza," Greyson says excitedly for Charlee's benefit, and he trails her into the kitchen with a soft smirk.

But what just happened there? That smirk? It doesn't help my racing heart at all. And my mind has immediately latched onto the vibrato of the single sound he uttered before *"I love pizza."* And *my god,* but I am in so much trouble here.

I follow them into the kitchen, clearing my throat and attempting to clear my mind, but my eyes zero in on his left hand without my permission.

Yep. Still there.

It's that reminder alone that settles my thoughts and emotions into an easy calm. For the most part, anyway.

"These are all our topping choices!" Charlee says, gesturing to the smorgasbord of them laid out on the counter before us. *"You can put as many on your pizza as you want,"* she adds, as if it's the best-kept secret on the planet, and I smile. She always insists we lay out as many topping options as possible even though she goes for pepperoni and pineapple every time, without fail.

And Charlee, as expected, decorates her pizza into a face with pepperoni eyes and a pineapple smile. I load mine with veggies and quietly watch as Greyson tops his with the same, before adding some pepperoni and pineapple at Charlee's insistence.

I laugh under my breath. She's a bulldozer, this one. And she already seems to be wrapping him around her tiny, six-year-old little finger like she has with the rest of us total suckers.

We throw our three pizzas into the oven and clean up our mess, and Charlee wastes no time dragging Greyson into the living room to set up for a first round of Mario Bros. 3.

Apparently, she and Greyson are going to play as a team, while I'll be stuck as Luigi on my own. Traitors, the both of them.

I suppress another smile as I set my sponge down in the sink and rinse my hands, gazing out the window and into my backyard. I take a grounding, steadying breath, watching my overgrown grass swaying in the wind. Up and down, and up and down, like the ripples in an ocean.

And my thoughts wander back to Greyson.

It feels like this—*all of it*—has been a long time coming. Years in the making. Inevitable, even.

Made even more confusing and obscure by that ring on his finger.

What is he doing here?

What does this mean? For him? For me?

Does his wife know he's here? Does he even have a wife? Is he married? One thought rolls into the next, and I feel suddenly impatient for the moment Greyson and I will be alone again—to air out everything between us. To finally rip the band-aid off and find a way to move on from here. *Whatever that means.*

I take another deep, calming breath and make my way into my living room. When I spot them both on the couch, game controllers in hand—Charlee giggling and him with an open smile—I stop to lean against the threshold, watching them.

I can't help but wonder if, in a different world, this could've been us. A family.

Or if now, in this lifetime, he already has one.

Forty-Seven *Before*

"JESSICA, STAY BEHIND, please. I'd like to speak with you for a moment," my photography teacher announced just before the bell rang.

I waited for everyone to file out before I stood from my desk and made my way over to her. Sara hadn't so much as glanced over at me as she left, so I doubted she was outside waiting for me.

I slowly stepped up to the edge of Ms. Greenburg's desk and watched as she pulled three large versions of a couple of photos I had taken from a manila envelope. She set them down on the desk between us.

"I hope you don't mind," she started, but I wasn't sure what there was to mind yet... "but I enlarged a few of your shots."

I slid them closer, glancing over them. Elizabeth in the kitchen, looking flustered as my dad kissed her cheek, Ashton and Reagan still wailing at her front and back in their carrier. Sara lying in the wildflowers behind our school, one held up to her nose as she closed her eyes and took a deep inhale. A football player with his head buried in his hands, the loss of his game written in the harsh lines of his features, highlighted by the dirt and grass stains that marred his uniform and arms. I'd played with the lighting and contrast, editing them in darker, muted tones.

Ms. Greenburg smiled as I looked back up at her. "You took a unique approach to this project. I appreciate your alternate view on the topic." I tried to grasp onto what she was saying, but I wasn't quite following. "Any of us can freeze-frame a snippet of time in a photo," she continued, "but what you've done here...there's a stillness in these shots that go beyond simple photography. You've captured *'Life in Action'* in a way we can all connect with. These quiet, private moments that propel life forward."

My mind spun around in a slow circle, sliding over each of her words. *She liked them?* Pride bloomed in my chest.

"These photos view like the work of an experienced and well-known photographer, Jessica. You have something beautiful here, and I'd like your permission to enter them into this year's DEMA Award. I know a few people, and they've already approved them for entry. All you have to do fill this out." She slid a paper toward me. "There's a ten-thousand-dollar scholarship on the line."

My mouth fell open. *What?* She was serious?

"It's an esteemed award, I know. But I think you truly have a shot here," she said. "It doesn't hurt to try."

I didn't know why, but it felt like she was handing me a lifeline that day. Another sliver of hope in a world opening itself up to me. It meant a lot, just that she'd thought my pictures were that good.

So I nodded, a smile pulling at the edges of my lips, and filled out the papers she'd handed me.

I was a little high in the clouds when I walked through the front doors of my dad's house after school that day. He was finishing up a call in the kitchen, his deep and steady voice traveling through the walls. I went to make my way upstairs but paused, turning on my heel and walking into the kitchen on a split-second decision instead.

I sat down at the table directly across from him and cleared my throat. *Now or never, Jess,* I swallowed. "I'd like to take you up on your offer…for counseling…if it's still on the table," I said, my heart racing a mile a minute.

He slowly slid his glasses down his nose and set them on the table in front of him.

I hadn't noticed before, how alike we looked. Our dark hair and dark eyes, the small freckles over the bridges of our noses. The features of my own face I could see in his older, worn ones. I guess it was the first time I'd actually taken the time to truly look at him.

And in that moment, he seemed...*relieved.* "Of course," he said. "Of course it is. I'll call and make an appointment for you right now."

I could've left it at that, said my *thank you* and walked away; at the time, I probably thought that I should've. But I still found myself asking him, "Was Mom always like that...an addict? When you knew her? When you guys were...together?" I realized that I didn't even know if they ever *had* been together. How sad was that?

But my mom didn't talk about much of anything of importance with me, and especially not the topic of my father. I'd learned a long time ago to drop the subject of him altogether. So, I honestly didn't know what their story looked like.

Had my dad been an addict too, at some point? And this was some old, sad and worn tale of two junkies who got together and accidentally had me? Or did he know a version of my mom I never knew? A sober version of her I'd imagined so many times but had never once truly seen? I honestly couldn't picture it.

He took a long time to answer me, long enough that I found myself fidgeting in my chair, uncomfortable I had asked in the first place.

But then he took in a deep lungful of air, his hand sliding across the table but hesitating, stilling in the space between us. "We grew up together—your mother and me. So, no. She wasn't always an addict. But we both...grew up in our own difficult situations. Your mother had a lot to be angry about; we both did...

"I'm not proud to tell you that we both ended up in the wrong crowd together, trying idiotic things we never should've been touching at any age, let alone at fifteen-years-old, to try and numb ourselves.

"We made some terrible, irreversible choices, and not a day goes by that I don't feel partially to blame for what happened to your mother. And to you." His eyes glistened with genuine emotion as he looked at me, as we sat across the table from each other and held the first conversation we'd had in seventeen years.

Way to dive right in, Jess. But was there an easier way to do this? I didn't think there was.

"I didn't know about you, Jessica," he said carefully. "Not until the day she passed away." He shook his head. "...I didn't know."

I believed him. I could see it in his eyes, in the hurt that bled through them. I could feel it in the way he grasped my hand and held onto it firmly, unwilling to let go.

And if I'd had any tears left to cry that day, I know I would have.

Forty-Eight *Before*

"**WE NEED TO** get a dress stat," Jaymes said, plopping down next to me in the grassy quad after stealing a bite of my burrito.

I rolled my eyes, pulling said burrito out of reach. "For what?" With Jaymes, who knew what he was about to say. I could imagine any number of things coming out of his mouth next: *So we can strap it on a mannequin and throw it in the ocean and watch people panic.*

For me, duh…I'm going to wear it to church this Sunday and ask to be baptized. See how many people freak and start praying for me.

A fishing net. A floatation device. A parachute.

Any of these things would have been fathomable in his mind, I was sure, but instead, he said, "The dress is for you. We're going to prom." He looked so sure of himself—and that statement—that it made me laugh.

"Ha. Funny. No, we're not," I countered, shaking my head and effectively wiping the smug grin from his face.

"Aww, don't be like that, babe." He turned me to face him, the knees of our crossed legs touching. "Picture it." He swept his palm through the air between us before reaching down and clasping his hands around my knees. "Booze. Grinding up on each other." He pulled me closer with a wicked grin. "You know, the superficial high school right-of-passage we can't allow ourselves to miss."

I honestly couldn't tell if he was joking. Especially when he looked at me like he was dead serious. But his dark eyes still twinkled with mischief.

I shoved his arm and laughed once under my breath. "Not that I think you're serious…But I'm okay with missing out. Honestly. Besides, there's always next year if I change my mind."

"Yeah, for you!" he shouted with an insufferable smile. "And I'm fucking serious. I won't let you rob me of this, Jess. These are *my* memories you're messing with, and besides, you're my girlfriend." He shrugged. "You're obligated. The second agreed to be my girlfriend, you agreed to this, so you might as well give in to me now."

"You know, I don't think I ever actually agreed to be your g—"

He pressed his finger up against my mouth. "Shh… Let's not let the technicalities get the best of us."

I almost choked on my bite of burrito. "You are so stupid."

"*Stuuuupid*, and going to prom with my girlfriend?"

I could've drawn out the ridiculous conversation I'd found myself in, but I mean…*what the hell?* "Sure, why not," I said, giving in to that incredulous smirk of his. I was sure he'd be over the idea by next week anyway. "But we're meeting there," I added. "And we're not doing the whole corsage, flower pin crap thing either."

He scoffed and pretended to pout about it for a second, before agreeing with a resigned, "Fine."

"*'Fine,'* what? What are you pouting about now?" Greyson asked with a chuckle, sitting down in front of us. "Hey, Jess," he quickly added before focusing his attention back on Jaymes again—all cool and casual.

"Nah, no more pouting," Jaymes responded, throwing his arm over my shoulders. "Jess and I are going to prom."

"Ah." Greyson nodded. His smile seemed a bit forced, but I could see that he was genuinely trying. I could give him that much at least. "What's that you're drawing?" He pointed at my forgotten notebook sitting behind me. I didn't know how the hell I'd left it out for anyone to see without realizing it.

I slapped it shut. "Nothing," I quickly answered. A little too quick.

Jaymes and Greyson wore matching expressions of suspicion.

"None of your business, okay?" I snapped at both of them, and then backpedaled with a, "It's nothing, just a random sketch." I forced a smile, hoping they'd back off. The sketch of Greyson's eyes burned a hole through my notebook and into my hands.

Had he seen what I'd drawn? Or worse, had the pages of my sketchbook opened up to something else *I'd drawn?* I stole a quick glance at him. Surely, I'd be able to tell if he had…right?

Jaymes shrugged. "Anyway, I've got to head out early. My mom needs some help trashing our old couch."

Aw, I kind of love that couch, I thought absentmindedly, my mind still stuck on my drawings, before Jaymes smacked a kiss on my lips and stood. "See you guys later."

Greyson diverted his attention elsewhere, his eyes scanning the library building and the rest of the quad.

We didn't say anything for more than a few minutes. It was the first time any silence between us felt off. Filled with something unspoken, or with too many things spoken.

He was focused on everything but me, but I still found myself focused on him. I studied his eyes, the way they felt contemplative, avoiding. I studied the sharp line of his jaw, the way it smoothed out and disappeared into his chin, curving up toward a pouty mouth of two full lips.

Lips I'd felt on mine; lips I had tasted. I swallowed thickly, diverting my own attention elsewhere.

"So, prom, huh?" Greyson asked after another minute or so, drawing my eyes right back to his.

And it was weird, this place we'd found ourselves in. We'd seen so much of each other, and yet…here we were, pretending to be nothing more than friends. If that's what we even were at this point. I honestly didn't know, but something between us felt forced. Forced to be *more than* or *less than* what we were, I wasn't sure.

"Prom…yeah, I guess so," I finally answered him.

But then he turned toward me, facing me dead-on, and gave me one of his most genuine, Greyson-trademarked, tilted smiles. "I hope you'll save a dance for me, then," he said, and the words—all of them—got stuck in my throat, my lungs completely forgetting how to give and receive air properly.

It didn't really matter, though, because Greyson stood up and walked away before I could've said anything back anyway.

And yeah, that entire last thirty minutes of my life had given me a severe case of whiplash.

I guess I was going to prom…

…with one boy when I still desperately wanted to be with the other.

Forty-Nine *After*

CHARLEE IS FAST asleep on the couch when the ending credits of Harry Potter and the Prisoner of Azkaban roll through the screen—her favorite of the series, of course.

"You impressed her, you know," I say to Greyson without taking my eyes off of her sleeping form. She's bundled up, taking up more than her share of the couch she and Greyson are sitting on.

"Did I?" he asks, and it feels like he's asking more than meets the eye. Hidden questions buried beneath unspoken words and even more questions. All of them concealed behind a pair of familiar green eyes.

And it hits me, that here we are, somehow. Hovering at the moment I've been waiting for all night—for what feels like an eternity.

It came too fast. But I'm not sure I'll ever be ready for this conversation if I'm being honest.

It's like reading a good book—the few and far between kind. The kind you open up and lose yourself in entirely, nearly devouring in a day, but at the same time, you spend half of the next picking it up and finishing it by only a sentence or two at a time because you can't bear for it to be over yet.

It's a lot like getting to know Greyson again.

The way he's pulled me right back into his orbit, digging up eight years' worth of buried feelings in a matter of weeks. Or minutes, really. The way the answers to what his life looks like now, *who's in it, what it's going to look like from this point forward,* have been at my fingertips all this time, I just didn't want to look.

I've subconsciously preferred the small amounts of exposure, the tiny slivers of who he is slowly presenting themselves to me without giving away how this story unfolds, because the truth is, I'm afraid.

I think I've known all along that once I find out the truth, I'll be forced to close these pages of my life forever. And I don't want this to be over. I'm not ready for whatever it is that still lives and breathes and *aches* between us to end.

"You did," I finally answer Greyson's question, attempting to suffocate the rest of my thoughts so they don't have enough air left to breathe. "I don't think we've ever made it to the last world without giving in and using the whistle at least once..." I say, still a little more than distracted, my mind spinning around all the possible outcomes for tonight. For this conversation. I will my heart to stop racing. And my thoughts, too. I push a hand against my chest, feeling the vibration of my breaths and my beating heart.

"Honestly, I think you might've reached hero status in her eyes in the span of one night," I force myself to continue, "and that is not an easy feat when it comes to this girl."

"Good to know," he says with a half-smile, genuine.

We both glance over at Charlee again, and the look I've seen a few times tonight flits across his face again—a curiosity in his eyes, and a hesitant tilt to his lips.

"She's a sweet girl." He clears his throat. "Is, uh..." And he clears his throat again, looking slightly nervous. It makes *me* a little nervous, or *more* nervous, though I'm not sure exactly why. "Is her father in the picture?" he asks.

His question takes me off guard. Confuses me. *What an odd thing to ask.*

"Um...yes. Fortunately," I answer him slowly.

He nods, looking mildly uncomfortable.

"He's an amazing father, actually," I add, though it doesn't seem to make him any less uncomfortable.

Charlie's dad really is good to her, though. He just happened to be a pretty shitty husband. He'd cheated on Maggie, and she'd been blindsided—hell, even I had been blindsided. Not one of us saw it coming. He didn't seem like the type. Not even close. But I guess we never really expect these kinds of things from the people we trust. So, we all lost a friend in him when it happened.

It was just after Charlee's third birthday when Maggie found out. She kicked him out, but he begged her to let him try and keep his family together, promising counseling and a whole other slew of empty assurances, so she took him back. Only to quickly find out he'd also been trying to mend things with the woman he'd been cheating on her with, and then she kicked him out for good.

"Shitty husband. But a great father—thankfully," I give voice to my thoughts.

Greyson's gaze snaps over to mine, his eyes wide and surprised. He clears his throat uncomfortably for what feels like the hundredth time tonight, looking uneasy on an entirely different level. "I had no idea you'd married," he says, his voice low and rough with emotion.

What? Me? "What?" Oh. *Oh!* And I draw it all together. "No." I laugh on an exhale. "Not *me*," I say with a hand pressed against my chest. I can feel my heart beating a mile a minute beneath my palm. "Charlee isn't mine." I shake my head. "Oh my god." And I can't help but laugh again. "Is that what you've been thinking this entire time?"

He nods, his eyes narrowed in confusion.

And I know I need to pull myself together and clarify, but *oh my god*, this is kind of hilarious, isn't it?

"No. She's my friend's daughter," I manage. "Maggie? *Her* daughter." And I look around the room, imagining toys and a little castle tent and a chaotic mess of things strewn across the space if she were actually mine. If I had a kid.

Someday, maybe, my living room might look like that. But today is not that day. I would've thought that would be a huge clue that she *wasn't* mine, but what do I know?

"Oh," he says, clearly relieved, taking a deep breath as he runs both of his hands through his dark hair. "*Have* you been married?" he asks.

"No..." I shake my head. "I haven't... But..." *And here we go*, because if there were ever a more perfect opening, this would be it. "I've noticed that you are," I point at his wedding band, finally giving air to the elephant taking up space in the room—in my mind, my heart. My future.

My throat tightens in anticipation of his impending answer.

"No," he says, looking down at the dark band, and then he laughs, too, bright and weightless, and our roles completely reverse between one moment and the next. Because now *I'm* confused. "I haven't been married," he adds. "Honestly, I forgot I had this on." He twists it around and around his finger before meeting my eyes again.

But mine pull together in suspicion without my permission, fully giving away my apprehension, because ring, plus ring finger, usually equals one thing: Marriage. If not in the present, then at least in the past. *Unless it's a purity ring,* I briefly think to myself. But I happen to know firsthand that that is *not* the case.

So I sit here and silently wait for him to elaborate.

He quickly does, much to my relief, leaning forward off the edge of the couch, his elbows resting down on his knees as he looks at me. "It was my grandfather's ring," he says. "He passed it down to my mother, and she held onto it to give to me.

"She gave it to me after my first tour overseas, actually."

Okay. I swallow, overwhelmed by the thoughts and emotions swarming through me all at once—relief, nerves, a shaky fluttering in my chest. I believe him, but...

"And you wear it now, because...?" I ask. *Because a girl could get really confused when you wear something like that on your finger. Clearly!*

And am I a complete idiot? Wasting so much time dreading the *what-ifs* when I could've just asked him as soon as I saw him again at the coffee shop?

I don't know.

Maybe. Probably. *Definitely.*

His green eyes don't stray from mine, and I watch as his lips tilt into a slow smile, as he chuckles softly and shakes his head. "I don't know how to say this without sounding like an asshole, but..." He shrugs. "It keeps me from being constantly hit on. Not that it deters too many women backstage."

I bark out an involuntary laugh. At him. At me. Who knows at this point? I sure as hell don't know, but my relief is palpable. "Must be nice." I sigh, pressing my back into my couch cushions and the heels of my palms into my eyes as I reign all my thoughts back in. "So they come flocking in by the dozens then, huh?" I ask with an amused tone, and definitely a tiny hint of jealousy.

"You could say that," he offers with a small smirk. "I'm not too interested in other women, though."

"You're not?" I manage to respond through my suddenly rapid heartbeats and shallow breaths. I don't mean to jump to conclusions or anything here, and assume what I think he's insinuating, but what else is that supposed to mean?

"No." His Adam's apple slides up and down his bare throat. I can't take my eyes away from the movement—until he says, "There's only one woman I've been interested in connecting with for the past eight years, and I think we both know that's you."

And my eyes snap back up to his.

Fifty *Before*

EXCEPT THAT I showed up on prom night—in a stupid, *awesome* black dress that tied between my shoulder blades—and neither of them were there. I'd curled my short hair into waves, had braided two dark chunks of it along the crown of my head. I had on *red freaking lipstick.* And neither of them was there. I couldn't spot Sara anywhere in the crowd yet, either.

You probably deserve it. Karma, much? I mentally flipped off my own subconscious.

I waited another half-hour in an unlit corner of our decorated multipurpose room, feeling like a full-blown idiot as I watched everyone laughing and dancing with each other, before deciding to storm off and punch Jaymes in the face as soon as I saw him.

His house was fifteen minutes away—walking distance. It was totally doable. Especially since I'd opted for a pair of high-top chucks instead of heels.

I was lost in a one-track mind: *Walk, find Jaymes, PUNCH HIM.*

I mean, I didn't even want *to go to prom in the first place!* I knew I should've stuck to my damn "no" when he'd asked me to go.

I felt the rumble of Lady's engine cut into my thoughts as much as I heard it.

"Jess?" Greyson called.

I kept walking.

"Jess!"

Yep, still walking. I was mortified. About all of it. Showing up, putting as much effort into dressing up as I had, Greyson catching me fuming on the side of the road, over *Jaymes.*

"Jess!" he yelled louder.

I stopped and turned toward him, my hands drowning in the lace pockets of my short dress. That's right, my dress had *pockets*. Rad, right? *I was going to punch Jaymes in the face so fucking hard.*

"What?!" I shouted at Greyson with more force than necessary.

"Why are you walking *away* from prom?"

"Because I'm going to find Jaymes and punch him in the face!"

He tried to hide his smile behind his fist, but I could see it anyway.

I started walking again.

"Get in, Jess," he called out to me. I wanted to be stubborn and refuse to give in, but I was afraid my anger would roll into attempted-murder status by the time I finally got to Jaymes.

So, I got in and slammed Lady's door shut behind me. I didn't miss the way Greyson cringed a little at that.

"Sorry," I muttered. "But can you please shove your fancy shoe into the floor and get us to Jaymes' stat?"

He laughed quietly. More a smile than a laugh, really. "Sure, Jess. You got it."

I'd been so lost in wanting to punch Jaymes in the face that Greyson in a tux had completely slipped my attention. Until now, of course.

And... *Holy shit.*
Holy.
Freaking.
Shit.

What in the actual fuck? And I'd thought Greyson in casual clothes left me breathless. I knew nothing about the way my airways could constrict until this moment right here. *Nothing.*

His long black pants were fitted, hugging his thighs; the sleeves of his white dress shirt kissed the tips of his wrist bones; and his maroon coat, with a sleek, thin black collar, and his slicked-back hair…fit in perfectly with Lady's timeless class.

I wasn't even going to get started on the black bowtie that hugged his throat…

"You look beautiful," he stole the words straight from my mouth.

I looked into the sea of his green eyes, and he smiled.

"You don't look so bad yourself," I said, and took my first full breath of air in what felt like minutes. I was smiling, too.

"So, why are we pounding Jaymes' face in?" he asked.

I looked out the window. We'd already pulled up to his house. *When did that happen?* "Because he stood me up when I didn't want to go to prom in the first place."

He nodded, amused. "Understandable."

I opened the door. "Thank you for the ride."

"You're welcome. Should I wait for you?"

I shook my head. "No, that's okay. You're already late. Go ahead and go." *Go be with whoever you dressed that heartbreakingly beautiful for.*

Even after everything, a small bit of jealousy stirred inside me.

It still felt like he was supposed to be mine.

"See ya, Grey." I closed the door, and he waved. Most of my anger had already dissipated, but I was still going to march into that house and give Jaymes a piece of my mind.

Fifty-One *Before*

WHEN I WALKED into his house and turned the corner into his hallway, though, I was assaulted by a sight I did *not* expect to see:

Jaymes and Sara. Up against the wall. Pants swimming around his ankles; pink, puffy dress lifted to her waist as he thrust into her.

Over, and over, and over again.

I cleared my throat, deciding right then and there that this wasn't going to be one of those scenes where I quietly snuck away and dwelled alone in my own hurt.

No. I wasn't that kind of girl.

Anger simmered in my veins, my fists aching for physical contact. I charged at them, tearing down the hall. Naked or not, I was going to beat the shit out of whichever one of them I could get my hands on first.

I didn't care that my feelings for Jaymes didn't run very deep. He was still my boyfriend. And my friend, or so I'd thought. I'd thought they both were. But *this?* This bullshit? This was exactly how much they cared about me, how much they respected me and valued *my* friendship.

Before I could make it even halfway toward their startled expressions, though, Greyson hauled me up and into his arms.

"Are you kidding me?!" I screamed. At the two half-naked traitors in front of me, and the boy behind me with a firm grip around my waist.

"It's not what it looks like," Jaymes said stupidly, quickly pulling himself together. *Seriously, what kind of idiot did he take me for?*

"Oh, please. It's exactly what it looked like," Sara said with a level of calm and disdain that stunted my speech for more than a few seconds. She smoothed her dress down. "How long was he supposed to wait for you to spread your legs, Jess?" She laughed, the Sara I thought I knew long gone.

I fought to break free of Greyson's arms. "What the hell is wrong with you?" I spat at her.

"You don't even like him!" she screamed. "But *I* do! I always have; you're just too wrapped up in your own stupid drama show to see it!"

Wow. I almost laughed. Almost.

So much for two people I thought were my friends.

It didn't even hurt my feelings, really. I expected these kinds of things from people. That wasn't anything new—the lies, the deceit, how fake they were. The world was sprinkled with bullshitters like them. So, no, I wasn't angry or upset with *them*. I was pissed at myself. Because I thought that after everything I'd been through, my bullshit-o-meter was a hell of a lot fucking better than that.

"You two can have each other." I smiled sardonically. "I'm happy for you both, really. You can go rot in hell together." I lunged forward. *Just one punch.* One punch would feel so damn good. Or a slap, a scratch. *Anything.*

But Greyson pulled me back and hauled me outside where I proceeded to kick and fight and push against him.

I worked my way out of his arms and shoved him away. "Don't touch me," I said, taking my anger out on him since he'd dragged me away from the two who actually deserved it.

"I get it, Jess. I do. But I didn't do this to you." *Didn't you, though?* my heart whispered. "Get in the car. Please. I'll drive you home, okay?" he pleaded.

And just like that, the fight fled from me, bleeding from my fingertips as I tried to grasp onto what was left of it. It was useless. I walked over to his car and got in, shutting the door and slanting my body toward the window.

Greyson slipped into his seat and turned the engine over, pulling away from Jaymes' house.

I watched the cracks in the sidewalks shift from dark lines to rhythmic shadows flitting past the faster we drove.

"Why'd you stay?" I eventually asked him.

"Honestly?" he said. "I had a feeling things might go that way."

I turned to him. "What's that supposed to mean?" Did he know something I didn't this entire time? Had he been keeping Jaymes' dirty little secret behind my back?

"Jaymes is Jaymes," he shrugged. "So I can't say I'm surprised." *Touché,* I thought, and let out a breath. "He's an idiot, though. The fact that he can't see what he has right in front of his face." He shook his head. "He's a fucking idiot."

I felt like turning his words around on him, telling him he was an idiot, too. Because if he could see what was right in front of *his* face? He'd see that he had me, so much more than Jaymes ever had.

"And what is that, exactly?" I asked him instead.

He looked at me questioningly.

"What is it that he has?" I elaborated.

He smiled a little. The right side of his lips, anyway. "I know what you're doing, Jess. Don't. Please."

I forced a smile back. "Right," I said, and we left the conversation at that.

Fifty-Two *Before*

WE DIDN'T TALK much after that, Greyson and me.

And I didn't really know why, except that sometimes it hurt just to look at him. The one thing in this world I'd desperately wanted but would never have. Yet another prayer gone unanswered.

There wasn't any animosity between us, though. We simply kept our distance. Smiling when we caught eyes or waving when we passed in the hallways. It was our acceptance, I think, that this was where our lives were meant to fork apart.

But still…it hurt.

Every time I looked at him. Every time I thought about him. Every minute of every day, every second I spent breathing, the thought of him leaving crushed me in a way I didn't know how to come back from.

I didn't understand it. Not really.

So I avoided it—avoided him. Just like he'd been avoiding me. Because if we severed most of our ties now, it wouldn't hurt as much later, right?

I could only hope.

So, I focused on school, on painting, instead. I focused on the therapy I'd only recently started but could already tell was going to help me. I focused on everything but the fact that Greyson was avoiding it, too: the tiny granules of sand falling through the hourglass, counting down the last days, hours, minutes, seconds we had left before we'd have to say goodbye forever.

Fifty-Three *After*

BOOM, BOOM, BOOM, goes my heart. A steady pulse in my throat; a whooshing in my ears. Too fast to track the beats, to differentiate one from the next. Just a steady, continual thundering that reverberates through my entire body.

Greyson gave me no time, no time at all, to linger on the relief of these revelations before slamming a new one down on me. The most insane one. *The most important one.*

"There's only one woman I've been interested in connecting with for the past eight years, and I think we both know that's you." No questions about it. Intentions clearly drawn.

I swallow thickly. Our gazes are still locked together, emotions running high. So high I can't tell which are his and which are mine as we look deep into each other's eyes, into what feels like our souls. I think we share them all—relief, curiosity, fondness, *yearning*.

I lick my lips and his eyes follow the movement, making my heart race even faster as his mouth pulls up into a slow smirk. Like he somehow knows and enjoys how much he still affects me after all this time. I open my mouth to say something—*what*, I don't know—but my phone rings in my lap, jolting me from the moment and effectively severing our connection.

I look down at the screen. It's Maggie. Maggie. *Answer it, Jess!*

"Hello?" I answer, breathier than I intended, but it's hard to speak clearly when my chest won't fully expand and allow me to breathe properly.

"Hey, girl. I'll be there in ten. And thank you again—so much. You're a lifesaver."

"Any time, Mags. You know that," I say, and I mean it. I love watching my little Charmander. Especially when it means helping out my best friend. "See you soon." I hang up.

"That was Maggie," I tell Greyson. "She'll be here in a few minutes."

He nods, coming to a stand. "I should probably head out, too. It's getting pretty late."

I can't deny the twinge of disappointment I feel at his words. I don't want him to leave yet. But at the same time, I feel like there's a lot to process here, and maybe I do need some time to sort these things out in my mind before we move forward—if that's what we're even doing here. Is that what we're doing? *God, I sure as hell hope so.*

And it's like he somehow knows it. That I need a little time to soak it all in and let my feelings settle.

Looking into his eyes now, I know with absolute certainty that I'm right, and my throat tightens, the walls around my heart completely crumbling.

If I hadn't already fallen for him eight years ago, I know I would've started just now.

Can he see that, too?

He reaches his hand down for me, and I slip mine into his, letting him pull me to my feet. I try to ignore the way my legs are slightly shaking. But again, he simply smiles, like he knows exactly what's happening inside my mind right now. And inside my heart.

I head for the door as he grabs his coat and his keys, watching as he slides them into his pocket.

"Thank you for having me over," he says with a smile that fully reaches his eyes.

"Of course." I pull my front door open with a matching fondness tilting my lips. "Anytime," I finish. It's not at all what I want to say. But...what else *is* there to say? "*Call me sometime*" seems incredibly anti-climactic. I know I don't want him to walk away without knowing when I'll see him again, but I sure as hell can't tell him that after only spending a handful of hours with him, I think I might still love him.

Even after all this time.

It's insane, psychotic even, because how is that even possible? *I don't know him anymore. Not really.* I'm only just starting to get to know him again.

Except...it feels like I do. It feels like time and space have shrunk themselves together, dragging eight years ago into the present and landing us right where we left off.

All it took was one look at him for it all to come flooding back, and it hasn't gone away.

My heart aches, twists and clenches at the thought of him leaving tonight and not knowing when I'll see him next. It makes my stomach turn. And I've only felt this way once before.

The first time I fell in love with Greyson Hayes.

He walks through the front door and into the nighttime air coating my porch, turning on his heel to face me, casually leaning against the doorjamb. His hand reaches out for my hand without hesitation, and when his fingers slide through mine, he gently pulls me toward him.

Awareness of our proximity slides over me, making my heart thrum through my body. But then his lips—*his lips*—lower down onto mine before I can finish a single thought.

A soft, intentional press of his mouth on mine, his warm scent enveloping me, and...

"We still have a lot to discuss," he says, pulling away far too soon.

"I know," I say quietly. *Why I left home. Why I changed my phone number. Why I didn't wait...* I know these are all things he wants the answers to.

The regret of that last one threatens to swallow me whole.

"Call me when you're ready," he knowingly says, and then he kisses my cheek and disappears into the night with a small smile.

And I'm not surprised.

Patience always was his best virtue, after all.

Fifty-Four *Before*

THE TIME FOR our poetry presentation finally came. It felt like a lifetime, yet no time at all, had passed between those first days with Greyson in class and now.

"Ms. Martinez, Mr. Hayes, you're up next," our teacher called.

We stood from opposite sides of the room and made our way to the front of the class. My heart raced as I stood next to him, all eyes on us. I didn't realize yet, that my heart was pounding away in anticipation of something else entirely.

Greyson cleared his throat and started our presentation, clicking through some of the slides we'd put together. I didn't hear any of it. I was standing there, feeling the weight of his presence beside me, hearing the tone of his voice carry across the room, but I couldn't, for the life of me, tell you what he was saying. I was too busy swallowing down the hurt that came with standing so close to him while feeling lightyears away.

He'd never felt more out of reach.

And then before I knew it, it was my turn. I swallowed, and I swallowed again. And then I recited the last few slides of our presentation through memory alone. Greyson ran through his closing statements, but still, I didn't hear any part of what he'd said. He turned it back over to me again. The entire class shifted and focused their attention on me, waiting.

I'd practiced my closing words over and over again, but in that moment, I couldn't find them. I tried, for a few stuttering seconds, to dig them up from wherever they'd ran off to and hidden, but it was a lost cause; they were long gone.

Instead, a new set of words spilled themselves forward, eager and ready.

"We disagreed a lot," I said, "on whether it was romanticism or insanity that Poe suffered from. I was so sure it was one way or the other. *Insanity, clearly.* Am I right?" I forced a laugh.

"But I sort of get it now...how they go hand in hand," I said, feeling the truth of it pressing down on my chest. "Because when you find the person that ultimately changes the core of who you are, and you feel yourself falling for them...you can't just *tell* yourself to stop. Even if you can see the train wreck and heartache coming from a mile away, even if you *know* there's no way that person could ever actually be yours...it won't stop you from loving them with all of your heart. It won't stop you from handing both *it* and a sledgehammer over to that person and sitting back while you willingly watch them—intentionally or unintentionally—smash it to smithereens.

"And that notion in itself...is pure insanity. I mean, it doesn't get any crazier than that." I laughed humorlessly, swallowing back the pressure of my tears surging forward, breathing against the weight that had fully settled in my chest. I looked up at Greyson, holding his gaze for a few agonizing seconds before tearing my eyes away from him, focusing back on our classmates again.

"Love doesn't care about any of that shit," I finished quietly. "It only cares about that single person who makes your heart beat faster just from looking at them. Everything else is collateral damage. And in Poe's case, it was his own sanity."

My heart beat wildly, reverberating through my body. Echoing in my ears. The *whoosh, whoosh, whoosh* was all I could hear. My hands were shaking, and my breaths were, too.

Because I was pretty sure I'd just told Greyson I loved him, without actually saying the words.

All it took was one look at him to know I was right.

Fifty-Five *Before*

THE BELL RANG, and I walked out of class as fast as I could without making it obvious. Through the door, and down the hall, and halfway into the quad before Greyson caught up to me.

"Jess. Jess, wait. Please. Slow down."

I slowed my pace and then stopped, slowly spinning on my heel to face him. I knew I couldn't avoid this; I'd willingly put my feelings out there, and now I was going to have to face them.

I didn't find myself regretting it, though.

Because I did love him.

It was stupid, and inconvenient, and the worst timing on the planet, *and God really must've hated me,* but there it was. I loved him. I couldn't have helped falling for him even if I'd tried.

And I think I had tried, but I still fell for him anyway.

I loved his crooked smile and his green eyes that easily swum into the depths of my soul. I loved the words he sang from his lips but the ones he spoke even more. I loved the way he viewed the world as if it were full of unlimited possibility and not all the ways it had tried to break him, and I loved his unfailing belief in a better future...his ability to twist all that negative into the positive.

Looking at him now, I knew it was the kind of love that would stick with me long after he left. All these little pieces of himself had slowly sunk their claws into me, burrowing themselves deep, altering the way I viewed life, too—the way I viewed myself—through a glass half full instead of one that was mostly empty.

"Jess?" Greyson stepped forward, hesitantly reaching his arm out. His fingers slid around my elbow as he stepped another foot closer.

I took a deep breath, and our eyes locked together. I had no idea what he was going to say, but his eyes…in his eyes, I saw a few things I was absolutely sure of: Resignation. Relief.

But what did that mean?

"I fell for you, too," he said, and his words stopped traffic. The thoughts and sentences and images that traveled through my mind in a blur just—*halted.*

"What?" I whispered, my breaths coming deep and fast. He always did that, made my mind spin and my heart race, *and it felt like I was floating, right up and outside of myself.* Was he actually saying what I thought he was saying?

"I tried." He swallowed, stepping even closer, sliding his hand into my hair and landing at the base of my neck. "I tried *really* hard to keep it from happening, but you made it too fucking easy to fall in love with you."

My eyes watered, threatening to spill over. Because *holy shit,* but I never thought I'd hear those words come out of his mouth.

They had looked so good, too, on his lips.

And his hand was now in my hair, and he was standing zero inches away from me, and I wanted to take the adoring way he was looking at me and bottle up the way it made me feel: like I'd found a slice of magic in an ordinary world—in my world.

But that same world around me grew dark without my permission. My sun hid behind heavy clouds, and rain started to pour while thunder sounded in the distance. Because I was smart enough to realize…that just because he'd fallen for me, too, it didn't mean that anything between us could change.

Fifty-Six *Before*

THE HOURGLASS WAS still bleeding sand from one glass orb to the other. Our time was still running out. He was still leaving.

We still couldn't be together.

I pulled away from the bubble he'd sucked me into. His bubble of: *We fell for each other, and that's all that really matters right now.* Because it wasn't all that mattered.

What the hell had I been thinking, spilling my guts like that back there? Making it so obvious how I felt about him?

I knew I definitely hadn't been thinking that he felt the same way. It wasn't even in my realm of possibility.

Liked me, sure. I knew that much was obvious. I'd have been an idiot not to have seen it. But he had a *really* effective way of shielding anything much deeper than that.

My mind spun for the second time in as many minutes.

This is a cruel, cruel fucking joke, Universe. I laughed darkly.

Greyson's eyes narrowed. "What's so funny?" he asked. His guard had gone back up, too.

I hadn't meant to laugh. *But seriously, God?*

"It just figures…" I said. "That I would finally get what I want without actually being able to have it."

He stepped closer, shaking his head. "That's what I'm trying—"

I stepped away from him again. "I guess that's one of life's greatest jokes, though, isn't it?" I interrupted. He took another step toward me, fingers brushing my arm as I moved another foot back. "Handing out love at the absolute worst of times," I finished, lost in a world of my own thoughts.

"I don't think so," he disagreed, and I pulled my attention back to him, studying every curve and line of his face. I could see that he meant it. He was insane. "If anything, I'd say it's the opposite. That it's one of life's greatest gifts…

"…It's when shit is at its worst that we need love most."

I let his words tumble around in my mind. Let them sink into my consciousness, tasted them on my tongue.

They were bullshit.

"No." I shook my head, the weight of our conversation fully hitting me. "I don't *want* to be here. I don't want to feel this way—*I don't want to love you when I can't have you.*" And *fuck*, but I knew I was going to cry if I stood here one second longer.

"You have me. That's what I'm trying to tell you," he implored. "*You have me.*"

"No, I don't!" I yelled, loathing the tear that rolled down my cheek. "Not forever. Not in the ways that I want to. Not in *any* of the ways that matter," I finished softly, my heart aching.

That made him angry. His jaw clenched, again and again, his hand balling into a tight fist and releasing. He stepped right into my space. "*This?*" he gestured between the two of us, taking a deep breath, "What we have here? It matters to me—*a fucking lot.*"

"Right," I breathed. *That's why you pushed, and pushed, and pushed me away this entire time.* I wiped away another tear. "I'd say prove it, but—" He gripped the back of my neck, pulling my body flush to his, and smashed his lips against mine. *Bruising. Consuming.*

Out in the open, in front of the entire school, for the whole world to see…he was kissing me.

I couldn't help it; I sighed, and it collided with his next breath.

He kissed me, and kissed me and kissed me, like it would last forever. Like it would never end.

I didn't want it to end, but at some point, it did.

He pulled away but kept his eyes on mine, hands wrapped firmly around my shoulders. "Why does it have to be written in the rules that we can't take the time we have left and make the best of it?" he said, adding a soft, "I'm willing to try if you are."

And, yep, there it was again. The drip, drip, drip of the sand creeping up on us. I didn't have any fight left, though; I didn't have anything left to say. I wanted him. Any piece of him, for any amount of time, for however much it would hurt later...*I wanted him.*

"The way I see it...it's going to suck either way, so why not be together *now*, while we can?" he asked, still holding onto me. "And after...when I leave...we can call each other, or write, or *something.*" He shook his head. "I don't know. But it doesn't have to be the end."

I swallowed thickly, slowly pulling at the strings of my acceptance. Dragging it through my doubt and fear and unease, and releasing it with a resigned breath...and a small, almost imperceptible nod. I knew full well I was more than likely agreeing to heartbreak, but the thing was...my heart was already breaking. It already ached for the day he'd leave. So, he was right. We might as well take advantage of the time we had left. And maybe, just maybe, I'd be lucky enough to get some time after that, too.

He smiled at me then. More genuine and heartfelt than I'd ever seen, and then he pulled me into his arms, simply holding me there for a long while. His breaths hummed in his chest, singing in my ears. *I could stay right here, all day—for an eternity,* I thought to myself. But the minute bell rang too soon. I peeled myself away from him and picked up my backpack that had somehow found its way to the ground, turning back toward Greyson after I slid it on.

"See you at lunch?" It was the only thing I could think to say. *Good one, Jess.*

"Yeah," he bit his lip, smiling shyly, "I'll take us somewhere off campus."

"Okay." I nodded.

But we both still stood there, trying and failing to hide our smiles like two scared, lovesick idiots, while the quad completely emptied out. My cheeks warmed, and my chest did, too. My heart was pounding like crazy. I felt our smiles melt into my bones and slink into my soul.

I forced myself to look down at my feet, sucking in an overdue breath. "Okay," I repeated, and I finally found it in me to turn and walk away.

But Greyson slipped his fingers around my wrist and gently tugged me back toward him. "Wait."

"What?" I asked nervously, a jittery feeling skating over my chest. *Since when have I been nervous around him?*

Probably since you admitted in so many words that you love him, and he chased you out of class and told you he loves you too, and then you yelled at him a little bit, but he kissed you anyway, and then you both agreed that you want to be together, and now he's looking at you like...that.

We'd gone from one extreme to another, and I didn't think a single one of my thoughts had even had the chance to settle yet.

"I was thinking that I'd like to kiss my girlfriend again before I have to go to class," he said, and his words stopped me in my tracks. Along with the heart-melting smile lighting up his face.

"Come again?" I said. I couldn't help but smile back.

"I said I'm going to kiss my girlfriend again," he repeated, and what was it with boys and them not asking me if I actually *wanted* to be their girlfriend? But why did I like it so, *so* much when Greyson did it?

I was going to say so—the former—just to give him a hard time, but his lips shut me right the hell up.

I might've whimpered. Just a little.

His mouth curved up in a secret smile against mine in response, and it immediately became my favorite thing in the entire world—his smile that I couldn't see but could wholly feel against my own.

And then the way his fingers dug into my hips as he pulled me right up against him…that became my second favorite thing.

The rise and fall of his chest on mine, the beating of his heart pounding against my own, the way he slowly tilted my head back and slipped his tongue between my lips and into my mouth, deepening our kiss*: third, fourth, and fifth.*

It washed everything else away.

But I still wondered, for a brief moment, in the middle of that kiss, how many favorites we would accumulate in the time we had left.

Fifty-Seven *After*

"OKAY, DEFINITELY THE *'fuck me'* heels with the ripped jeans and white tee, and...the leather jacket!" Kat claps. "Yes!"

"Totally agree. Even I kind of want to bang you in that," Sita adds, looking way too serious about that statement, and I can't help but laugh.

"Thank you?" I say.

"You're welcome!" She perks up from her sprawl on my bed. "Now. Hair and makeup."

"You guys know I could totally handle this on my own, right?" I ask, even though them being here has helped ease any nerves I know I'd otherwise be feeling, and I'm more than grateful for their diversion.

"But it's your first date with Greyson," Mags offers with a smile.

"I don't think I'd call it a date—"

"Oh, don't be obtuse," Sita cuts in.

"It's totally a date," Kat says with a smirk.

"But even if it was," I roll my eyes playfully and continue, "It still wouldn't be our first date. We did go out in high school, you know."

"Girl, that doesn't count," Kat says.

"Why not?" I respond.

"*Because it doesn't!*" Sita shouts. "You were in *high school*; you're different people now!"

Touché. But Sita should probably slow her tequila roll, or I'm going to walk out of this house looking like a hot mess—if her overexuberant shouting has anything to say about it.

"We've hung out a few times now, though," I push back against their words anyway, because this is what we do: banter, and laugh, and try to make light of the heavy.

"A bar with all of your friends and a Nintendo night with Charlee doesn't count either. Now sit." Sita gestures to the stool in front of my vanity.

"Yes, ma'am." I shake my head with an amused smile and sit down in front of her, meeting her gaze in the mirror. "You sure you haven't kicked back too many to see my face straight, though, Miss Feisty?"

"Psshhh. You know there's no such thing as *too many* drinks in my world. But even still, I've only had *one*." She gathers a chunk of my dark hair and starts in with the straightener, using it to make the subtle, beachy waves I love.

"Speaking of drinks!" Kat says. "You should definitely have one in your hand right now." And she and Maggie quickly slip out of my room and into the kitchen, the sound of laughter and glasses clinking and my fridge opening and closing making its way down the hall.

"I'm just excited for you, babe. You deserve this," Sita adds, her tone shifting from the playful of a moment ago to serious, and I catch the glimmer of genuine emotion in her eyes before she focuses her attention on my hair again.

"Thank you," I say, feeling my own emotions suddenly knotting my throat. "That means a lot to me."

And here's the thing: It's not like I've been a saint or anything. I've dated plenty in the past eight years—some relationships lasting longer and turning more serious than others. But it always felt like something was missing. And as much as I consciously kept myself from comparing one man to another, I could never silence the little voice in the back of my mind whispering that we didn't quite fit together. Not as well as we could have.

But seeing Greyson again was like feeling that last, lost puzzle piece slide back into place. Different, and slightly warped by distance and time, but still an effortless match.

I think that's why my feelings for him came flooding back the instant I saw him again at the coffee shop. There's no escaping a connection like ours. I would know; I've spent the last eight years trying to convince myself otherwise.

Maggie and Kat stroll back into the room, drinks in each of their hands, and I'm pulled away from my thoughts. Kat passes one to Sita, and Maggie sets one in my lap.

"Thank you." I curl my fingers around the glass, lifting it to my mouth, and take a sip of the crisp, cool mojito Mags managed to scrounge the ingredients together from my kitchen for. It tastes amazing, and I'm reminded once again of one of the major benefits of having a bartender for a best friend.

I sigh into my cup, *"So good,"* and Maggie laughs.

"You're welcome," she says, leaning her hip against the counter in front of me, digging through my makeup bag. She finds whatever she was looking for and turns back toward me, makeup brush in hand. "Okay, close your eyes."

I take another sip of my mojito and do what she asks, shutting out my view of the room.

It's not long before the soft sweeps of eyeshadow across my eyelids and Sita's fingers gliding through my hair make me relaxed enough to want to fall asleep. And I think I could, if only there weren't this knotted ball of anticipation and excitement churning in my stomach.

Greyson's texts unwittingly slip into my mind, fueling these feelings further, and a small, secret smile curves my lips.

He went less than twenty-four hours of waiting for my call before deciding to text me himself. A short, sweet, heartbeat inducing:

I'm finding that I'm far less patient than I used to be. I'm dying to see you again. Come to my place this Saturday, 7pm?

Followed by his address.

It didn't take me long to agree. A slightly embarrassing thirty seconds, maybe. But hell, if he isn't here to play games then neither am I. And every cell of my body rages with the need to see him again.

My mind has gone haywire with the possibilities.

I force in a deep breath and push those thoughts away from the forefront of my mind, gently shoving them back into a dark corner for later, and focus on my girls. Their banter, their laughter.

The way it fills my heart with light and happiness.

It's forty-five minutes later when they've finished their assault on my wardrobe and face, and I'm all ready to go, looking next level thanks to my three best friends. My long, dark waves, smoky eyes, and nude lips are a definite step up from my own capabilities, and at the risk of sounding completely into myself: *I look pretty damn good.*

"Thank you, guys! I love you!" I yell from where I'm now standing in my front yard, arms wrapped firmly around my tree. A deep breath in and a deep breath out while I wait for my Uber to show.

"It's nothing." Sita waves me off. "But get your tree-hugging-ass back inside your house for a sendoff shot," she finishes with an amused laugh.

"A sendoff *toast*!" Maggie adds.

"Is she seriously hugging her tree again?" I hear Kat say, and I can't help but laugh, the sound echoed by my girls.

It's an ongoing joke—the tree-hugging. But they're used to it. My entire neighborhood is probably used to it at this point if I'm being honest. But hey, none of them should be knocking it until they've tried it. Because let them wrap their arms around a solid tree like this one and tell me that that shit doesn't bring them some inner peace.

I tear myself away from my front yard with a laugh, make my way back inside, and scoot onto a stool at my bar top as Sita slips me a shot of tequila, a smile still curving my lips.

"To Jess!" she cheers. "And a night of rekindling." She winks, and my stomach fills with warmth, with all the possibilities I tucked away earlier.

"To Jess, and a night of reconnecting," Kat adds, and I blow her a kiss. *I love you,* she mouths, and I mouth it back with a smile.

"And to Jess," Maggie says last, eyes shining with emotion as her lips curve into a smile of her own. I find myself holding my breath as she continues. "And the beginning of what we all hope is your happily ever after."

Her words immediately choke me up, hitting me somewhere deep and vulnerable. I blink back my tears—my hopes, my fears, my expectations. But along with all of that, her words carry in the current of nerves I've managed to keep hidden away for the past hour. A rush of butterflies and excitement, too.

The beginning.

Or the ending, maybe. The ending to an upside-down, backward, *beautiful* happily ever after that already began eight years ago.

Fifty-Eight *After*

I DON'T THINK he did it intentionally, but Greyson taught me that I was worth something.

He taught me to dream, beyond the simple kind of hope I knew. He taught me to live.

And he loved me—in his own way. Patient, reserved. Valuing me and my feelings, and what he thought was right for the both of us, above anything else.

It was the kind of love that made me see myself in a new light. The kind that made me grow to like myself for the person I saw in his eyes. The kind that taught me to love myself for exactly who I was, pain, and scars, and past included.

He taught me that my circumstances did not dictate my future, because he'd been through a childhood of darkness, too, but every day, he chose happiness. He chose a smile, and kind words, and the belief in a future for himself that was different from what he knew.

And I had noticed it right away—how happy he was. It was just that it had taken me a while to realize he was actively choosing that happiness every day. That he was fighting to rise from his circumstances instead of allowing them to drag him under.

It was the bravest thing I'd ever seen. And it was the most important thing he ever taught me.

I never thanked him for that.

It's the one thing I absolutely plan on telling him tonight, though, among too many other things. But he deserves to know that. At the very least, he deserves to know that he is one of the greatest gifts this life has ever given me.

And that I am so, *so fucking sorry,* I ever let him go without telling him that.

I force in a deep, shaky breath and finally gather up the courage I need to exit my Uber, shutting the door behind me as I glance up his driveway—only to find him patiently standing there in his doorway with a soft smile, the light from the inside of his house illuminating him like an angel.

Like the angel he looked like the very first time I saw him. Golden halo and all.

Fifty-Nine *Before*

WE SPENT ALL of our time together after that. Hanging out, taking long drives to nowhere, talking under the stars and the moon like we used to. Watching movies, going out to eat, swimming—in his pool, and in mine, too—working on homework, drawing, writing.

Holing-up in our rooms, doing all that making out I'd dreamt about too many times.

I think he'd kissed my mouth in all the ways possible by now.

And things had been…more than a little heated between us these past few days. I'd felt a lot of him, against a lot of me. Shirts and pants went pretty quickly at this point, too, and so did our hands, roaming up and down, and over and around, and grasping, and sliding over, and feeling.

Feeling, feeling, feeling.

Things always stopped there, though. One of us inevitably and reluctantly hitting the breaks before the other one did.

I wasn't sure I could handle giving him that part of myself, though, just to watch him walk away with it. And I think he felt the same way, too.

So here we were, having slipped back into our clothes for what felt like the hundredth time this week, still catching our breaths. He'd handed me his notebook, and I was slowly flipping through it.

I landed on one mess of a page titled, *"Jess,"* and looked up at him, eyes wide.

He dipped his head with a shy smile, his silent *go ahead.*

My heart raced, and my mind spun. I didn't know what to expect, but I know what I definitely didn't expect:

I think of kissing her at least twice a day,
*   or maybe twice an hour,*
but give me two seconds of her lips,
*   and I can fill an hour,*
singing about the way
*   one kiss can reach inside your soul,*
can feel brand new yet entirely old,
*   can fill a hole in your chest*
you didn't know should exist,
*   until the touch of her kiss,*
and the taste of her lips
*   left me yearning for this.*

I stared at the page long after I finished, afraid that if I looked up at Greyson, I'd pounce on him and rip off his clothes and give him everything I knew we both desperately wanted.

Because there were so many other words on that page, too.

Her eyes show you the stories of her past
*   she doesn't want to tell.*

And,

I found a future in her smile.
*   I want to stay there a while.*

And,

I don't want to let her go.

And,

I wish this pencil in my hand could draw her mouth.
*   I'd draw the shit out of her mouth.*

I laughed out loud, somehow breathless and full of life at the same time, and handed him one of my sketchbooks. He sat up against my headboard and opened it, his eyes widening at the first drawing: *his mouth*. And then it was his turn to laugh.

"I see you conveniently omitted that you're obsessed with me too," I said, "when you teased me relentlessly about *that*." I gestured to the collage of pictures on my wall. I didn't know how I'd forgotten about them the first time he walked into my room. But there they'd been, and I'd been slightly mortified, seeing as how he didn't drop it for *two days.* Or ever.

But also…I remembered how he'd stepped closer that day, taking a deeper look and getting lost in the sea of other pictures I'd taken. The way he'd looked at me in awe, a lot like Elizabeth had, before asking if he could keep one of them.

"Sure," I'd told him, assuming he wanted one of his team shots, but he'd plucked down one of me instead. A black and white of me sitting still on a swing, cheek resting against the chain. I was looking directly into the camera, eyes dark and filled with a myriad of emotions.

Sara had taken that one.

"Yeah, but now I have *Exhibit B* of your obsession with me," he waved my sketchbook in the air, pulling me from the memory. "Should I be worried?" he teased. "You're not gonna, like, hogtie me and keep me in your closet, are you?"

"Shut up." I shoved his shoulder, but he wrapped his fingers around my wrist and pulled me closer.

I landed in his lap, and we both quickly inhaled, all humor fleeing from our eyes, our minds, the room.

And then he kissed me, and I kissed him back, and I thought to myself, *I could do this forever.* But the darkest corners of my mind still whispered back: *you're on borrowed time.*

Sixty *Before*

BUT WERE WE? On borrowed time?

It didn't feel like it. Not after we'd ripped ourselves open in the middle of the quad, spilling how much we wanted to be together. Not after all the time we were spending with each other—laughing, and kissing, and talking, pretending like the rest of the world didn't exist.

But there was still this nagging feeling, a clawing weight in my stomach telling me I was wrong. That good things like this didn't last.

That they couldn't; that they *wouldn't*.

A whistle blew, loud and reverberating, tearing me away from thoughts I didn't want to be dwelling inside of anyway. I welcomed the distraction with open arms, fully focusing my attention on Greyson and his teammates out on the football field.

I knew I'd once said I hated his football pants—that they were stupid. *Irritating. Obscene.* Or something along those lines—but I was lying. I was a dirty, *filthy* liar, because those pants—*those pants*—were anything but.

I pulled out my sketchbook and immediately started drawing him, in full gear—like the total creeper I was.

But if no one besides Greyson ever knew I had an entire sketchbook full of drawings of only him, did it still make me a creeper?

Does a bear shit in the woods, Jess?

I don't know. Does it?

I couldn't help but laugh at myself, but my smile slowly melted away as I pressed pencil to paper, getting lost in the art of it.

Small flicks, and curved strokes.

A heavy hand on the shadowing around him, pulling him center-focus.

Everything else faded out. I was adrift, floating somewhere outside of reality. In that drawing, in the contrast between the quiet breeze blowing through my hair, the soft sounds of my pencil scratching against paper, and the echo of loud grunts and tackles on the field below making their way up the bleachers.

After a while, or what had felt like only minutes, really, another whistle blew in three short bursts. I pulled my attention away from my drawing to find everyone walking off the field and toward the locker rooms.

Everyone but Greyson, of course.

He slid his helmet off and called me over, beckoning me with a single finger.

I didn't know what it was about that one move. Whether it was simply him, attractive and all sweaty in uniform, or if it was the intense look in his eyes and the subtle tilt of his lips as he watched me fumble with my things, but...it did something to me.

Kicked my heart into overdrive. Forced my breaths to stall somewhere between my lungs and my mouth.

It should've been impossible to feel all the things I felt for him then, but I did.

I made my way down the bleachers one slow and measured step at a time, willing my heart to calm, and didn't stop until I was standing right in front of him. Less than a foot away, looking up into his green eyes.

His smirk twitched at the corner of his mouth. "Want to learn how to kick a field goal?"

"What?" I said, somehow excited and confused and lacking oxygen all at the same time.

"I'm going to teach you a little something about football, and then in exchange, you can show me how to draw," he said.

"Okay." I laughed. "I mean...why not." I shrugged, as if I wasn't excited about it. As if there wasn't a giddy version of me laughing and giggling and rattling pom-poms inside my chest.

He smiled. A knowing smile—crooked and perfect.

"But let's not expect me to be good at this," I added with a finger pressing into his chest. "Because then you're just in for disappointment."

"We'll see about that." He pulled me by the hand to the far end of the field, dropping the ball to the ground and turning to face me. "So, first...kicking the ball is all about body position, and follow through. If your ball is here..." He bent down and positioned the ball between his hand and the ground before letting it fall again, getting all serious on me between one breath and the next. "You're going to want to be here..."

His hands slid over my hips, wrapping around them as he walked me back three steps, and another two to the left. His fingers dug into my skin between my jeans and my shirt, the breath of his words falling over my lips.

He was explaining things.

Angles and degrees and body positioning, but all I really heard was the steady *whoosh* of my heart pounding in my ears. Completely overreacting to our proximity—to his hands on me.

His fingers curved over the front of my jeans as he moved behind me, one hand sliding down and gripping my thigh.

What was he saying?

"...eyes on center goal, and kick."

I nodded. "Okay." I was pretty sure I'd heard at least enough to give it a try. Right? *Keep telling yourself that, Jess.*

He kneeled down and held the ball in place as I positioned myself where he'd shown me to. "Perfect," he said with a smile.

I stood there and stared at that smile for a few lingering seconds, my own lips curving higher before I shook my head, and focused on the ball in front of me. And then I went for it, running the short distance and kicking it as hard as I could.

It flew out straight ahead, crashing right into the center pole of the field goal, maybe two feet up from the ground.

I snorted out a laugh. *Oh well. I tried.*

I found the same laughter dancing in Greyson's eyes as he attempted to smother his smile, teeth biting into his bottom lip. "Okay, how about something a little easier?" he eventually asked.

And by the end of that hour, I had learned how to properly hold and throw a football, what each position on the team was responsible for, and why football pants were so distractingly tight.

Turns out, there was a reason for this—other than my own viewing pleasure, of course.

Greyson laughed as he explained knee and thigh pads and the way his pants held them in place, but a quick google search later that night confirmed my thoughts exactly:

It was all about the bulge.

"Eyes up here, Jess," he said, and I tore my gaze away, shrugging unapologetically.

He chuckled, humor lighting his eyes. "I'll go get showered and changed really quick, and then we'll head over to Maddie's?"

"Okay." I nodded, watching him walk away and disappear into the locker room.

It wasn't too much later that we were sliding into a booth at Maddie's Diner—the same booth as the first time we'd been here, I was pretty sure.

And as I sat beside him, watching him talk and smile and laugh, his arm wrapped firmly around me, it wasn't lost me that I was just as desperate for him now as I was back then, all those months ago.

Desperate for one touch, one kiss, any piece of him I could get.

Only now, I was desperate for so much more—*for all of him.* For all of the pieces I'd collected, and for all the pieces I had yet to see. I wanted to own them all, forever. I wanted to sweep them up, and slide them into my pocket, and never let them go.

Sixty-One *After*

"HI, JESS," GREYSON greets me with a kiss on my cheek, and then a second pressed softly to the corner of my mouth. "You look beautiful," he says, and it does things to me, his words and the touch of his lips singing through me.

The feel of his mouth on mine lingers, and I so badly want to turn my face to his and steal some more of this feeling. Of his lips. Of the way they make me feel alive, the way they send a buzz flowing through my body, flooding my thoughts.

The need to do it rushes over me, overwhelming. We could skip dinner, skip all the talking, and I think I'd be happy with that alone.

I reign all these thoughts in and wring them out, forcing out an unintentionally breathy, "Thank you," instead.

"Come on in," he says quietly with a knowing smile—more of a smirk, really—and I laugh under my breath, stepping into his house for the first time.

The intoxicating aroma of something cooking in his kitchen assaults my senses, overshadowing my nerves. "Oh my god, what is that?" I ask without much thought.

"Chicken marsala," he answers, half-smile, half-smirk still firmly in place. He guides me through his entryway and over to his kitchen with a hand at my back, steering me toward a set of barstools sitting along his kitchen island. I sit down and quietly take in the space around me.

It's beautiful. And it very much suits him.

Raw, wooden floors and cabinets, crème walls, and black window and door frames accenting the otherwise muted furniture and décor. It's somehow both simple yet intentional. Comfortable, yet intimidating.

Much like Greyson.

Especially when he studies me like he is now, his eyes raking over me, over the features of my face, carefully reading my reaction to his home. Or to being *here*, *in* his home.

"Your house is very...*you*. I love it," I tell him honestly.

"Thank you," he replies, and if I'm not mistaken, there's a slight blush tinging his cheeks as he turns toward the stove to dish up our plates.

"You cooked this all yourself?" I ask him.

"I did." He nods, and I nod my head back in response even though he can't see it. But this is not something I knew about him. It seems ridiculous, but...I didn't know he could cook. Not now, and not before. And this is where my mind has decided to wander instead of forming the words for an actual response, because this tiny piece of information is entirely new, and it hits me...how desperately hungry I am for more of these revelations.

Hungrier than I am for the mouthwatering dinner Greyson is now carrying over to his dining room table. He places both plates at one end rather than on opposite sides, and I decide that I like this about him, too.

Intimacy over formality. Intention forward. I like it a lot.

"Would you like a glass of wine?" he asks, drawing my eyes back to his.

I unwittingly scrunch my nose. Honestly, I don't mean to, but I feel like such a child every time I have to explain this aberrant piece of myself.

"I feel like you may want to revoke my adult card after I say this," I start, "but…I don't understand wine. It tastes like an accident not meant to be consumed, and no matter how much I try, I can't understand why people like it." I immediately cringe at my response. *A simple,* no thank you *would've easily sufficed, Jess!*

He laughs, the sound of it making my chest warm. "A beer then?"

"*Yes, please,*" I practically hum the words, and he laughs again, amused, the sentiment reaching his eyes.

"Coming right up."

I walk over to his table and sit down, scooting my seat forward just as he places two beers onto the table between us. A couple of napkins and a large bowl of salad, too.

"Thank you," I tell him.

"Of course," he says, and with that, we dig in, a comfortable silence washing over us. Nothing but covert glances and small, addictive smiles are exchanged between us as I continue to eat and take in the space around us.

The view through his windows is breathtaking. Greenery stretches as far as I can see at one end of his house, but on the other, the city full of lights shines and twinkles in the distance below.

It gives his house all the color it needs, and the aesthetic of his home makes even more sense now. Definitely intentional. A piece of art in its own right.

"I have so many questions," he says, chuckling softly as his words slice through my thoughts, "that I don't know where to begin."

"Oh?" I swallow, fully accepting that this is the moment we're finally going to dive in and dig through our past, deciding where we go from here. But instead of the expected nerves or the upheaval of my heart, I feel an easy calm wash through me. *I'm ready.* "What would you like to know?" I ask.

"How were you discovered? Your art, I mean," he starts simple.

I take a sip of my beer and set it back down onto the table. "My first year at WSU, actually. I was working part-time at a restaurant that was starting on a remodel, and one thing led to another and my paintings ended up on their walls. A gallery owner asked about them a few weeks later, and…the rest is kind of history." I shrug.

And I tell myself I don't believe in luck.

Holding onto the belief that something will happen, manifesting it into fruition? Sure. But luck? That, I'm not so sure about. I don't want to believe that everything hangs in the balance of *chances* and *maybes.*

But sitting here now, next to Greyson, looking into his familiar green eyes…

Maybe it was a stroke of pure, insane luck that the right person saw my paintings at the right time and liked them enough to ask about them.

Maybe it was a lifetime's worth of luck paid forward that Greyson walked into my favorite coffee shop a few short weeks ago, and that somehow, I've ended up here with him tonight.

I don't know.

But I still wouldn't like to think this is all a matter of simple luck. I'd rather believe there's something larger at work here. A deep, soul-path kind of thing, where his and mine were always meant to realign and no amount of luck or chances could've ever veered our fate off course.

"Wow. That's amazing," his response cuts through my thoughts, and my line of vision clears as I refocus on his eyes again. "But you deserve it. I can see why so many people are drawn to your work."

"Thank you," I say. I can feel myself blushing, heat spreading through my cheeks. "Right back at you, by the way...I always knew you'd make it."

He smiles, and it warms my insides.

"You still owe me an autograph to the face, though," I add, attempting to slice through the increasing number of butterflies filling my stomach, but he laughs—unrestrained—warming me even further, and then my heart starts beating faster, too. I can't take my eyes off of his—the warmth in them being directed right back at me. It makes it a little hard to breathe.

I swallow thickly.

I need to find a breath of fresh air. Out his back doors and into his backyard, maybe. Or I could climb over this table and into his arms and steal some of his breaths for my own.

He clears his throat, somehow aware of the direction of my thoughts—if the heat in his eyes has anything to say about it. "Would you like a tour?" he asks.

"Sure." I nod, collecting myself with a not-so-subtle breath. "I'd love one."

"Great." He stands, and I follow his lead, letting him guide me out of the room with his fingers wrapped around mine.

Sixty-Two *After*

"**HOW LONG HAVE** you lived here?" I ask him.

"About a year now," he answers, glancing back at me as he leads me into his living room, hand still wrapped around mine.

A year? My eyes widen in surprise.

"I was on tour most of that time," he adds. "We're just finishing up now, with a few shows in-state over the next couple of weeks."

"Oh, cool." I nod. "And then what?" I ask as my eyes sweep over his spacious crème couches and dark, wooden coffee table. Only a single green plant, a black, marbled bowl, and a few books decorate the space, sitting directly on the coffee table.

But then he points above his fireplace, and I see my painting. Or *his* painting now. It complements the room perfectly, and vice versa. I can see why he chose it—if not for the somber reason he already admitted to.

And I won't lie. The knowledge that a piece of me has been taking up space in his home well before I walked through those doors tonight warms my insides. Makes my heart flutter in my chest.

"I like it," I admit, though I'm sure it comes off as a simple compliment rather than the marking of territory my ego clearly intends it to be. I can't help it, though. Some part of me likes it very much.

"Me too," he says, his voice rough, and I'm immediately proved wrong. His eyes communicate what his words don't—that he knows exactly what I mean, and he wholeheartedly agrees.

"Come on." He pulls me outside with a soft smirk caught between his teeth, through his back doors. And the warmth I've been feeling tonight spreads somewhere else entirely.

His backyard manages to redirect my attention, though. For the most part, anyway.

"Wow, what a dream," the words come out on a breath. Because this view is...*breathtaking*. It's all of the most beautiful parts of Seattle, right here in his backyard. From the overgrown trees hovering above his guest house and pool to the view of the city below—it's incredible. "How do you ever drag yourself out of this house?" I ask him, more than serious. I'd never leave.

I mean, we live in a world where everything I would ever need could be brought to my front door in a matter of minutes—hours, days, tops—so I actually don't think I would ever leave.

He chuckles softly. "I've thought about it a few times. But there's a lot of life to be lived outside of these walls, too."

"This is true." I smile. "I still think I'd like to try and bring that world back here, though, so I'd have to leave a whole lot less."

A deep, insightful look passes over his features. "Note taken," he says, and he clears his throat with a small smile. "Let me show you the rest of the house."

I nod, swallowing thickly as he leads me back inside, the warmth of his hand enveloping mine. With a deep and slightly shaky breath, I will my nerves to disappear.

We make our way down his hallway, and I pull him to a stop to admire the pictures of him and his band hanging on the wall. There are four of them, spaced a good distance apart. I study them one by one.

A candid of them backstage. A posed photo in front of an old, crumbling building in Los Angeles. And two from mid-show, in a House of Blues somewhere. One from the front of the band, and one from the back of them—looking out at the impressive crowd full of excited eyes and mouths held open, frozen in time, singing along to one of their songs.

"What's that like?" I ask him, genuinely wanting to know the answer. I can't imagine what that kind of success feels like. So many souls connected to yours in that way.

He thinks it over for a few moments, taking his answer seriously, and I add this to the growing list of new things I like about him. That, and the emotion that passes through his eyes. I can see how much he recognizes the weight of the gift he's been given, and it's obvious he doesn't take any of it for granted.

"Indescribable," he answers with a layer of awe and appreciation, and I know without a doubt he means it.

I'm happy for him, *so* incredibly fucking happy for him. He deserves all of his success and more.

We continue down the hallway, initiated by the slight tug of my hand in his. "How long have you lived in Seattle?" he switches gears.

"Almost eight years now." I swallow, pushing past the weight of that fact, and his head dips down in a nod of understanding as he pulls me around yet another corner of his house.

We go on and on like this, walking through each room of his beautiful home, asking and answering small questions, getting to know each other again.

His guest rooms are spacious and minimalistic, with small plants here and there and a single piece of artwork hanging in each room.

"You said you went to WSU?" he asks.

"Yep." I smile.

"What did you major in?"

"Business. With a minor in Arts," I answer, one of my smiles melting into the next.

He nods again, his body angled toward mine. "Do you plan to open your own gallery someday?"

"I don't know..." I consider his question, sliding my hands into my back pockets. "Maybe." I shrug. The idea has been there for a long time, lingering in the back of my mind, but it's always felt like a farfetched dream rather than a realistic goal.

"And how's your family?" He completely switches gears again.

"Good. They're really good." I smile again—for the millionth time tonight, really.

"Do you see them often?" He returns my smile, and I desperately want to kiss the tilt of it, starting at one perfect corner and ending at the other.

I take in a deep breath instead, releasing it as I follow him out of the room. "I do. They live here in Seattle too, actually," I tell him, and his eyes widen in surprise, his mouth held open for just a breath.

"Oh, wow. I had no idea. That's great, Jess."

"Thank you...It is pretty great." The thought of my family fills my heart with joy. They've lived here for about five years now, but they visited me every year before that. I've loved having them close. Especially since my little brothers are getting so damn big now. They almost make the past eight years feel like they've flown by.

We walk into Greyson's office next, and it washes away those thoughts. It's probably the busiest room I've seen so far. Paperwork is strewn across a mahogany desk; there's a bookshelf that spans one wall, filled top to bottom with books; and then there are the framed pictures and articles that cover the majority of the other three walls.

"And how's your family?" I bounce the question back at him.

"Good. They're good as well." He answers with a purse of his lips, thinking something over. "My parents are divorced now. For the better," he adds.

"That's…good?"

"Yeah." He nods, a slow smile forming on his lips.

"Do you still talk to your father?" I ask carefully.

"Just recently, actually. So, yes, I do." He leans back onto his desk, gripping the edges with his hands. "We've been working on building a relationship—slowly," he says.

"That's good." I nod in acknowledgment. "I'm glad to hear that." And I mean it, I do. But I still can't keep my gaze from lingering on his tensed forearms. From trailing up his biceps and across his chest, up to his face. The echo of our words drifts away, and his eyes feel like they're penetrating mine, begging me to come closer. To close the three or four feet of distance that separates us.

I almost give in to the need, but the look in his eyes tells me it'll go much further than a kiss, and there's still too much of our past hanging between us to allow that to happen.

I clear my throat and divert my attention. "Did you like being in the military?" I ask.

"I did," he answers, and a thought occurs to me. He said his mother gave him his grandfather's ring during his first tour. His *first* tour.

"How many tours did you do?" I ask him.

"Two." He takes a deep breath and releases it. "I did two tours."

The darkness that briefly settles over his features quickly forces me to steer away from that topic. "So, why Seattle? How did you end up here?" I want to reach over and smooth the crease from his brow, but he offers a shrug and a slight smirk, completely wiping away the darkness of a moment ago.

"I made some friends in the army who grew up here, and we started a band together. But there's nowhere else I'd rather be," he says, and the intensity of his stare sends a warmth spreading through my cheeks. I try my best to ignore the way it keeps spreading, traveling lower.

He leads me into a game room next and flips the light switch on. I take in the dark pool table at the center of the room, the few classic arcade games resting against the back wall, and a leather couch positioned in front of a big screen tv and a few different gaming consoles.

"Charlee would go absolutely nuts in here," I say.

"Then you should bring her sometime," he suggests with a smile, and I can't help but smile back. Honestly, it's getting harder and harder to keep my distance from him.

I follow him out of the room, and we trail our steps back down his hallway, my eyes sweeping over the back of him without restraint.

Tanned neck, muscles shifting beneath his dark shirt, black jeans hugging his backside. His bare feet on his tiled floor make me feel completely at home somehow, and *holy hell,* but I'd really like to have my way with him now. This man is perfection. Every piece of him, inside and out, is absolute perfection, and I ache to run my hands over every inch of that perfection.

The temperature in his house spikes a few extra degrees—or ten. It certainly feels that way, anyway.

He looks back at me, catching me mid-ogle, practically drooling all over myself, and his lips tilt into a crooked smile. My heart can hardly take it.

We head back out toward the foyer and up a flight of stairs, into a bedroom that takes up the entire upper floor.

I keep waiting for the questions to come. *The* questions. But they never do.

And then it hits me, with the weight of a thousand intentions, that this is his bedroom we're now standing in.

His bedroom.

Nerves settle in, breeding butterflies in my stomach.

It's a dark room, overlooking his yard and that amazing view. An oversized bed rests against the main wall, facing the windows, and...I can't help but wonder how often it gets used. The thought feels like a slap across my consciousness.

Have you seen the man, Jess? It probably gets used often— very often. I swallow down my thoughts and my irrational jealousy, and a handful of other things while I'm at it. Like the intense need to erase those memories of his with some new ones of our own.

I'm not left to contemplate these things for long, though, as he makes the reason for being in here embarrassingly clear by guiding me through a door I hadn't noticed until now and into what looks like a recording studio.

"*Wow*," I say, looking around the small room. "This is rad." I don't know much about recording studios, but this one looks pretty damn legit. Instruments and microphones sit behind a windowed wall, and a hundred different flips and switches on a soundboard rest in front of it, in the half of the room we're standing in.

"It's my favorite room in this house," he comments with a smile. That crooked smile of his that never ceases to take my breath away. The smile I so desperately would like to kiss right now. I've fought the urge to do it all night, and it's a battle I'm fully ready to lose at the moment.

Soon, I silently admonish myself.

Talk. We need to talk first; we *have* to talk first.

Get it together, Jess.

"I bet." I take in a deep lungful of air, willing my feelings to settle, and spin around on the balls of my feet, but my eyes land on a single photo that quickly steals the breath right back from my lungs. Not a single one of them remains.

Because...*holy shit.*

I swallow thickly, pushing against my tears that surge forward, threatening to fall. Forcing half-breaths in and out of my mouth.

He kept the picture.

He kept it.

And it's hanging right there, on his studio wall. Blown-up, and framed, and resting in a spot you couldn't miss from anywhere in this room, and *holy shit*.

I stare at my sixteen-year-old self, sitting on a swing, entirely consumed.

Relief curls itself around my heart and cradles it with hope. Emotion lodges itself in my throat.

And my tears, they just want to fall, and fall, and fall.

Sixty-Three *After*

I FORCE ANOTHER shaky breath in and out of my lungs before turning back around to face Greyson, meeting his gaze. His eyes sink into the depths of mine, and they glisten with the same emotions I'm feeling, and I can't help it.

I walk straight into his arms.

He wraps them around me with zero hesitation, and I let out an audible sigh of relief at the exact moment that he does. And *this*. This is exactly where I belong. Where I've always belonged.

Somehow, a sixteen-year-old version of me knew it before I ever could've comprehended what the weight of that meant. Like my soul saw his and took its first breath in centuries. Like it whispered *hello,* and his whispered back *I've missed you,* and then they sat back in contentment, willing to wait until we came to the same conclusion:

You are mine. You are mine; you are mine; you are mine. You have always been mine, and you will always be mine.

Greyson's arms envelop me, his scent permeating the air around me, and I breathe it in. Let it settle into my bones. The familiar smell of mint and chocolate and Greyson—mixed in with a feeling of home I want to linger inside of forever.

And right now, in this moment, I think I could.

One breath against his chest turns into four, and four turn into a hundred, and I'm still wrapped up in his arms. I don't want him to let me go. Not now, not ever.

But he deserves his answers. He deserves an explanation for the decisions I made all those years ago.

I start to step away, but his arms tighten around me, and a smile breaks free on my lips, slipping past the myriad of emotions I'm feeling—fear, uncertainty, contentment, *peace*.

A hundred, a thousand, a million others.

I look up at him, my chin resting against his chest, and his green eyes meet mine, locking them in place.

"I am so sorry, Greyson," I finally say the words that have weighed on me for so long. They come out a lot softer than I intended them to, though—a quiet, broken admission. A world of regrets and *what-ifs* laced carefully through them.

But he shakes his head, releasing a breath. "You don't have anything to be sorry for," he says, and a tear unwittingly slips free, sliding down my cheek. He wipes it away with his thumb, curving his hand over my shoulder and sliding it down my back, holding me against him as he continues, "I've had a lot of time to think things over, and I—I think I've always trusted that you had your reasons. That they were important to you...

"I think I just need to hear them," he says, his brow creasing as if he's still mulling over his own thoughts, "from your lips. This one time, so we can move forward."

I nod, swallowing past the lump in my throat. I did have my reasons. And they *were* incredibly important to me. I had things to prove to myself, a world of hurt to recover from, and a past to prove wrong, and I think I knew, on some level, that I had to do these things on my own before I ever could've given someone like Greyson the love he deserved.

It's something I know with absolute surety now.

But still...I never should've— "I never should've left you like that." I shake my head against his chest, somehow managing to hold the rest of my tears at bay. "But I was afraid," I whisper. "I was so fucking afraid that I would give up everything for you, and it would be for nothing. That something would change for you, and you wouldn't be waiting to come back to me anymore.

"Because I would've done that. I would've given up so much—too much, maybe—to wait for you, if I'd known for sure that you would come back."

I don't realize I'm staring down at my feet, chin trembling, until Greyson lifts my face in his hands, forcing my gaze back to his. I blink back my tears, and the look in his eyes tells me he'd like to end this conversation right here and pull me into him and crush me against his chest, And I want that, *I do*, but I force myself to continue anyway, because he needs to hear these words, and I need to say them more than I ever thought possible.

"I wanted that, Greyson. More than *anything*," I continue, swallowing thickly. "You have to believe that I did. I just didn't think there was any way in hell it would actually happen," I say, shaking my head. "At the time, I was sure it wouldn't, so...I left.

"I ran away, because I thought..." I almost choke on my own words, on the sob building in my throat. I take a deep breath and push past the shakiness in my chest—in my heart, in my voice. "I thought you'd leave first. And it felt like—for once...like I was in control. That life couldn't screw me over and push me down its own path like it always did because *I* had made the choice to walk away." The shakiness in my chest intensifies, my heart thundering. I rub my hand against it, willing it to settle, fighting back my tears.

He takes a deep breath and releases it, closing his eyes. It's a few breaths, a few heartbeats, before he opens them again, his gaze meeting mine. "I'm not going to pretend that it didn't hurt—*that it didn't fucking hurt like hell*—but I understand, Jess. I do. I get it." His gaze bores into mine. "I was afraid, too...

"But my fears became my reality."

"I know," I say, barely audible. I press my face into his chest, and the rainstorm of tears finally fight their way free, falling down my face one by one. "You have to know how truly sorry I am."

His hands slide up my back and into my hair; he rests his chin down on the top of my head. "I know, Jess. I do," he says, followed by a deep and quiet sigh. My head rises and falls with the movement, more tears sliding down my cheeks.

I didn't think this would make me so emotional. Or...hell, maybe I did. Maybe that's why I kept running from this very conversation. But now that I've found myself in the middle of it, now that I've finally spilled the words from the place they've been hiding all this time, I feel a thousand pounds lighter.

Even with the unknown still sitting before me.

"You're here now. That's all that really matters to me," Greyson says, slicing into my awareness, and if I wasn't already crying, I think I would completely break down with the relief that washes through me. "We have now," he continues, his voice vibrating in his chest, humming against my cheek, and I press myself closer to him. "This moment—you and me—and what I hope is a lot more time spent together to make up for the years we lost. That's all I want, Jess," he finishes quietly.

His fingers gently tug at my hair, forcing me to look up at him. His green eyes swim before me. "*God*, I've missed you," he breathes, brushing the streaks of my tears away with the back of his hand.

"I missed you, too. So fucking much," I whisper, and then I lift up onto my toes and press my mouth to his.

Our lips slowly move together, soft and hard all at once, and the ache in my chest smooths away and shifts into something else entirely.

Because this kiss. It doesn't care about expectations, or disappointments, or mistakes. It doesn't care about regrets, or the past, or eight years lost. It only cares about the fact that I've loved this man for a lifetime, and that I plan on showing him exactly how much I've missed him—missed this—

—*missed us*—with anything else but words.

Sixty-Four *Before*

"**LIKE THIS,**" I said, stroking the paintbrush outward in short, curved flicks against the canvas. I pulled my hand away from Greyson's and watched him finish the tip of the wave on his own.

Someone knocked on my door, and Greyson practically pushed me out of his lap. I glared at him, attempting to hide my amusement as my dad walked into my bedroom.

"Jessica, Greyson," my dad greeted us with a smile. He loved Greyson. They all did. Elizabeth, and especially the twins. One dinner was all it took. Greyson, somehow, had kind of been like the unofficial starting point for us all. The safe buffer we needed to start fresh and finally get to know each other.

"This came in the mail for you," he continued, setting an envelope down on my dresser. "Elizabeth and I are heading out. But we'll bring dinner home in a few hours. Are you staying for dinner, Greyson?"

"You bet," he quickly said, making my dad chuckle.

"Alright, see you two in a few. Behave yourselves." He motioned with two fingers, pointing them between Greyson's eyes and his in that silent *I'm watching you* gesture. I rolled my eyes.

"And Greyson?" he added.

"Yes, sir?"

"I sure hope you're not planning on following Jessica into a career of painting. That canvas looks like a sad, smashed blueberry pie."

"It's the beach," Greyson laughed.

"Tomato, tom-ah-toh."

I snorted. "*What?*" That shit didn't even make sense. And I finally understood what all that *Dad Joke* business was about after these last few weeks. My dad thought he was hilarious. Unfortunately for me, I was starting to see where I'd gotten my personality from. Or fortunately, maybe.

"Don't listen to him, you're doing awesome," I told Greyson.

"Love is blind," Dad quipped. "And on that note, I'll see you kids later," he said as he walked out the door.

"He's a mean one," Greyson said with a smile and turned back to his painting. "*Blueberry pie.*" He chuckled.

I swiped the envelope off my dresser and opened it, pulling out the letter folded inside.

Congratulations, it read, and the rest of the words were completely lost on me. Except for: *$10,000 scholarship.*

No fucking way. I read the whole thing again, hands shaking. "No fucking way."

"What?" Greyson turned to face me.

"I won. *I won!*" I shouted.

"Won what?" He smiled in confusion.

I laid it all out for him, telling him about my pictures, and Ms. Greenburg, and the form she'd had me fill out, and the contest, and that somehow, *somehow*—by some miracle—*I'd actually freaking won it.*

"What?!" He stood up, eyes wide and as excited as mine, and walked toward me.

I matched his quick pace and jumped up into his arms as we collided. "Holy shit! I won!"

"Holy shit," he reiterated.

"*Holy shit,*" the words came out on a breath as I looked over at my wall of photos. It was surreal, the moment where I realized my pictures were actually good. Not just to me, but to somebody else in this world who mattered.

I never, *not in a million years*, would've thought they were worthy of something like this. But here I was, holding this letter in my arms as Greyson held me in his, and...*holy shit.*

"You deserve it," he said quietly, forcing my eyes back to his.

"Thank you," I whispered, and I got lost in his gaze like I had a thousand times before. I swallowed thickly as his eyes bore into mine.

And just like that, our excitement shifted into something else. Something that threw fire into our eyes and coiled deep down inside of me. Our breaths matched, heavy and fast.

I looked down at his mouth, and he looked down at mine as he pulled his bottom lip between his teeth.

And that was it; I couldn't take it anymore. I closed the distance between us faster than I could count to one, had my mouth on his before I could've ever have gotten to two.

My hands quickly caught up to the speed of my lips and slid around his neck, desperately pulling him closer to me even though I was already in his arms.

It didn't matter. There was no way I could ever get close enough. But also...*this was so much more than enough*—his arms around me, his lips sliding over mine, tongue teasing, teeth biting.

I lost myself in that kiss, in Greyson, before he pulled away, breathing hard. And I could see it in his eyes then, how this time was wholly different from all of the others. More intense. Consuming. Entirely unstoppable.

I think he could see it in my eyes, too. He sucked in a deep breath before walking us over to my bed and laying me down, climbing on top of me and settling his body in between my legs.

I could hardly breathe. My entire body hummed with awareness—hands tingling, heart soaring. I'd never felt this way. So alive. So aware of the way my body cried out for someone else's. For his.

And then his lips sunk down and slowly pressed back into mine, heightening the buzz that traveled through me. He kissed me—*he kissed me, and he kissed me, and he kissed me*—shifting between light brushes of his mouth over mine and deep, lingering kisses that ignited a fire deep down in my soul.

And then somewhere along the way, our kisses went from soft, and *slow*, and exploring, to frenzied and impatient. Hurried and demanding—almost desperate. From zero to sixty, and neither one of us were interested in finding the brakes. We weren't going to stop until we crashed together and burned.

He ground himself into me, and I pushed back against him, kissing him harder, pulling his hair between my fingers.

His hands were under my shirt, fingers gripping my waist. I slid my hands up to his elbows and, together, we slowly moved his palms up—*higher*—until I could move into his touch.

He groaned into my mouth, and I gasped into his, and we swallowed each other's sounds as our clothes hit the floor. One by one, piece by piece.

His finger was tucked beneath the waistband of my underwear as he sat back on his heels, out of breath. It was the most beautiful sound. His breaths echoing in the quiet space around us. Knowing I'd done that to him. Knowing I'd affected him that way.

We hadn't gone this far before, and the way he looked at me then, silently asking for my permission, almost broke me.

Because I couldn't help but be conscious of the fact that it was the first time I'd ever wanted more, even though I'd had plenty of pushy offers before. From men two, three times my age.

The first time I'd ever been kissed, was by one of Mom's boyfriends. The first time a boy had ever asked to see me naked, was forever replaced by the memory of a grown man asking the question.

But it felt like Greyson was wiping away all of that. Because with him, it was the first time everything felt right, *easy*. The first time I'd wanted everything I saw in someone else's eyes. The first time I ached for someone to strip me bare, and see me, and touch me, in all the ways he was making me crave.

And he was still sitting there, patiently waiting. I fell even harder then, all the way to the bottom.

"Take them off," I whispered.

He swallowed thickly, eyes glued to mine, before sliding my underwear down my legs and tossing them to the floor.

And I had a thought, that maybe I *should* be nervous, or scared, but in those moments with Greyson, I felt nothing but comfortable.

Eager. Filled with a burning desire.

And then he pulled off his shirt, and my mouth went completely dry. I'd seen Greyson shirtless before, but there was something about knowing where this train was headed that made the sight of him that much better.

I ran my hands up his stomach, and he visibly shivered before lowering back onto me and unhooking my bra, slipping it off my shoulders and down my arms.

And then went his boxers, and we were skin on skin, and I didn't think anything had ever felt better. Except for maybe the way he looked at me then. Like I was the most beautiful thing he'd ever seen.

Because that was the thing. He'd seen all these beautiful, broken pieces of me. Had brought most of them to light when I had never cared to see them before. And now it felt like he owned some of those pieces, like he'd left his mark on them before putting them back inside of me.

"I love you," he whispered shakily, and I breathed it back into his neck as I kissed my way up his throat.

And with a sharp intake of air, I handed him the very last piece of me. The most important one. The one he would own forever.

Sixty-Five *After*

GREYSON HUMS A half-sigh, half-groan into my mouth before deepening our kiss, his tongue stroking mine.

Beautifully. Blissfully.

Washing away everything but my need for him.

I slide my hands up his chest and around his neck, feeling the soft scratch of his hair against my fingertips, and I love it. The way the tingle of it spreads up my arms and through my chest, heading straight down into the core of my stomach. A warm flurry of desire quickly building.

Building, and building, and building.

He picks me up and presses me back against the wall, his body flush with mine, and my breath hitches. I'm sandwiched between him and the wall of his dark studio in the most delicious way, the pressure of him hitting me exactly where I need it most.

My chest heaves against his with heavy breaths, and I can't seem to find enough air, but his tongue swirls around mine, and I'm lost. Completely and utterly lost.

In his hands. And his mouth. And his chest crushed against mine. In the way it sparks a fire inside me that lights up my soul.

I cross my ankles behind his back and pull him even closer with his shirt in my fists as his mouth continues to move over mine—slow, exploring, reacquainting. Matching the weight of his hands sliding over the curves of my body.

And it feels like our lips somehow remember each other's. Two old friends falling into a wordless conversation of breaths and tongues and the tug of my bottom lip sliding between his teeth.

I moan against his mouth, and he swallows the sound, and my entire body flushes with warmth.

And my heart, it feels like it remembers his, too. Pounding against his. A steady and wistful *hello*. Tugging itself another inch closer.

It was that first day in English class all those years ago that I felt that invisible string weave its way around my heart. Over and under, and through and around—around, and around, and around, it wove itself into me, connecting my heart to his.

And over the course of days, and weeks, and months of time spent together, it drew them closer together, and then pulled them further apart. Together and apart, and together and apart, with all of our ups and downs.

But that connection always remained. Strong and sturdy. Strengthening over time, until it couldn't be severed.

When I saw Greyson again, after all these years, it was the first time I felt that string tugging against my heart again. I'd almost forgotten what it felt like. That connection.

But here, with Greyson, his heart firmly beating against my own, that connection feels more like a lifeline, calling me back home.

His lips trail over my mouth, across my jaw, and down my neck, effectively reeling my mind away from these thoughts and back into the present moment.

Here. Now. With Greyson. *My* Greyson.

He carries me out of his studio and straight into his bedroom, and I let out a sigh of relief as he lands us both on his bed, the large frame of his body settling in between my thighs.

I can feel him everywhere. Literally, figuratively.

From the pressure of his lips at my neck, to his hardness pressing against my core, to the tips of my toes now trailing up his calves, my heart still racing against his.

The weight of this moment, the intensity of it—of Greyson and me, here, in his bed, our eyes locked together—burrows itself deep down into my bones, leaving me breathless.

And then his mouth crashes against mine once more, and there's no air left to breathe but his. We share every single one of his breaths as his tongue glides over mine, his hand making its way up my leg, wrapping it around his hip while his other hand keeps his chest hovering just above mine, and I'm lost in him all over again.

I let my hands roam over him. Over every inch of him. His arms, his neck, his chest, his back. *Lower.*

Firm, solid muscle I ache to dig my fingertips into.

So, I do. And he groans. Thrusting his hips into mine as he kisses me deep into oblivion, and I nearly lose my mind.

I have this muted, faraway thought, that maybe I should attempt to slow things down and savor them a little longer, but I'm far too impatient. My body is too impatient, screaming out for more of his. And thankfully, that impatience seems to match his impeccably.

He pulls away, breaking our kiss to slip off my jacket, and I practically rip his shirt from his chest.

My shirt goes just as quickly. He pulls it over my head, and then his lips are on mine again, and...

"*Oh, god,*" I breathe against his mouth, skin brushing over skin.

His lips trail away, following a path down my neck, across my chest, and over the swell of my breasts.

I slide my fingers through his hair, through the longer part at the top, my heart steadily pounding out of my ribcage.

Pounding, and pounding, and pounding away. Matching the rhythm of the deep ache between my legs.

"I really want—" Greyson pulls away, breathing heavily. "—but should we—" he swallows, and I lose myself in his eyes; green, and careful, and wanting, "—should we hold off? Do you want to wait?"

I shake my head quickly back and forth. "No. No fucking way," I say, breathless, and he smiles, lip caught between his teeth.

"Thank God," he says, between one breath and the next, and I reach for his pants at the same exact moment he reaches for mine, and we both start quietly laughing. The breath of our laughter collides between us; the vibration of it hums against my chest. And I can't tear my eyes away from his, from the lust and need and adoration shining in them. It seizes my breaths.

Because *holy shit,* but I love him. I definitely still love him. Absolutely insane or not, entirely out of my mind or perhaps the sanest I've ever felt in my life—the feelings are there. Climbing up my throat and desperately wanting to spill from my lips.

They're right here. On the tip of my tongue. But Greyson kisses them away, his mouth sliding over mine achingly slow. So I swallow them back and push them forward through the touch of my lips instead, searing the eight letters into his skin.

Up his throat, and against his mouth, I will him to feel them through our kiss. *Can he feel them? Does he feel this, too?*

Or am I just crazy?

"Fuck, I...I—I need you to stand up." He breathes heavily, his bare, muscled chest expanding and contracting, and I don't need him to say the words; I can see them playing behind his eyes. Steady, sure.

I press a soft kiss to his mouth and slide out from beneath him, standing up against the edge of his mattress. My heart still races as he steps off the bed and gently turns me around with his hands at my waist, nipping the space between my neck and shoulder with his teeth as I watch his fingers slowly unbutton my jeans. And then he kneels down—on the wooden floor of his bedroom—to slip off my shoes and slide my pants down my legs, and it's, hands down, one of the hottest sights I've ever seen.

And *my god,* but it's been way too long since I've felt this way—wholly and utterly consumed. There isn't a single thought in my mind that doesn't entirely exist for the way Greyson is making me feel.

The way he slowly kisses his way up my spine, his fingertips trailing behind, making a line of goosebumps break out along my skin. Along what feels like the surface of my soul.

I reach forward and help him out of his pants, out of his black boxer briefs, and lead him back onto the bed, climbing on top of him. I lower my mouth to his, and if he didn't feel how much of myself, and my heart, I put into that last kiss, I know he feels it now, his hands gripping my hips tight as he pants a, *"Shit, Jess,"* against my lips.

"This is…" He shakes his head beneath me. "This isn't only me, right? You feel this too?" he rumbles, breathless.

"I do," I nod, breathing the words into his chest, and I feel our hearts winding themselves even closer.

I kiss him. *Harder*—deeper—than before.

He rolls over me and finishes undressing me, until I'm completely bare beneath him, and it's just him, and me, and the sound of our heavy breaths crashing between us.

His gaze sinks further into mine, and…

I love you, I wordlessly tell him, with my heart, and my eyes, and my hands raking over the taut muscles in his back.

I feel it reciprocated in the way he holds me against him, the way he smooths my hair away from my face and curves his hand over my cheek. In the way he slowly swallows with too many emotions to name as he eases himself inside of me.

I clench down around him, fingers biting into his skin as pleasure immediately sings through me, and—

"Fuuuckk," he groans. It's easily the sexiest spoken word I've ever heard in my life, but then his mouth crashes against mine, his tongue matching the rhythm of his hips, and he moans it again into my mouth, and I think I liked it even better that time.

Tension coils itself inside me, too fast, pulling every cell, every nerve ending, to the center of my being. Dragging my heart all the way back to his, all the way back home.

I feel them beating together, thundering against one another.

And then he tugs my bottom lip between his teeth. Slides his fingers up my throat and grasps my jaw, my chin. And proceeds to kiss me deeper than I've ever been kissed before, thrusting and groaning into me. And I'm gone.

Completely, and entirely, gone.

We come together—a hot, heated, tangled mess of sweat and limbs and teeth digging into flesh.

And I could stay inside of this high forever.

But eventually, after some time, the outside world slowly trickles its way back in, and my body settles back into itself. I sink into his mattress with a deep and contented sigh. A sigh mirrored by his own, and we both quietly laugh into the calm that surrounds us.

The sound mingles with our breaths and teases the silence away, and there's nowhere—*nowhere*—on this beautiful green earth, or any place beyond it, I'd rather be.

Sixty-Six *After*

THE WORLD SLIPS into my consciousness piece by piece. Breath by breath. One sliver at a time.

The soft, clean smell of Greyson's comforter.

The daylight streaming through his tall windows, beams of light streaking across his wooden floors.

Warm, muscled arms wrapped around my naked torso. His heartbeat calmly thudding against my back. The soothing sound of his steady breaths blowing across my neck.

I twist around in his hold and press a kiss to his bare chest, and another to the base of his throat.

He stirs and pulls me closer, still asleep.

I take in a deep breath. Soak in the silence. I let it slither in between one breath and the next. Let it snake around my bones, and coat my thoughts, and hug my skin.

It's blissfully quiet.

A kind of peace I'm not sure I've felt before.

It settles over me fully.

And it's that feeling of absolute peace that has me holding onto Greyson tighter, burrowing myself deeper into his chest and arms, breathing him in.

Because when you've grown accustomed to losing the things you love most, you can't help the niggling feeling that everything is temporary, that anything can be ripped right out from under you without warning. And when you've lived half your life this way, it's hard to remember that giving away pieces of your heart can be an investment, too.

The thing is, Greyson seems to take and take and take these pieces without permission, without even knowing he does it.

He always has.

And I'm left scrambling. Holding tight to the pieces I don't want to let go of. I gave him so many pieces of my heart last night, that it feels like I ripped the entire thing from my chest and handed it right over to him.

But when his arms tighten around me, and his lips find my skin, his breathy *good morning* sending chills down my spine, I willingly and easily, finally, let these things go.

He can have my heart. The whole thing.

He's always owned it anyway.

Sixty-Seven *Before*

THOSE TWO WEEKS flew by. Funny how time did that. How when we prayed for it to speed up, to zoom past us so we could pull ourselves together, or heal, or grow, or finally find ourselves in a better place in life, it crawled by instead, oozing past us in slow motion. But when we wanted to ram a fist into it and stop it altogether, it passed by so fast it gave us whiplash.

So, no. Not funny at all. Not really.

—*two days*—

Two days were all we had left, and then I was going to have to face reality. Face all the thoughts I'd been ignoring and keeping buried deep where I couldn't see them.

So many truths I was going to have to acknowledge, even though I didn't want to. It was the last thing I wanted to do, but...

It didn't mean this was the *end,* end, right?

It didn't have to be. Greyson had said as much himself.

This could continue.

I could believe that, couldn't I?

I thought I could.

But all I really heard was, *liar, liar*—

Liar.

Sixty-Eight *Before*

"**WELL, ISN'T THIS** fucking precious," Jaymes seethed from behind us, and my back stiffened.

I guess we'd gotten away with not having this confrontation for long enough; it was bound to happen. But I didn't want to do this today. *Not today.*

Greyson's arm slipped from my shoulders as he turned around, leveling his stare on Jaymes. "What?" he snapped.

"You heard me."

Greyson stepped forward, and I wrapped my hand around his arm to keep him from going any farther.

Jaymes laughed, a slow *clap, clap, clap* of his hands as he cocked his head to the side. "Fuck me, but I never pegged either of you as backstabbers. Makes sense, though."

Was he for real?

"You're clearly delusional," I spoke up. He was the one who'd finally gotten what he wanted, only to completely piss on it by sleeping with Sara behind my back. "You cheated on *me*, remember?" I ignored the tiny little detail that, technically, I did cheat on him, too.

And he laughed again. "You know, I actually liked you, and that's saying a lot for me. But you know me, Jess. You *know* me." *Know that you're an epic dick and an asshole? Yeah, I do...* "I might've called you my girlfriend, but we weren't going to be official until you were willing to make it official," he said.

And yeah, I wanted to punch him. I'd never gotten the chance to the last time, thanks to Greyson. But it wasn't worth it. The truth was, I still didn't care that much. Especially not now. Not when I had the one thing I'd wanted, standing right here in front of me, defending me, straining not to punch Jaymes in the face himself.

Jaymes pointed his finger between me Greyson and me. "Can't say this surprises me, though." He laughed. "You've got a type, don't you? Sad, little depressed bitches…just like your mom."

My next breath got stuck in my throat, frozen in my windpipe. *What the fuck?*

I didn't know if it was the stress of him leaving tomorrow, or the purely fucking shitty things Jaymes had just said about his mom and me, but Greyson…

He just fucking lost it.

He pulled out of my grasp and had his fingers around Jaymes' throat faster than I could blink. His fist reared back and swung across Jaymes' jaw. Once, twice, nailing him hard in the face.

But Jaymes just laughed the entire time. Dude clearly had some serious issues.

I grabbed at Greyson's shoulders. "Come on. Let's go. He's not worth it. I don't want to spend our last day like this," I said, and that immediately snapped him out of it.

He stood quickly, chest heaving, anger still simmering in his eyes. If he could've killed Jaymes with a look, he would've right then. There would be a pretty little outline of Jaymes' body on the ground where he laid.

Greyson gave him one last shove. "Back the fuck off," he spat, and turned back toward me, grabbing my hand and leading me away.

"I'm sorry," I whispered.

He shook his head. "Not your fault."

We walked through the campus and down the front steps of our school in silence.

Greyson stopped us in the parking lot, in front of his car, and pulled me into his arms, letting the weight of the world settle onto his shoulders with one breath. "I don't want to leave you tomorrow," he said.

I hugged him tighter, swallowing past the lump in my throat. "I know. I don't want you to leave, either." I pushed my face into his chest, breathing him in. "I don't want you to go."

We stood there, for a long time, holding onto each other tighter than we ever had. Maybe if we refused to let go, the Universe would obey, would freeze time and hold us in that moment forever.

I would've given anything to have that one prayer answered.

Sixty-Nine *After*

"**THREE S's, AND** Jess, *baby*, you know you're going first!" Sita exclaims.

I laugh, shaking my head. "Nope. No way. I'm definitely saving the best for last tonight."

A groan, a whine, and a laugh trail from the lips of my three best girlfriends.

"Touché, bitch. Touché," Sita throws back with amusement, swallowing down a shot of tequila before diving into her Three S's with a mischievous smirk. "*Something new*—you definitely slept with Greyson last night, I can see it in your eyes," she points at me, talking in Sita-hyper-speed. Which for Sita, is really saying something. I hold back my smile. "*Something positive...*" she continues, "I'm positive it went well, because, girl, I've never seen you look so 'cat caught the canary' in my life. And *something to expel*—I feel like I'm going to die of anticipation if you withhold this information any longer!"

Kat shakes her head with a grin as she starts to say something, but Sita quickly bulldozes over her words. "Wait, wait, wait!" she says, looking both Kat and Maggie in the eyes with exaggerated seriousness before continuing, "You two better make this fast, or I'll strangle you myself."

They both laugh in response.

"Calm down, crazy pants. I already planned on it," Kat replies.

"Same. We're here for the juicy stuff, and we all know it," Maggie says, but now she's the one who looks like the cat that ate the canary.

I narrow my eyes at her, and she smiles a secret little smile. Okay, *interesting*. Definitely coming back to that.

"So," Kat starts in on her Three S's. "Sorry-not-sorry, Sita, but I can't hold this in any longer—the hubby and I have decided we're officially trying for a baby!" she rushes happily.

"Ahh! Yay!" I gush, and Maggie echoes my excitement as we sandwich her in a three-way hug.

"This is amazing news! I cannot wait for *squishy baby cheeks!*" Maggie squeals.

"Truly amazing, love." Sita slides her hand over Kat's with genuine happiness, the sentiment shining in her eyes.

We all express a few more rounds of excitement over this amazing turn of events before Kat says, "And I'm absolutely positive Sita might actually explode if we don't move this along, and I'm not looking to become collateral damage in that mess, so let's do this..."

We take a collective breath and turn our attention to Mags.

She smiles another mysterious, mischievous smirk and says, "I'm going to ask Sam out tonight."

"Wait, what?!" Kat and I both scream at the same time. Probably a little too loud for the rest of the bar, but I don't really care at the moment.

"Yes!" I shout. "When? Now? Do it now. You have to do it now, Mags." I'm not giving her the chance to back out. No way, no how. I feel like I've been waiting for this moment for...well, *forever*. My entire life, maybe.

"Oh, you just had to go and do it, didn't you?" Sita complains.

"Do what?" Maggie mocks her, feigning innocence.

"Come up with literally the *only* viable distraction good enough for Jess's Three S's to wait. You better not let me down, girl! This is happening. And it's happening right now."

I crack up. We all do.

And it's sort of perfect. Because I kind of, desperately—selfishly—want to keep the details of last night, *and this morning*, to myself for just a little bit longer anyway.

Seventy *After*

"WAAAAAAOOH!!!" I SCREAM alongside my friends. Alongside a good-sized theater packed with contagious excitement.

It's incredible—*mind-blowing, surreal.*

Greyson, down there, on stage. A crowd of enthusiastic concertgoers loudly chanting his name.

"Holy shit, he's like...*famous*," Kat says, wide eyes looking down at the space filled with people. Greyson gave us some kind of special access passes, so we're up here on a private balcony with the rest of the band's guests—some family, and some friends.

I don't recognize much of anybody, of course, but I do catch eyes with Brienne, the drummer's wife, and wave at her with a small smile. She flashes a brilliant smile back, and my lips tug up even higher.

An excited and out of breath Maggie redirects my attention.

"Hey, guys!" she says. "Sorry we're late." She points up at her date's chest. "You already know Sam. I mean, of course you do, but I feel like I'm supposed to officially introduce everyone or something...like...that..." she trails off, blushing slightly, and Sam pulls her closer into his side, holding out his hand to us.

"Sam, officially." He smiles widely.

Sita and I laugh at Maggie's expense and exchange introductions with the man who's poured drinks at our favorite bar and restaurant for over two years now. And yes, Maggie has crushed on him that entire time.

I'm not surprised that after only a single date they completely clicked and have been almost inseparable since. They fit together really well, like they were made for each other. Two halves of one whole. And it's nice to finally witness the smile she can't seem to wipe away from her face. And his, too.

I blow her a kiss as Ricky tugs me back over to the edge of the balcony, where Greyson's band is just starting to play their first song of the night.

The drums *tap, tap, tap* to life, and the guitar starts in with an addicting melody, entangling itself with the beat of the music that begins to pour from the speakers.

But nothing is as addicting as Greyson's voice, the way it floats across the space between us and slides over my skin.

I pushed, you pulled,
    right from the start,
to shield and win
    a broken heart, he croons, and it melts my insides—my heart, my soul.

The longer I stand here and watch him, the more I slowly start to fall into a world of my own. I don't even realize it's happening until it's just him, and me, and a lifetime ago—where I sat on a small stool in a tiny pub and watched him sing to a crowd for the very first time.

The difference between then and now, the before and the after—these images flash in my mind, one replacing the other again and again. A young and nervous Greyson perched on a stool with his guitar in his lap. And this one. Stage-dominating, confident.

It takes my breath away. *He* takes my breath away. The contrast between the Greyson I knew, and this man on stage who commands and enraptures an entire theater full of people.

He swaggers across the stage without arrogance. Belts the words of his song without an ounce of restraint. And stands up on a speaker and flashes a tilted smile that makes the theater go wild without even realizing he's doing it.

I didn't think it was possible to be more attracted to Greyson than I already am, but his stage presence is...

It's something else. Something otherworldly.

The way his fans absolutely adore him. The way they eat it up as he toes the edge of the stage and waves his arm back and forth. The way anyone in this room can clearly see that he's living his wildest dreams come true and is enjoying every fucking second of it, not taking a bit of it for granted.

The crowd quickly mirrors his movement and a sea of arms sways side to side in perfect synchrony below me. I watch the wave of them flowing back and forth, and back and forth. And it's mesmerizing.

It's almost too insane to wrap my mind around. All of this. But above it all, above anything else, I feel so—*wildly, insanely, immeasurably*—proud of him. Of all he's done. All he's accomplished. Who he's become in the process. It's beautiful.

Ricky takes my hand in his and spins me around in his arms, and my thoughts seem to fly away with the movement, falling from my mind one by one. My eyes meet his excited ones, and I can't help but feel that excitement too.

It seeps into my consciousness until it flows through my veins, and I smile. Big, and unrestrained, and full of all the happiness, and joy, and love I'm feeling.

Because *holy shit*. But that's *my* Greyson down there.

Ricky swings me around, again and again, and we dance the rest of the song away. We dance, and we dance, and we dance, and one song rolls into the next, and I don't ever stop.

I switch from Ricky's arms to Sita's, and then Kat's, and Maggie's. Brienne and her friends come over and join us, too.

And I don't think my smile leaves my face the entire night.

Especially not after Greyson's attention focuses up on our group mid-song, and his eyes find mine, winking at me once before singing,

You blow my mind, girl.

You blow my fucking mind.

Because ditto, baby. Ditto.

Seventy-One *After*

I SLIDE MY legs up and over Greyson's, turning to face him on the black leather couch we're sitting on. We're in our own little world. An imaginary bubble separating us from the rest of the backstage crowd.

Ricky and my girls are around here somewhere, mingling with the band and their friends. I hear their laughter drifting across the room, but my focus is all on Greyson.

"That was insane. *You're* insane. Does this not blow your mind every single day?" I gush. "Like, do you wake up in the morning and look yourself in the mirror and go, 'holy shit, I'm Greyson Hayes'?"

He laughs, pulling me closer, shaking his head. "Not exactly. But something like that, I guess. The awe of it all."

"Wow," I say on a breath, sinking back into the cushion beside him, looking up at his face. "It's one thing to know you've done it—made a name for yourself. But it's an entirely different experience to witness it firsthand." His eyes meet mine. "It's amazing, Greyson," I continue. "You're absolutely amazing."

"Thank you," he blushes the tiniest bit and clears his throat, "but nothing feels as amazing as this right here," he says, lifting my chin in his fingers. His lips land on mine, and the entire night's worth of excitement buzzes through our lips, through my fingertips grasping his shirt and his tongue stroking mine.

He breaks our kiss a few minutes, or hours, or days too short. *Would it be rude to ask if it's time to go now?* Back to his house, or mine, I don't really care.

"You know...tonight's the first time I've truly felt like it's all come full circle for me," he says quietly, redirecting my attention entirely.

"Yeah?" I say, looking up into his eyes.

He nods. "I know I wasn't the best at articulating my feelings back then," he continues, "but it meant the world to me that you were there for that first performance."

I swallow, sliding my fingers through his as I push back a swell of emotions.

"Made me nervous as hell," he laughs, and I smile at his words, looking down at our hands folded together, "but you just sat there beside me, this calm force that settled most of those nerves back down." He swallows, too, before saying, "I think that's when I knew that I was falling for you…

"It scared the shit out of me more than anything."

I squeeze his hand tighter between my fingers, my gaze sinking back into his. "Honestly, Greyson, I think I've loved you since the first second I saw you."

His lips tilt into a smile. Captivating, shy.

"In fact, I think one of my first thoughts about you was something along the lines of, *I want to marry him and beg him to let me have his babies someday*," I add.

He laughs, shaking his head. His laughter rumbles through my shoulder and into my chest, squeezing at my heart, constricting my airways.

My gaze is still glued to his as something hits me with overwhelming surety, and I ignore the nerves swirling in my stomach and fluttering in my chest as I quietly say, "I'm not sure I've ever stopped loving you, Greyson."

"No?" he says, just as quiet.

"No." I shake my head. "Not even a little bit."

His lips slam down on mine between one breath and the next. He kisses me harder, deeper, than before. And I get lost in it, in him. As far as I'm concerned, we're still alone on an island of Jess and Greyson—just him, and me, and a blur of sounds that don't even register.

His tongue grazes my bottom lip, and I sigh into his mouth, my hand sliding over the scruff along his jawline.

"*The* Jessica Martinez!" someone says, but I don't want to take my lips off of Greyson's to see who.

But also, I'm a mature adult, so I force myself to do it anyway, breathing heavily as I tear my mouth from his.

"It is a pleasure," the voice continues, and I look up at a tall, dark, and handsome man—the bassist, I'm pretty sure. "Ah, there she is! I didn't recognize you with your face attached to my man's there," he extends his hand out to me, "Seriously, it's a pleasure."

I bite down on my smile and slide my hand into his. "Jess."

"Trey."

"It's really nice to meet you, too," I say.

My hand slips out of his as he brings his hand to his chest. "First off, thank you for fueling ninety percent of G-man's songs and helping make us famous."

Greyson kicks his leg out and it hits Trey in the shin.

He rubs out the pain with a mock scowl. "Right, right. Breaking bro-code. Anyway." He straightens. "Second, where are we all heading to after this? Because I've got a shit-ton of questions."

I laugh. I like him already. I like him a lot.

"You up for going out?" Greyson asks, his mouth an inch away from my ear, sending chills up and down my spine, down the length of my arms.

"Yeah." I smile, my bottom lip caught between my teeth. "I'm totally up for going out."

"Woo!" Trey hoots, and the sound is quickly followed by my friends' whoops and shouts of excitement.

And that's how we end up here, at none other than our favorite place: Toca Madera, of course.

Two rounds of shots have already been passed through the group of us—all thirty of us.

Me, and my girls, and my Ricky, and our Sam, and Greyson and his band and their people—and what I'm quickly learning is his tight-knit, makeshift family.

We talk about anything and everything. Sports, art, music. The military. Recording. Touring. College. Highschool.

Greyson and me.

My friends, and his.

Laughter flows in abundance along with the drinks, and in the span of a single night, our worlds completely shift. Fusing Greyson's and mine together.

It's one of the most beautiful things I've ever seen.

Seventy-Two *Before*

I FELT THE darkness beckoning before I even woke. My limbs were heavy, weighted to the bed, to Greyson.

Everything, every piece of me, was heavy. My chest, my breaths, my heart. Every cell, every thought, every bitter and broken and devastated one, felt like a thousand pounds dragging me down.

I was slipping, so fast, into the dark.

The suffocating pressure strangling my throat, the cage around my chest imprisoning my breaths, the sharp pain spearing through my body—I thought I was prepared, for the emotional upheaval, but I had no idea, *no clue,* it would hurt this much.

It took effort just to breathe through the pain without breaking.

How? How was I supposed to get through this day? How was I supposed to say goodbye and not feel like I was dying inside?

I'd known all along God was never going to let me keep Greyson. Even after everything we'd shared these last few weeks, I knew that. I just hadn't realized he was going to rip my heart out and force me to watch him walk away with it, too.

I didn't know how to survive it.

So I turned my face away from the sun and held onto him for dear life, counting at least a thousand breaths before I sat up in bed and wiped away the tears that fell down my cheeks, forcing myself to focus on something—*anything*—else.

We still had time. Hours, minutes. *Focus on that.*

But Greyson stirred beside me, pulling me back into the warmth of his arms, and I split open. Everything I held bottled inside rushed free, spilling into my arms and onto the bed between us.

This was goodbye. I knew it with every bone in my body. And it would've made sense, if I'd looked down at my hands and had found them bleeding. It hurt that badly.

I cried into his side, broken. I was gasping for air, but I still couldn't get enough. All the minutes in the world wouldn't be enough, and I only had a handful of them left.

"Hey," Greyson whispered, lifting my chin in his fingertips. His eyes glistened with the same sadness I felt in the core of my being, and I cried even harder, sobs wracking my body.

I wasn't sure they'd ever stop.

"Baby, *please*," he said, broken, too. "Come here. *Come here*." He tugged the sheet up and over our heads, shielding us both from the world, and kissed me softly.

"I love you," he whispered against my lips and kissed me again and again.

I love you. I love you; I love you; I love you, I said through my tears. Between each one of our kisses. As we slowly slid each piece of clothing from our bodies.

We hid there for a while, in our safe haven. Whispering goodbyes across our skin with soft kisses and light touches.

Careful, devoting…*devastating.*

Seventy-Three *Before*

THERE ARE CERTAIN moments in life, certain images that burn themselves into your brain, and no matter how much later—a month, a year, ten years—you can still pull it up from the vault within your mind and see it with startling clarity.

This was one of those moments. One of the images I'd never be able to erase, to hit the delete button on.

The image of Greyson walking away from me for the last time.

He pulled away from the curb and disappeared down the street, and I fell to my ass in my driveway, throwing my face into my hands.

I hate this, I hate this, I hate this.

I hate you, I wanted to scream at God.

"This isn't goodbye. We're going to see each other again. Tell me you understand that," Greyson had said. Only minutes ago, though it felt like hours. I didn't know how much he truly believed his own words, because it felt like he was trying to convince himself, too, as he'd said them.

"Yeah," I'd whispered back, trying not to break again even though I'd already completely shattered.

I stood from my driveway, attempting to shake off the memory as my tears fell free. I felt the anger I'd let go of seep its way back into my bones, feeding into my bloodstream. I clenched my hands into two tight fists, nails biting into my palms.

Fuck this.

But when? I'd thought to myself. And who would we be then? In four years? I knew we would change. Things would change. We'd be different people then.

It's not that I didn't trust him. It's just that people abandoned me. Time and time again. How could I be sure this time would be any different?

I couldn't. I couldn't be sure, and that was the point.

He could easily meet someone. Could make friends and decide to move somewhere else when he finally got out.

Time had a cruel way of helping you forget, and even though I knew I would never forget him, he could easily forget about me—and the promise he was trying to make me.

All these thoughts I'd kept buried had clawed their way to the surface, forcing me to acknowledge them. But one stood out above all the others:

I couldn't spend the next handful of years of my life waiting around on a maybe. *I owed myself a hell of a lot better than that.*

I turned on my heel and stormed into my house, tearing my way up the stairs and slamming into my bedroom, chest heaving with hyperventilating breaths. I hated this. I hated everything about this.

I've been so fucking stupid.

The words of our last conversation assaulted my mind again and again. I wasn't sure I'd ever forget them.

"I'm not going to sit here and wait around for you, Greyson. I can't do that," I'd finally said. The words had been sitting around in the back of my mind for a long time, I'd just been too afraid to say them. *"I have plans of my own,"* I powered through them anyway. *"I've waited my entire life to start over, too, you know."*

"I know." He shook his head. *"I'm not asking you to do that. I'm just..."*

"Just what, *Greyson?"*

"I don't know," he sighed. "I just know that I care about you. So much. And I love you…

"But I'm not asking you to wait for me. I know I can't ask that of you. I'm just hoping for something—anything. Anything but the possibility of never seeing you again."

I spun around in my room, wanting to thrash all my shit against the walls. Wanting to ruin every piece of furniture in that goddamn room.

My eyes landed on one wall in particular.

I shook my head, tears rolling down my cheeks. "I love you, too. But I don't see how that's possible."

"We call each other," he said right away, "whenever we can. And we stay friends… And in a few years, when I get out, we see what happens."

I knew that wasn't possible. I couldn't do that and not still love him. I'd hold onto it, and it would keep me from living my life—from learning, and growing, and finding myself. And again, I owed myself better than that.

I picked up the bottles of paint that sat on my easel and twisted off the caps one by one. Red, black, blue, green, too many other colors to care. There were so many pictures on that wall that I wanted to ruin. That I wanted to forget.

But I took a deep, shaky breath, and nodded my head anyway. "Okay," I'd whispered. Despite all my feelings. Despite all my misgivings, and doubts, and fears. Despite all my convictions.

It was the most devastating lie I'd ever told.

I launched each of those bottles across my bedroom with all the anger I felt burning inside of me. Watched the paint spill and splatter and drip all the way down each one of those photos, erasing each memory.

Only tiny slivers of those real bits in time poked through.

Just enough to still remember.

Seventy-Four *After*

LADY'S DOOR SLAMS shut, jolting me out of my daze, and a giggle unwittingly pours out of me. I may have, probably, definitely, had a bit too much to drink tonight.

But I'm not mad about it. Because tonight was a blast. One of the best, ever. And I'd do it all over again.

Greyson slides into his seat, shifting my focus to him as he turns the engine over. I trail my eyes over his strong hands, languidly moving them up his muscled arms and broad shoulders before landing on his face. It's a good face. A really good face. And those lips.

Fuck, those lips. They do so much more than the average lips, don't they? The way they sing, and speak, and kiss, and laugh.

"Let me paint you," I blurt. "I could paint you so hard."

"Come again?" those lips reply with a smirk, and it takes everything in me not to climb across this car and kiss it from his face.

"You heard me. I'm painting you," I decide for the both of us, a smile spreading across my lips. "You can't say no," I add with a shrug, and he laughs in response.

"I wasn't planning on it," he says.

"No?"

"No." He shakes his head. "I look forward to it," he adds, and I smile even wider.

"Okay. Thank you."

He glances over at me, eyes shining with amusement, his lips matching the sentiment, and says, "I want to be a dragon."

"What?" My face scrunches up in a weird way that feels funny and ridiculous, but I know I must've had even more to drink tonight than I thought I did, because did he just say *dragon?*

He wants to be a dragon.

What? "What?" my words quickly echo my thoughts and give voice to the expression on my face.

"We are talking about body paint here, right?" he says, seemingly dead serious. "So paint me into a dragon."

A laugh bursts out of me. "Oh my God, I love you."

He smirks. "Joking."

"I know." I smile. "I mean, that does sound like a lot of fun—believe me, it does—but I think I'll stick to what I know."

"Sounds good." He's still smiling, too.

"Doesn't mean you can't still get naked," I add. "Just so we're clear. Naked portraits are my specialty."

He raises his brows. "Are they now?"

"Yep."

"Funny, I didn't catch any of those at your showing."

"Well, of course not. Those are personal." I'm barely holding back my laughter. I mash my lips down on my smile in an attempt to anyway.

"Mmhmm." He smirks. "We'll see about that."

And I know I'm only joking—I've never actually painted anyone naked before. Not from a real, live model, anyway. But the thought of painting Greyson that way feels suddenly, absolutely, and *obscenely* necessary.

Yeah. It has to happen. I'm going to make sure it does. And I don't even try to hide my smile at that thought.

Greyson laughs in response, probably already knowing where my mind has headed. "Did you enjoy yourself tonight?" he asks, switching gears, his tone shifting into a more serious one.

"I did. Probably a little too much," I say, sighing and sinking back into Lady's seat. "But your people are awesome."

"Yours are too." He chuckles.

"Yeah, they are," I say, and my eyes drift closed. Lady rumbles beneath me, soothing. "I'm so happy you kept her."

"Hmm?"

"Lady. I'm really glad you still have her."

"Yeah? And why is that?" I can hear the smile in his voice.

I shrug, a small lift of my shoulders. "Remember that day you drove me down to the beach?"

There's a beat of pause before, "Yeah, of course I do."

"I never thanked you for that."

"You didn't need to, Jess," he says quietly. His hand wraps firmly around my knee and squeezes once, reassuringly.

I open my eyes and nod, but I feel the need to thank him anyway. "It helped me," I say. "I'd never really allowed myself to sit with my feelings like that, until that day. To sort through them and see where they laid. You gave me a safe place to do that, and I...

"I finally started healing that day. So, thank you." I smile for the millionth time tonight, but this one feels wholly different from all the rest.

His eyes meet mine. "You're welcome, but that was all you," he says.

"No." I shake my head. "You helped me more than you know. In so many ways."

He smiles, too, and nods, his eyes back on the road as he laces his fingers through mine. "You helped me, too, you know."

I squeeze his fingers tighter and turn my body in my seat to fully face him. "Yeah?"

"Yeah." He swallows. "Talking to you about what happened with my parents...with my father. It helped me move on from it, too."

"I'm glad," I tell him, and I mean it with every fiber of my being. After all I've felt like he's given me, it's nice to know that I was able to give him something, too...

I don't realize we're here until Greyson gently shakes me awake, and I startle a little in Lady's seat.

"Sorry." Greyson softly chuckles, and I smile into a yawn. "But we're home." He glances out the front windshield and up to his house with a crooked tilt of his lips.

Home, he said, and I like the sound of it.

I like it a lot.

Seventy-Five *After*

I'M PAINTING—GREYSON. Naked. In the flesh. Mirroring the image of him onto the canvas in front of me.

Painting is my passion, my dream, my breath of fresh air, and my slice of freedom in a chaotic world. But right now, there are a million other things I'd rather be doing with that naked body.

He laughs, already knowing where my thoughts have been bathing for the past half-hour. Soaking in the dirtiest corners of my mind like a hot, bubbling bath of depravity.

I close my eyes and shake my head. *You're better than this, Jess.*

Am I, though?

I take a deep breath and focus on the task at hand, dipping my brush into the black paint and adding more detail to the hairs that trail down his stomach and head straight toward his—

"You know what, I can't do this. You're too distracting," I say, setting the brush down on the tray of paints, a little less than gently. The tray rattles and the brush rolls down it, hanging precariously over the edge before I catch it and set it down on my easel.

"Come on, Jess." He laughs again—unwittingly. Moving. Parts. Of himself. It draws my attention straight to those parts. He clears his throat, dragging my gaze back to his. "I want my custom Jessica Martinez work of art."

And then it's my turn to laugh. "If you thought this was going to be hanging anywhere but my bedroom wall, you were sorely mistaken."

The sound of our mingled laughter bounces off my studio walls.

"Here," I say, standing up and grabbing my camera from the shelf beside me. I switch it on and make a few adjustments to the ISO and shutter speed, before lining up the perfect shot. I peer over my camera at him. "This okay?" I ask.

He clears his throat, green eyes intense. "I'm good with whatever you want, Jess."

I lick my lips, biting down on the bottom one with a smile. "Okay," I say quietly. And I take the shot.

I set the camera down on a small table set against the wall and walk over to Greyson, holding my hand down to him. "Come on." I swallow thickly. "Your custom Jessica Martinez will be on its way to you soon. Now let's find our way back to my bed."

The intensity in his eyes increases tenfold, and I almost climb on top of him right here and now, before we could ever make it to my house, let alone my bedroom.

Turns out, we only make it just outside my studio doors.

And my favorite place to ground? The one smack-dab in the middle of my self-made meadow? That's where we collide together and strip, and taste, and feel.

I'm pretty sure it isn't written anywhere in the rulebooks of how it's done, but I can say this: I've never felt more grounded in my life.

Seventy-Six *After*

I WATCH GREYSON, quietly, as he makes his way around his kitchen. His back and arms flexing as he reaches up into his cabinets for two bowls. His fingers wrapped around a matching pair of spoons before setting them down onto his marble countertop.

The way he licks his lips as he lifts the lid from an ice cream container—his green eyes catching mine watching him as he scoops said ice cream into the bowls sitting in front of him.

I smile, not at all ashamed of being caught. He's something to watch, this man. The ease and surety in which he moves about a room. The calmness that seems to emanate from his every pore.

Just being in his presence puts me at ease. Calms something inside of me, too.

He winks at me with a soft smirk before looking back down and continuing to put together our desserts. Chocolate brownie, vanilla ice cream, caramel drizzle, crushed almonds, whipped cream, and a cherry on top.

He knows me well—I bite back another smile, hiding the evidence of it behind my clasped hands—and he is too, *too* good to me. If this dessert has anything to say about it. "You're too good to me," I voice my thoughts.

He shakes his head with a hidden smile of his own. "It's just dessert, Jess."

I quickly suck in a breath, wide eyes and feigned shock that borders on disapproval. "I cannot believe you just said that to me.

'Just dessert.' Who are you?" I slide my bowl from the counter and spin around on his stool, making my way toward his back doors with my dessert in hand. "Dessert is everything," I finish.

He laughs, shaking his head. "Of course it is, babe. Of course it is," he relents. "Forgive me."

I try not to smile while pretending to think about it. "*Hmm*...Okay. You're forgiven. I guess." I shrug and roll my eyes.

He laughs again, and we slip into his backyard, settling into the two oversized chairs at the side of his pool facing his view of our shared city.

"You think we could find my house from here?" I ask, even though I know it's impossible to find my own little speck of a home in the cluster of at least a thousand others.

But he points out in front of him somewhere, in the general vicinity of where I live. "Approximately... There," he says. "Seventeen-minute drive time, thirty-two with traffic." He says it as if he's dead serious, and I snort with laughter.

"Should I be impressed, or slightly afraid for my life?" I ask, taking a bite of my dessert.

He shrugs a shoulder. "These are important, need-to-know things, Jess."

"Really."

"Absolutely."

I can't keep my laughter from spilling forward. But Greyson quickly draws my attention back to him, his eyes on mine as his spoon slides out from between his lips.

"Okay," I follow the movement, taking a breath of clarity, "So...did you follow me to Seattle, then?" I ask with a subtle smirk.

He relaxes back into his chair, kicking his legs out in front of him. "I think so. Intentionally, or unintentionally," he pauses for a moment, eating another spoonful of ice cream before continuing, "Life sort of worked out in my favor that way, but I think I would've ended up here either way...in the hopes of finding you again."

I nod, feeling a sudden swell of emotions as I say, "I don't think it was a possibility—in any version of our reality—that I wouldn't have found my way back to you, Greyson."

The air around us grows thick these emotions, squeezing at my airways. Because...

I love him. So fucking much.

And I can see the sentiment mirrored right back at me through his eyes. Can feel it in the soft graze of his thumb against my cheek. It slips in, slinking past my awareness and into every cell of my body, warming me from the inside out.

He picks my hand up in his and presses a kiss to the center of my palm, before caging it against his chest as he digs back into his dessert.

I look out at the view, soaking in this moment. The quiet surety of it all. It's what startles me most, I think. What throws me a little off-kilter—how I seem to know without a doubt that this is exactly where I'm meant to be. In the right place, with the right person, and finally at the right time. *Finally* at the right time.

"I still don't know how you ever leave this place," I slice through my own thoughts and the handful of others I see playing behind his eyes, too.

The right side of his mouth pulls up into a smirk. "A wise and *very beautiful* woman once told me, in so many words, that I should try to bring my world here, so I won't have to leave half as much."

"Mmhmm," I hum on a half-smirk of my own.

He sets his bowl down onto the small table beside him and turns to face me dead on. I watch as his Adam's apple slides up and down his throat, his eyes intent on holding me in place, right where I am.

For eternity, maybe.

His next words breathe life into those very thoughts. "Move in with me," he says, and time stops. The world stops, the earth stops spinning on its axis, and my smile slowly but surely breaks free.

I could launch myself into his arms and kiss him into oblivion; I could scream, *"Yes!"* from the depths of my soul, and kiss him some more, and never come up for air; I could somehow find my words, drag them up past my thundering heart, and give him the answer I know we both want to hear.

But I can't seem to do anything but smile.

Smile, and smile, and smile.

"I love you," I say through the curve of my lips, and he says it back, and his returning smile is the soulmate to my own.

Seventy-Seven *After*

"**MOVE IN WITH** me," Greyson says again. It's more of a statement than a question, really, and my heart is still racing. Pounding out of my chest.

With excitement. With all of the excitement and none of the nerves; there are no nerves to be found, but I decide it's absolutely necessary to mess with him anyway. "Move in together? That's an awfully big step so soon," I say, barely hiding the smile I can't seem to wipe away from my face.

He pulls my hand into the warmth of his. "Jess," he replies, with a seriousness that borders on amusement. "I love you; I've loved you for eight long years. And for every minute of that time, I've known—without a doubt—that you were the one that got away."

I lean over my chair, across the small distance between us, and press a soft kiss to his mouth, already fully ready to give in. I was ready before he ever said the words—*move in with me, move in with me, move in with me.* I think they're my new favorite words ever spoken.

"I'm not letting you get away again," he finishes quietly against my lips anyway.

Giddiness rushes through me, sparking in my body like fireworks. I want to keep the teasing going, say something along the lines of: *Are you sure? This is kind of fast.* Or maybe a: *I don't know...*

But I can't help myself. I can't contain it any longer. And I think it's pretty obvious how I feel about the situation anyway.

"Hell yes, I'll move in with you!" I give in, with a smile on my face and tears sliding down my cheeks, and then I launch myself into his lap like I've wanted to do since the second he uttered those words.

His arms snake around me, and I feel his smile against my lips. I graze it with my teeth before pulling his bottom lip into my mouth, and he groans, pulling me into his chest and deepening our kiss, slowing everything down. Tongues, and lips, and teeth exploring. Indulging, savoring. Celebrating.

By the time we come up for air, the sun has fully set, goosebumps breaking out along my skin from the cold breeze rushing through.

"So, *'hell yes,'* huh?" he says the words with a soft smirk, a little breathless, his chest visibly expanding and contracting before me.

"Hell yes to anything with you, Greyson. To everything with you," I say, my breaths matching his.

"Anything?" he asks with a devastating smile, brows raised in question.

"Anything," I answer, and his mouth crashes down on mine once more. He lifts me as he stands, my legs wrapping around his torso as he walks us across his backyard, through his house, and up his winding staircase while hardly breaking our kiss.

We land on his bed in a tangle of limbs and laughter and clothing half hanging off our bodies. I finish undressing him, sliding his pants and boxer-briefs down his legs, and he slips the last of my clothing down my arms in return.

And I pause here. Beneath him. Breathing heavily as I try to catch my breath, but it's no use. My chest rises and falls against his, and it's clear he's just as affected as I am. His green eyes, the ones that have always seen every beautiful and broken piece of me and loved them anyway, shine with every emotion I'm feeling, too, and...

"I love you," I whisper the words into the space between us.

His eyes drift shut, and a smile tugs at his lips. He bites down on it before bringing his mouth to mine. "I love you, too, baby. So fucking much," he says into my mouth, and I swallow the words down. I lock them away where no one else can ever touch them as he pushes himself inside of me with a soft groan.

His lips find mine again, and our mouths move together beautifully, and our bodies do, too, and I'm already gone. Completely lost in him and the way he makes me feel.

His hands skating across my skin, fingers tightly gripping my waist—and my hips, and my thighs. His mouth moving over mine, tongue penetrating deep.

Our breaths and the sounds we make mingling together.

I sink my fingers into his muscled back, heels digging into flesh as I climb higher and higher, and I gasp for air. Frozen, as my back arches and I cry out, release washing through me in endless waves.

Greyson soon follows, groaning into my neck as his hands hold me tightly against him, and we're two bodies molded into one.

A lifetime passes before my breaths settle and my bones feel like they're no longer made of liquid.

I look over at Greyson, and he shifts on the bed beside me, turning to face me fully. He rests his head down on his folded arm beneath him, and we lie here, staring at each other from across our pillows. Quiet, smiling. Chests rising and falling with slow, contented breaths.

"So...about that anything..." he says after some time.

"Yeah?" I pull my bottom lip between my teeth, my smile growing even wider than before.

He clears his throat, eyes shining—with love and adoration and a hundred other things I can't quite name at this moment—and I want to curl myself up in his arms and stay inside of this feeling forever.

"Does that mean you'll marry me then?" he asks, and my heart skips a few beats, and then a few more. I lick my lips and trail my eyes over every inch of his face, gauging exactly what he means, his intent behind the question.

What I find are green eyes, and full lips, and strong features arranged in a beautiful way that anxiously and honestly await my answer.

"Will you marry me?" he asks again. His intention is clear, his voice rough with emotion, and I release a soft breath and smile.

And I kiss him, and I wrap my hands firmly around his neck as tears fall down my face, but I don't think I've ever been so happy in my life. It overwhelms me.

I suck in a deep, emotion-filled breath as he leans forward and kisses my tears away, one by one. The soft touches send chills up and down my spine, fill all of the leftover spaces in my heart with pure, unfiltered light and warmth, and my answer is easy...

"Okay," I whisper against Greyson's lips.

Because I've known it all along. I've known it since the very first moment I saw him—that he was exactly what I wanted the rest of my life to look like.

ACKNOWLEDGMENTS

Call it manifesting, call it high hopes, call it wishful thinking, but I'm hoping that someday, sooner than later, more than a handful of you will own this book. And if and when that dream comes into fruition, I want—no, *need*—you all to know how thankful I am. (I promise to make this quick.)

So, first, thank you to YOU. To the ones that picked this book up and read it, and gave it, and me, a chance. I thank each of you with all of my heart for handing me a piece of my dream come true.

Thank you to my husband, for believing in me. (Relentlessly believing in me.) There is no way in hell I could've done this without you. The book thing, and the life thing, too.

I love you so much it's insane.

Thank you to my little loves, my babies, for filling me with the fight to chase my dreams, so that one day you'll know how important it is to fight for yours, too. You are my light, and I love you beyond words.

Thank you to Kara, the best friend, aunt, auntma-to-my-littles, co-author, and everything in-between. I know we don't even remember how we started this author journey together, which is crazy, but it's only further proof that it was meant to be—you and me. I love you *more*, always.

Thank you to my sister, Ashley (*the best sister on this planet!*), for being the most amazing auntie my babies could ever wish for, and for watching them for countless hours while I was out writing, and daydreaming, and clawing my way through this book.

Thank you to Angelica, for your support, and your friendship, and for always getting me. I have no doubt that the Universe nudged us together for so many beautiful reasons. My life would not be the same without you. Not even close.

Thank you to Emma, my Dilemma, because first, you'd kill me if I didn't include you here, but second, because you are my friend who has always been more like a sister.

Thank you to my Cakie and my SIL, because you're two of the raddest humans I know, and you care that I write which makes me feel pretty rad, too.

And to my Mama. ILY.

ABOUT THE AUTHOR

Michelle Chamberland is a whiskey-loving, moon manifesting, daydreaming author, wifey, and mama to two rad kiddos, living in sunny Southern California. She is the Michelle half of the Watty Award-winning author duo, Kara Michelle on Wattpad, and is an absolute lover of losing herself between the pages of new worlds and clawing her way out on the other side with the worst (in the best way) book hangovers.

You can find her on Instagram and TikTok @iamtheauthormc

Made in the USA
Las Vegas, NV
16 June 2021